Death of a Spymaster

A New Ukrainian Spy Thriller

from

Russell R.Miller

BeachHouse Books

Saint Charles Missouri

USA

Copyright

Graphics Credits:

Cover design by Dr. Bud Banis using a background image, Pripyat01.jpg from Wikimedia. The Pripyat Ferris Wheel, as seen from the City Centre Gymnasium in the exclusion zone in Chernobyl. Author: Keith Adams, February 2006 License details: Released into the public domain (by the author).

Egyptian hieroglyph figures on page 272 are from www.discoveringegypt.com/pics/hiero.jpg

ISBN 978-1-59630-092-7- BeachHouse Books Edition, 2014

Publisher's Cataloging-in-Publication

Miller, Russell R., 1928-
  Death of a spymaster / Russell R. Miller.
    p. cm.
  ISBN 978-1-59630-092-7 (regular print : alk. paper)
  1. Retired executives--Fiction. 2. International Executive Service Corps--Fiction. 3. Americans-- Ukraine --Fiction. 4. Illegal arms transfers--Fiction. 5. Ukraine--Fiction. I. Title.
Library of Congress PCCN reference number   2014950558

BeachHouse Books

Saint Charles, Missouri
USA

(636) 394-4950

www.beachhousebooks.com

To the Family

Elsie
Cheron, Mike, and Paul
Mark, Margaret, and Cindy
Melinda, Timothy and Nicole

"We have to build up a picture. It's like a jigsaw,

but with key sections missing, and pieces

from other jigsaws mixed in."

Sir John Sawers — head of the U. K.'s
foreign spy agency MI6

A man's gotta do what a man's gotta do.

John Wayne

1.

Langley, Va.

Rain pelted the office window. Ray Riordan turned to the sound. The storm had started that morning coming out of the East, first as a light drizzle gradually intensifying as it crossed Chesapeake Bay, then gathering force as it passed over the Capitol. Now, a full-blown ugly storm was menacing Langley.

Riordan's mood matched the bleak sky. He had been thinking about his career at the Agency. His background was different from most; he was military. In the beginning, he was just a common grunt in the infantry. Then they moved him to the Rangers and sent him to Nam. When he got wounded, it was back to the States for recuperation and discharge — they didn't need him anymore. On his way out the door, a little man with thick glasses motioned to join him in a small room just off the main corridor.

When the man offered him a job with the CIA Riordan barely knew what they did, but what the hell, he didn't have anything else to do, and he needed the money. So it was off to Langley for a little while. From there it was to what they referred to as *The Farm*, an out of the way location within Camp Perry, somewhere outside of Williamsburg, Virginia.

He soon realized that he did not fit in with most of the other recruits. They were all from some expensive Ivy League School, and he was from Fort Leonard Wood. When they found out what he knew, and what he could do with what he knew, he got along with the others just fine. After he completed the course they sent him immediately into the field, rather than back to headquarters for additional

1

training. They needed agents, and they could not wait to get him deployed.

In the beginning, as he moved from assignment to assignment, he had progressed if not rapidly at least steadily. After eventually becoming a deputy director, actually Deputy Director of Operational Intelligence, it had all definitely stalled—not going anywhere—just plodding along on the same level plane. He was not an old man, much too young to retire. Maybe getting a little thin on top, but not a lot really.

At least, he consoled himself, at this level he was more involved. The world was getting more dangerous by the day, and he had a birds-eye view—whether he wanted it or not.

It was funny though, at first, he could care less about his career, but after he had a wife and kids it was different. Now he had to figure out......

"He's dead!"

Riordan whirled toward the intrusion, as his assistant Bill Brady entered the office without the usual knock.

"Dead?" Who's dead? What the hell are you talking about?"

Brady already regretted his action. It was obvious that his boss was in the midst of one of his more frequently occurring funks. "Valentine, Emmett Valentine. The old man is dead. You know your guy in the basement office."

"He's not my .... Where--how did he die?"

Brady sat down across from his boss. He was tired. He had stayed out far too late the night before entertaining a new hire from the Crypto Section at Chadwicks in Georgetown. He was trying to impress her with how many people he knew. Now he was paying the price, and he was

2

fully aware this conversation was not going to be either easy or quick.

"Not here," he assured his boss. "He didn't die here in his office." He knew that would be the next question asked.

Riordan was relieved.

"They found him at home. He didn't show up at his regular time in the morning. You could always set your watch by him. By lunch, his administrative assistant was worried. He tried calling Valentine's place, but no one answered. So he grabbed a sandwich at the cafeteria and took off for the old man's flat.

"When he got there he knocked, but no one answered. He tried the door, and found it locked. Now, he was certain there was a problem. The old man had not shown up for work as usual, and he wasn't answering his door. The assistant didn't panic; he has been around here long enough not to call the police."

"Thank God for that," Riordan exhaled. "So?"

"So he called in the *housekeepers* and told them it was urgent. He knew that was what they are here for, to fix things. A couple of them showed up within fifteen minutes. They jiggered the door without a problem, and looked around the apartment. They found Valentine sprawled face-down on his desk."

The rain had stopped but neither man noticed.

Riordan felt bad. The old man was...well old. Valentine had already lived longer than most of his contemporaries, but somehow you started to assume he would live forever. "Well I suppose you had to expect that he would die sometime. You know a man of his age."

"It wasn't old age that he died from. He was shot—"

"Shot?"

"--and it was not suicide," Brady assured him, anticipating the next question. "He was shot in the back of his head. He would have to have been a damn contortionist to do that. It looked pretty bad. His assistant recoiled at the sight, he admitted to me."

Riordan considered what Brady had told him. Shot in the back of his head. He supposed that the old man could do that to himself if he had wanted to. He knew him well enough to know that he could do damn near anything he set his mind to. But why do it?

"The gun?" he asked, abandoning the possibility of suicide.

"There was no gun, at least none anyone could find." Brady had wondered about that himself. "Whoever did it wanted us to know that it was murder—not suicide. Whoever did it could have made it look like suicide, but he didn't. It was a hit.

"It also had to be someone Valentine knew, at least well enough to let him into the apartment. There was no damage to the door, or the lock, and there was no sign of violence, except for the blood covering the papers he had been reading. Other than that, everything was as neat as the proverbial pin. Whoever it was locked the door behind him when he left."

"Anything missing?"

"We have no way of knowing. The housekeeping guys looked around the apartment, but they really could not tell if anything was missing or not. None of them had ever been there before."

That was understandable, Riordan conceded. He had never been there either, and he was closer to Emmett than most. "What did they do with the body?"

4

"They called me on my cell. I told them to wait until it was dark, and then bring him back to the Agency. They rolled him up in a carpet, carried him down the stairs, and put him in their van. We think that no one saw them, but we are going to have to tell someone what happened, and then the funeral...."

The phone on Riordan's desk interrupted their conversation.

"Linda, what is it? No not now. Get his number and I'll call him back later. Also, get the managers together and bring in the organization file. Ok? Please," he added as an afterthought.

Riordan replaced the receiver, and turned to his assistant. "The first priority is to figure out who to tell---and then who not to. It doesn't look good having someone from the Agency knocked-off in his own home.

"By the way, what about the papers?" Riordan asked.

"Papers?" Brady's headache had returned, and he massaged his temple to keep it at bay.

"Yeah, the papers. You said that he had bled all over the papers he was reading. Did you get the papers? Maybe there is something on them that will give us a better idea about why he was killed."

"I'll look into that," Brady quickly assured him as Barbara Richards, the senior staff analyst, entered the office. Her scent immediately penetrated the stuffy room, creating a sense of nostalgia, unconsciously reminding both men of every woman they had ever known.

She is beginning to show her age, Riordan thought. Still good looking though. Dresses like a professional, unlike some of these kids around here. Acts like a professional as well. Did a damn fine job in Beirut before they had to pull her out.

5

Barbara took her usual place at the conference table, bestowing a slender smile first on Riordan and then Brady.

Riordan's office was starkly decorated. A long conference table T-boned the mahogany desk that contained none of the obligatory pictures or expensive pen sets. Its feature attraction was a walnut frame that held a variety of small national flags. No one ever inquired about it, just assumed that it was representative of a man whose career spanned the globe. Actually, it was nothing like that. Each flag represented a country where Riordan had successfully laid at least one of its female residents. Occasionally, he could be seen twirling one of the small flags between his fingers while smiling to himself in recollection.

The next to enter the office was Ralph Gross. Riordan was glad to have him on his staff. He was tough. He was the muscle. You could count on him. The Agency had temporarily detailed him to the shadowy Global Response Staff in Benghazi, until everything hit the fan. Afterwards, they had to draw out all of the GRS people that were still alive, and hide them away from the congressional investigators.

Riordan noticed Gross was putting on a little weight though. Too much time in the office, and too long from the field. It happened to all of them if they weren't careful, Riordan knew that from his own experience.

Riordan watched as Gross took a chair across the table from Barbara Richards. He had to walk around the table to do it, but Riordan knew that he always liked to look at her.

Gross had a stocky build, with broad shoulders that made him appear shorter than he actually was. Deep-set crow's feet bracketed watchful gray eyes. His ham-like hands were rough, like a man who had spent his life doing manual labor. He and Riordan, the ex-soldier, felt comfortable with each other and given a set of facts, the two of them usually arrived at the same conclusion.

Ken Madden, an IT whiz with a cyclist's slender frame, was the newest member of Riordan's organization. His friends at the bicycle club referred to him as "lean and meek" behind his back. After entering the room, he tentatively chose the chair next to Barbara Richards and across from Ralph Gross.

The young man provided the organization with a window on the cyber world. Riordan needed him to translate the complex into concepts that a man of Riordan's generation could comprehend. He told Madden, at the outset, not to bother explaining how everything worked, Riordan only wanted to know what the numbers did either for, or against him.

As he studied the two men seated across from each other it was painfully obvious to Riordan that they represented opposite poles of the individual spectrum. The analyst and the activist. Mind over matter so to speak.

Riordan, normally not a reflective man, caught himself studying them and wondering if he was observing the past and the present; the changing of the guard from the older more experienced field agent to the remote cyber-spying that was typified by the younger man. And, if that was so, where the hell did he fit into the shifting equation.

Enough of that crap, he decided, he would think about that tomorrow.

After they settled, Linda brought in a manila file with ORGANIZATION marked in block letters on the cover. Back when Riordan joined the Agency the organization had been relatively simple to understand. Since 9/11, all government agencies having anything to do with intelligence or security had expanded exponentially. New organizations were formed then reformed, others folded into the new ones, and old organizations that had once been disbanded were now revitalized. The file-folder bulged as a result. Riordan shoved it to the side, as if it were a distasteful object. He would look at it later, but now he wanted to bring his staff up to date before deciding how to proceed.

"Last night we lost a man, Emmett Valentine," he began.

"Valentine—who is—was Emmett Valentine?" Madden blurted. It was not his style to inquire about things that were not computer systems related. He was too new to the organization to chance that, but the statement had taken him by surprise. Staff meetings typically involved budgets, data system modifications, or new projects--not death for god's sake. He fidgeted nervously in his chair.

Riordan tried to decide how to answer without revealing too much. Valentine had been his guy, and he had been the one who convinced the Director to bring him back one last time and to carry him off the books. Now the old man was dead. Shot dead. He was going to have to tell the Director. No doubt of that, but if in the end it became some kind of a bollixed operation, as these type of things often do, he knew his career would be as dead as the old man.

The other assistant directors would be all over him like white on rice. He couldn't afford that right now. He had to either clear it up, or stomp it down. The question was how to do that?

Riordan looked around the room, attempting to find the right words--perhaps written on one of the pallid walls that framed his office. When that proved unproductive, he shifted his gaze to the bank of clocks on his right that told the time of day in the major cities of the world. They failed to provide an answer as well.

He realized he needed to acquaint his people with the problem in order for them to help him form a strategy or, if not that, at least to become accessories. He was well aware he would have to make them part of the problem so they would not be able to abandon him when the going got rough—as it most surely would.

"Emmett Valentine," he took a deep breath as he began "was the last and the best of the old cold war warriors. He goes way back, joining the Agency before it even was an Agency---back in the days of the old OSS during the big one—back there with Wild Bill Donovan."

He looked around the room at the expression on the people's faces, trying to see if he had lost them. You could never be sure now when you mentioned the old days. Probably ancient history for most of them, but they did seem to be riveted on what he was telling them.

"He began running agents into France as the war was winding down. He seemed to have a knack for it, and he caught the eye of the powers that be.

"After the war, when they converted the Office of Strategic Services into the Central Intelligence Agency, Emmett was one of the boys they held over."

After unthinkingly referring to Emmett Valentine as a boy, Riordan chuckled to himself. Such a thing was almost inconceivable to him now.

"He was also here during the Cold War," Riordan continued warming to his topic. "Emmett knew how to run agents so they sent him to Hungary. He set up a network establishing *assets* under the nose of Ivan and did a damn fine job of it. He was in Budapest when the Russian tanks rolled in, and the Agency ordered him out. He knew too much for them to risk his capture. He did not want to leave his people, but had no choice. Finally, he made his way to Switzerland and from there back to DC."

"And he has been here ever since?" Barbara Richards asked incredulously. The others had wondered the same thing, but did not want to show their lack of knowledge.

"Not exactly," Riordan replied. "When the Berlin Wall fell, the Cold War melted away overnight. Afterwards, the Soviet Union had to revert to its Russian roots as their former controlled countries chose independence. The KGB morphed into the FSB, and one of their former agents eventually became president of the country.

"Here at the Agency, it was eventually decided that they no longer needed the old Russian hands, and they were *requested* to turn in their chits and retire. Emmett was one of them.

"Then 9/11 happened and the Agency was at war again, only with a different enemy. Having got rid of most of their former specialists, they began to build-up once again with a new type of guy... or gal," he added quickly in deference to Barbara. "They needed people with different experience--not the old Russian hands. That was yesterday's war."

"You stayed-on though, didn't' you?" his assistant asked, more a declarative than a question.

"Yeah, yeah, I did," Riordan, acknowledged. "Actually I had been hired by Valentine a while before he left. Afterwards, I drifted around and eventually spent time as station chief in Tel Aviv. Then the Agency brought me back here to the big-time," he smiled sardonically. "I was put in charge of running agents of a different type.

"The only problem was, while we were concentrating all of our resources in the Mideast, Putin's people were not accommodating and wanted to take advantage of our lack of attention."

He picked up the phone. "Coffee Linda," he barked, then added a perfunctory "please" before replacing the receiver in its cradle. He moved the bulging file folder further aside to make room for the anticipated tray.

"I talked to the Director," Riordan continued. "He, as you all know, goes back a long way too." They all smiled faintly in acknowledgement.

"We both agreed we needed some coverage of what the Russians were doing while we were concentrating on the Mideast. They got their asses kicked out of Afghanistan. It was a national embarrassment. Afterwards, Putin began to quietly build-up his security services. We knew he was not doing it for the fun of it. You don't use your resources to build a weapon unless you plan to use it, and he was building one hell of a big weapon. Their new security organization was funded with their oil resources, which had become far more valuable."

Occasionally Riordan would hesitate, groping for the right words. Telling, but not telling all. Only what he had to in order to enlist their assistance.

"The Director and I agreed we needed some coverage, but didn't know how to pay for it. That was when I got the bright idea of bringing back Emmett, and hiding him in the organization charts."

"I didn't know you could do that," Ken Madden blurted. "Wasn't that against regulations?"

Riordan ignored the question. "Emmett jumped at the suggestion. He had been going nuts in retirement. An old fire horse without a fire, he told me once."

Linda brought in a decanter of coffee on a tray, setting it next to her boss. He motioned to Barbara Richards to serve while he continued talking.

"We put him in the basement office, and he started to work. Valentine had run spies all his life—an experienced spymaster—and he did more with nothing than most organizations here do with hundreds. He knew more about how the Russians operated than anyone else at Langley.

"On top of that, the old man was cheap. He was already drawing a pension so we bumped him up a bit and put him in a basement office without a staff. We have so many new people wandering around here now nobody questioned who he was or what he was doing. We just gave him a tight-lipped assistant, and what help he could occasionally wrangle from other departments."

As he concluded the explanation of his very secret agent, Riordan felt fatigue engulf him, along with considerable remorse over the death of a friend. He looked directly at the group, shrugged his shoulders and reached for the coffee before it turned cold.

When he finished and put down his cup, Riordan opened the folder and spread out the charts. "Now let's try to figure out who we have to share this with—and more importantly who not to," he grinned.

They gathered around him and stared intently at the contents of the folder containing complex drawings filled with circles and squares, tied together with lines that seemed to go everywhere yet nowhere.

The CIA was presently under the Director of National Intelligence. Under the DNI, the chart also made room for the FBI, NSA, Homeland Security, and still squeezed in the Drug Enforcement Agency, along with a variety of armed forces intelligence agencies. All of them had the responsibility of gathering intelligence that theoretically was to be shared with other appropriate agencies. While the organizational lines of authority appeared reasonably clear, the definition of *appropriate* was far more murky.

12

"What about talking with one of the Homeboys?" Barbara Richards ventured pointing to a box labeled Homeland Security. "They seem to have an involvement with almost everything under the sun."

"Not there" admonished Ralph Gross. "Perhaps someone within the FBI. They are in charge of domestic intelligence, and Emmett's death certainly was a domestic matter."

Bill Brady, Riordan's assistant, tanked that suggestion. "Once you go to those guys we would never get them out of our pants."

The Deputy Director was equally reluctant to share the killing of Emmett Valentine with any of his contemporaries within the Agency itself, much less any other outside organization. Since coming to Washington, he had been through enough organizational battles to last a lifetime. He had lost a man, which was bad enough, but he was damned if he was going to lose his job as well.

The group spent the next hour bickering among themselves over who in the intelligence community had a need to know, and more importantly who did not. Eventually, the room became deadly quiet. They all realized that the decision could have a profound effect on their own careers. Finally, they concluded they would share the information relating to Emmett Valentine's death only with the Director himself, and of course, whomever else he might suggest.

"We need a complete blackout on Valentine's death. Nothing is ever to become public about him, about his past, what he was doing or how he died. If he was never officially here, he can't be officially dead. We put a hat on all of it," Riordan summed up.

The meeting had run much later than anyone expected. Brady, helpful as always, stayed on after the others filed out.

He was tired, but it was an assistant's role to ask the hard questions that no one else asked. "Now, how do we go about finding who actually killed Valentine? We have to do that without alerting the entire District of Columbia. We also need to find the killer before he takes out someone else. For all we know we could very possibly have a mole hidden deep within the CIA itself."

Riordan stared straight ahead. At the moment, he really had no idea how to go about doing that.

"I'll think of something," he replied dryly, turning back to the window.

His assistant quietly left the room, leaving his boss alone.

2.

Chicago

At the sound of his wife's voice, Charlie Connelly turned with an inquiring shrug of his shoulders.

"Charlie," she repeated, then added, "it's *them*."

"Who?"

"*Them*," she informed him disgustedly. "You know *them*, I can always tell *them* by the sound."

He dropped his pruning shears and, wiping his hands on his khaki trousers, entered the house.

Once inside, he reached for the phone. "Yes?" he inquired cautiously. His wife Beth stood by, while her husband held the receiver tightly against his ear.

After a long silence Charlie finally asked, "when did he die?" and listened for the answer. The question provoked an extended silence, that was followed by an uncertain, "I see." Beth drew closer when she heard her husband say, "No" then a long pause followed by "no, no I can't do that right now."

He turned his back toward her, shielding the phone even more tightly against his ear, for fear his wife would interrupt.

As the conversation continued, Beth watched him intently. There were times when she wondered if she really knew her husband at all. Even though they had been married for what seemed like forever, and had three children together as well, she sometimes wondered who Charlie Connelly really was.

He could be maddening at times, but he was still a handsome man. His tanned face was framed by pewter gray temples. One of his outstanding features had always been his deep blue eyes that could look right through you. Penetrating, they called them. The creases forming on his forehead only added to the picture, and gave people immediate confidence in him. Rightly so, she decided. He was a good man with a strong will, but damn it he could make her angry at times.

She had a good idea what was happening on the other end of the line, and who it was that was calling. The man had given his name, but she had paid little attention. It made no matter, she knew from experience it would not be his real one. It never was. It would be one of those nameless, faceless people her husband had met when he was still in the corporate world.

Finally, Charlie spoke after a prolonged silence. "Where is it?" he asked, then listened intently before putting down the receiver.

Turning to his wife, he confirmed, "You were right Beth. It was *them*."

"Charlie, you promised, we are not going through that again. You told me—you told them you were done. No more, no way, you said never again," her voice rose with each phrase.

"I know I did Beth, and I meant it. It's not like that. Not this time. You remember me telling you about Emmett Valentine?" She reluctantly nodded her acknowledgement. "Well he is dead, and they thought I would want to come to the funeral. That's all, just a funeral of an old friend."

"Another of your stories," Beth admonished. "You *have* come to like it haven't you? The deception and deceit I mean. It is beginning to define you, and now you can't let it alone. Even with me.

16

"How did he die?" Beth asked, knowing she was losing the argument.

"*How* did he die" he repeated the question. "I don't know," he replied with a shrug of his shoulders. "They didn't say, and I didn't think to ask. He was an old man, and he just died I guess. Old men do that all the time."

"So now what? What do they want of you now?" Beth asked, trying to stare through him.

"It's not like that dear. They don't *want* anything. Just trying to be nice—thoughtful I guess. They thought I would want to attend the funeral."

"And?"

"And I do. He was always good to me. He had my best interests at heart. At least I always thought so," he added, with less conviction.

"So now what?" she repeated her earlier question that remained unanswered.

"So now I am packing an overnight bag and catching a flight to Washington. Would you like to come with me?" he added as a too obvious afterthought.

"To go to a funeral of someone I hardly know? Not hardly. Anyway, I have other things to do, and I would rather do anything more than attending a funeral of someone I have never met."

Charlie went upstairs to pack a bag. He took his blue blazer and grey slacks from the rack, and stuffed in a sport shirt and three dress shirts, He paused before adding a couple of ties, underwear, and a lightweight sweater, along with a pair of athletic shoes, and finally a jacket.

Beth came into the room as he was preparing to close the bag. "Why are you taking all of those clothes Charlie?"

she asked pointedly. "I thought you were just going overnight?"

"Just an old rule of the road hon, always be prepared,"' he smiled.

"That's the Boy Scouts Charlie," she replied irritably. "You're not telling me everything are you?" The old friction between them was rising up again. It seemed it had always been this way back when he was head of international marketing and traveling the globe for Apex Electronics. Then, after he retired and was doing consulting work overseas, he would take off for a week and it would end up to be months before he returned. Particularly after *they* got in touch with him.

"Should I call for a reservation?" she asked, giving in. She was tired of fighting the same old battles she never won.

"They have a private plane waiting for me at Midway," he told her kissing her cheek. She reached out to him, but he was already hurrying down the stairs.

Outside a taxi was already idling at the curb.

Beth watched in dismay as the taxi, and her husband, pulled away from the house.

It was a beautiful day in Chicago. A crystalline blue sky shielded the melancholy advance of a Midwestern fall. The driver's radio blared a peculiarly discordant version of *la Paloma*. Charlie failed to notice the loud music, as his cab wound its way past the neat row of bungalows lining the street. His mind was focusing on Emmett. What in the hell happened to the old man? Charlie had not been entirely candid when he had told his wife that he didn't know how he died. He didn't, but they seemed to be unnecessarily vague about his death when they called.

Charlie could think of quite a few people who might want Emmett out of the way, he decided after a moment more of consideration. Not specifically, but in the abstract as the spooks liked to say. Or as *they* like to say, he thought, mentally mimicking his wife.

On the other hand, he thought, why didn't they just say that Emmett had died a natural death? He was certainly entitled to that, at his age. Why beat about the bush like that. Maybe it was just the Agency, after awhile they instinctively have an aversion to stating anything directly. Perhaps that was it.

He was uncomfortable not telling Beth what he thought about Emmett's death. He felt he should be more open about the situation, but it would only lead into the old mine field about his association with the Central Intelligence Agency, and there was no time for that now. Maybe when he got back they could discuss it more thoroughly. Maybe.

He and Beth had met in college, fallen in love, and had been together ever since. There had been good times and bad times, but very few in-between times as they shared the life of corporate nomads, moving from job to job and town to town. That was what people like them did during those days. Beth was the glue that held the family together while Charlie worked to support the financial demands of a growing family.

As they passed from one suburb to another, Charlie had to admit to a feeling of exhilaration, much like an actor might feel when he discards the coat of normalcy and dons the cloak of an adventurer. He had often felt the transformation back in real life before he retired. There was an element of the unknown surrounding the telephone call from Washington. Sure, it was nice they called to tell him about Emmett's death, but he knew he had not had a previous association with anyone named Ray Riordan. Then, to have a plane waiting to take him to Washington for the funeral seemed to stretch the bounds of empathy — as well as his credulity.

He knew Beth would be wondering about that as well. But, what the hell, he was on the road again, heading into the unknown and away from the damned roses, and there was a lot to be said for that.

Charlie stared out the cab's window. A woman was watering the flowers in front of her home as the taxi went by, while two houses further down the street an old man struggled with his balky lawnmower.

The traffic began to increase, and the neighborhoods became more gritty. The driver slowed as the taxi approached the smaller of Chicago's two airports. Charlie was unfamiliar with the layout. He usually traveled out of O'Hare on his international flights.

The street soon clogged with cars letting off their passengers at the terminal. Charlie leaned forward. "Over there" he pointed, and repeated the directions he had received earlier over the phone to make sure the driver understood. The man nodded his acknowledgement, and veered down a narrow side road behind a row of smaller hangers and toward a line of executive jets.

Charlie tapped the driver's shoulder and pointed toward an unmarked plane with tail numbers matching those Riordan had mentioned. The cab pulled to a stop, just as a heavyset man in a suit and tie lumbered down the plane's gangway. Once on the tarmac he pulled a small snapshot from his pocket and glanced casually as Charlie approached him. They shook hands at the bottom of the gangway, and walked together up the stairs and through the open doorway.

Immediately after Charlie was inside, the plane began to taxi toward the runway. The pilot had requested clearance when he saw the approaching cab. Charlie suddenly realized that his flight was taking precedence over the commercial flights already waiting on the line. The pilot's instructions had been clear, and whoever the passenger was, it was important for him to be in Washington as soon as possible.

After his traveling companion entered the pilot's compartment, Charlie tried to get comfortable in his seat by adjusting the well-worn leather armrests. Failing that, he leaned toward the window staring at the rooftops below. As the Learjet circled the field before heading east, Charlie tried to identify his own neighborhood. He was unable to locate his house. He never could, but he always tried.

The plane sliced through the overhanging clouds, while Charlie tried once again to get comfortable and possibly doze off. He had no luck with that. He tried, once more to adjust his seat, but it was already reclined as far as it would go. He had not thought to bring a book, and there were no magazines in the rack next to the cabin door.

Left to his devices, Charlie's mind wandered back to when it all started. His extramarital affair with the Agency had begun innocently enough, then had gradually become almost like an illicit thing that both parties agreed to keep hidden from everyone else, while mutually agreeing to continue.

At the outset, the association had begun very casually, with just an introductory contact by some of the Agency people visiting his office at Apex Electronics. They had only wanted an insight to usual things like the import restrictions in Peru, or the economic stability of Sri Lanka, or some other seemingly reasonable request regarding a tedious business detail occurring in some far-off place. Then things began to snowball, and he soon found himself dealing directly with Emmett Valentine, or one of the people in Washington working directly for him.

He had actually found his little errands flattering, and he was initially pleased to be asked — to be trusted as it were. But, gradually he found himself getting in deeper and deeper, occasionally feeling in over his head. He usually felt more like Maxwell Smart than James Bond. Even then, he had to concede, it made him feel important that he could develop the skills that were so alien to his normal areas of proficiency.

In time, he learned how to check to see if he was being followed — tailed as they referred to it. Then came the elementary dead-drop routines, and brush passes. Later, he was instructed on the ways to use simple encryption; as well as ways to contact certain people in Washington, if need be, without anyone becoming suspicious. Following that, in the intentionally opaque parlance of the intelligence community, he began working as a NOC (someone under non-official cover) and learned how to modify his identity and purpose without detection. It was almost like a truncated on-the-job training program in some kind of crazy corporation, with the Mad Hatter acting as CEO.

Even after he left Apex, the association with the Agency continued as he became an occasional economic advisor for one or another of the multitude of international organizations that were attempting to assist developing countries through the advancement of their private sector.

With too much time on his hands, he developed a form of intense restlessness, like an itch he couldn't scratch. He had to admit, the occasional contact from a shadowy figure in Washington added a little spice to an otherwise bland diet, providing a dollop of melodrama to the more sedentary life of a recent retiree. However, he fully realized he was at best a knowledgeable amateur in a world where there were none. At least not for long.

Now they had contacted him again. What for he wondered? To attend Emmett's funeral they said. He didn't believe that for a minute. But he was curious what they really wanted. It wouldn't hurt to find out. Besides, he did feel obligated to attend the old man's burial. What was it Emmett had told him once, something about old fire horses chomping at the bit? Charlie chuckled. That sounded like the old man all right. Suddenly he wondered, did it possibly describe himself as well? No, of course not. Hell no, not him. Not even close, he decided. He shut his eyes tightly to eradicate the thought, as the private plane continued on its direct route to Washington.

3

Fairfax, Va.

A Black Buick pulled up to the side of the small hanger at an obscure landing strip outside of Fairfax, Virginia. A casual passerby could barely see the car, much less its two passengers seated behind the darkened glass. Inside, Ray Riordan checked his watch—again. "Shouldn't they be here by now? The funeral will be starting in a few minutes."

"Their flight plan said two o'clock. It should give you enough time," his assistant Bill Brady assured him, looking once more at the schedule. Bill had checked with the pilot before he took off from Chicago, but you could never be sure out there. The weather changes by the hour.

"Why are you bringing him to Washington anyway?" Brady inquired, partly to take his Boss's mind off his damned watch.

"Connelly, you mean?" Riordan turned away from the window.

"Yes, of course, Connelly. It's kind of a stretch, isn't it?"

"Probably, but I thought if Emmett had been murdered by someone within the Agency I didn't want to take a chance on accidentally getting that person involved in finding the killer. By using an outsider that can't happen.

"Anyway, it seemed like a good idea at the time. Valentine had used him before. Several times as a matter of fact, and the guy always did a good job. The old man was high on him—for an amateur. Connelly had—has the advantage of not being directly associated with the Agency. He's a corporate guy. He looks like a corporate guy. Walks and talks like what he is, a corporate guy. No one would think otherwise. No one would think that he was one of us."

"A clean face," Brady observed.

"Yeah that's right, a clean face." Riordan assured him. "Valentine never had to construct a legend for him. No hokey story about him being something that he wasn't. As that cartoon guy used to say 'he was what he was, and that was all he was.' "

"Popeye," Brady confirmed.

"Yeah, Popeye." his boss chuckled.

"So when Valentine got hit, you all agreed that we had to figure out who did it, and then deal with it ourselves, none of the other agencies, and no one outside of our own organization. So, what does that leave us? Our people are all tied up trying to figure out who the hell sprang the *Arab Spring* on us, and what to do about it before we all get snowed under. Much too busy to get involved in the death of an old cold warrior.

"On top of that, I can't assign someone to find out who killed someone who was never here can I?"

After a short pause, Brady asked, "Could you repeat that?"

"It gets complicated doesn't it?" Riordan replied, gazing once again out the car window,

"That leaves us Charlie Connelly," Riordan concluded.

"So he has agreed to help us?"

"Well, not actually agreed. As a matter of fact, I haven't really mentioned that part to him. I just told him that Emmett Valentine had died. I can't remember if I mentioned exactly how he died. We constantly deal in so many big lies that sometimes I lose track of the small ones. Anyway,

25

because of their long relationship, I thought that he might want to attend the old man's funeral."

"And he bought that?" Brady asked skeptically.

"He's on the plane isn't he? Actually, I don't care if he bought it or not. I just want to have a chance to talk to him and see if he will agree to be our mole catcher."

"I didn't think that you were convinced that it was a mole that shot Emmett," Brady replied, surprised.

"I'm not. It just sounded good when I said it. It may not have been a mole — probably not actually, but right now that doesn't make any difference if Connelly goes along with it."

"How are you going to bring him in if he does agree?" This time it was Brady who was nervously checking his watch.

"I haven't fully thought that out," Riordan replied. "But, we will kind of figure it out as we go along. That's what we are good at isn't it? If the Agency wanted thinkers, they would hire professors. That's what they are good at. We are the doers. Now we have to do something without other people finding out. We do that all the time."

"Yeah maybe," Brady replied, "but usually not hiding it from our own people."

Riordan ignored the comment. "You can handle that. We can't bring him in through the usual process. Takes too damn long. This way he just shows up one day. Another face among the thousands walking around. You manufacture some fake ID, you know, we do that all the time for our agents. We're good at that too. He becomes a specter among spooks, an organizational will-of-the-wisp so to speak," Riordan concluded with a self-satisfied grin

The two men fell quiet. Brady knew that his boss didn't like too many questions, particularly when he didn't have all the answers. It was becoming quite clear that Riordan was winging it more than he liked.

Riordan began to fidget. It was the damn waiting that he hated. But this wasn't really that bad. Waiting for a plane outside of Washington was nothing like waiting for a joe to appear in a dark night in Beirut or Istanbul. There had been plenty of that in his life. More than he liked to think about. He stared blankly at the clear sky. Nothing up there. Not a damn thing. He looked at his watch once more.

His mind drifted back to that night in Belgrade. He was waiting in a dark cold doorway for his guy to appear. His *asset,* as they referred to them in the dehumanizing vernacular the Agency loved to use. Only this time his guy was a girl. Not a Joe, a Joan. And not just an asset. He hated that reference when it came to someone he had come to love.

They had been together for several months. He had forgotten exactly how many. They had met at an embassy party. He was head of commercial services in the American Embassy. That was his cover. He knew as much about commerce as Connelly knew about spying. Maybe less — hopefully a lot less. She was an encryption clerk at the Russian Embassy.

There was a spark between them, and they began to see each other. He soon learned that she actually hated the communists, and he recruited her.

She had said that she would be walking by that night on her way to the Plaza Bar. He would walk toward her going in the opposite direction. As they passed each other, their hands would touch. When they did, she would pass him a tiny piece of microfilm containing a revised list of Serb agents working undercover for the Russian Embassy.

In the trade, the process was referred to as a brush pass- -tradecraft 101, learned it the first week at the Farm. He had done it hundreds of times before. But, it wasn't that clinical when she was involved. He had come to love her.

She never came. He waited. And again the next night. That was standard protocol—but he would have done it anyway. Waited longer than the night before, but she never showed. He found out later that she had been *unexpectedly* shipped back to Moscow. Out of the consulate—must have caught her--never heard from her again. Never will.

It was his last love, before he met Audrey that is. He and Audrey had married, and he never loved another. But, he never forgot the girl in Belgrade and thought of her often.

"Is that a plane?" Brady asked, interrupting Riordan's reflections. A small dot in the sky was becoming larger as they watched.

4

Langley, Va.

The service had begun by the time Riordan weaved their car through the narrow lanes of the secluded cemetery. No one looked up when the three men joined the small group at the graveside. They were all concentrating their attention on a black robed cleric intoning a litany of prayers, as the others stood with bowed heads.

The funeral was more modest than he expected, Charlie decided studying the small cluster of mourners around the open grave. No one seemed to be with anyone else, each maintaining a discreet distance from the other. There were no knowing glances, no whispered conversations, no apparent family relationship; just a group of individual strangers. Standing away from the rest, was a lone slender woman in a severe gray suit and matching felt hat, clutching a patterned umbrella—even though the sun shone brightly.

Charlie had thought the service would be larger than this. Perhaps Arlington, caissons, military color guard, taps certainly. Good God! Not even a flag. He hadn't known what to expect really, but certainly something with more ceremony would have been fitting for a person of Emmett Valentine's stature. The old man had given so much to his country for so long. But, Charlie decided, when a man lives in a clandestine world he is bound to die in the shadows. He felt a slight chill at the thought.

The priest sprinkled holy water on the mahogany casket. Six men in the dark suits of professional pallbearers strained as they lowered the vanishing remains of Emmett Valentine into the waiting grave. When the priest finished, he turned to bestow a final blessing on the mourners who, as soon as it was completed, quickly melted away. Most of them hurried to their nearby cars, while the gray-suited woman strolled to a waiting taxi.

"I thought there would be more to the funeral than this," Charlie put his thoughts into words directed toward Ray Riordan. Brady had gone ahead to bring the car from the outskirts of the cemetery where it was left. "There were only a handful of people in attendance," Charlie added, shaking his head.

"Not many people are aware of his death," Riordan shrugged, guiding Charlie toward the waiting car.

"He wanted it that way?" Charlie asked, surprised at Riordan's response.

He was even more astonished when Riordan answered, "No, I wanted it that way. There is a lot we need to talk about when we get back to my office."

Connelly started to speak, but thought better of it.

Traveling back to Langley, Riordan described how Emmett was found, and how he had died. Charlie listened in shocked disbelief. He wasn't surprised that the old man had met a violent death, it came with the territory. What did shock him, however, was that the death had occurred in his own home.

"Who did it?" he asked finally, as Riordan finished his explanation of Emmett's death.

"Don't know. Wish I did," was the brusque reply. It wasn't easy for him to appear without answers to an outsider, even when the outsider was Charlie Connelly.

"KGB?"

"No, I don't think so," Riordan replied after a slight pause. "Not directly, at least, that's just an opinion, not a fact you understand. The KGB, the SVR or the FSB, or however the hell they now refer to themselves, are typically more brutal when they decide to do away with an enemy. More blunt — more crude. Soft-nosed bullet that would blow off most of his head. This was a smooth, relatively clean hit. Mafia style."

"The Family? Why would they want to do away with Emmett?"

"I don't know," Riordan answered, gazing out the car window. "I really don't think it was them. I was just thinking out loud."

"OK, Ok," Charlie answered exasperated. "Why *was* he killed?"

Riordan replied more quickly this time. "Damn it! I don't know that either. I know you want answers to your questions Charlie. Don't you think I want them just as much — even more than you. It literally came out of the blue. I think his death was meant to send a message, but I don't have any god-damned idea what the message was, or why it was sent."

Afterwards, the three men rode in silence, while Brady maneuvered the Buick through the growing traffic.

Finally, Charlie spoke. "All right I can understand, I guess, that you don't know who killed the old man, or why, but what the hell are you doing about it?" He turned to look directly at Ray Riordan.

"Well *that* I do have some ideas about. We can discuss it when we get to my office," Riordan crossed his arms across his chest effectively ending the conversation.

Despite his inability to answer some of Connelly's questions, the conversation had gone just as Riordan had planned. He felt as sorry as Charlie to see a man with such an illustrious career as Emmett Valentine's end in such an ignominious fashion. He deserved more than just a brief service, with a limited number of mourners, taking place in an obscure cemetery, and miles away from the center of power where he had spent so much of his career. Riordan knew that, and resented being reminded by a relative walk-on.

What were those words he wondered, trying to recall a poem he had learned in grade school? That was it, he finally remembered. It was *The Lay of the Last Minstrel* that contained the phrase he was searching for 'doubly dying shall go down, unwept, unhonored, and unsung.' That didn't quite apply to Emmett though. It described someone devoid of any love for country, but the words were certainly descriptive of the old man's funeral, Riordan concluded.

On the other hand, while he was depressed about the brevity of the service, he was pleased that he had successfully gotten rid of the body. Before the funeral he had arranged to have it hidden away in the cold storage annex, deep in the bowels of the mammoth office building.

Emmett's was probably not the first body hidden away at Langley--either physically or organizationally-- Riordan chuckled to himself. Nor the last, he concluded wondering again about his own career, as their car approached CIA Headquarters.

"Almost there," Brady commented to no one in particular.

Charlie had visited Langley once before at Emmett's request. He was surprised again at the size of the sprawling building they were rapidly approaching. People might think, given the clandestine nature of the Central Intelligence Agency, that it would be housed discreetly and inconspicuously on some back street, hidden away in a remote geographic cranny of the Federal District. This may have once been the case, and probably was, in the formative years of the organization. But, things have changed considerably since then. The present CIA is centered in a mammoth beehive of a structure, somewhat similar in dimension to that of the Pentagon.

As their car approached the entrance, a pair of broad shouldered Marine guards signaled them to stop for inspection. Riordan and Brady displayed their badges to one of the Marines, while the other stared at Charlie. "Visitor," Brady told the guard, reaching out for the necessary form that would allow Charlie to gain entrance to the building. After returning the documents to the guard, a temporary visitor's pass was produced and handed back to Connelly before the group was waved through. Once past the gate, Charlie clutched the armrest as their car suddenly dove down a steep ramp to an underground parking lot and Riordan's designated slot.

As they strode toward the elevator, Charlie stretched his shoulders and flexed the muscles in his back. It had been a long day, and he felt the stress of the unexpected trip, and funeral. He watched Riordan slide an ID card through a small reader by the elevator. The heavy steel doors cracked open, casting a slender column of light on the grimy garage floor.

Seconds later, the doors slid open once more, revealing a large marble-lined lobby. Riordan and Brady, with Charlie in tow, strode toward a larger bank of elevators lining the opposite wall. On the way, Riordan paused, pointing to a statue dominating the entranceway. "That's old William J. 'Wild Bill' Donovan. The founder of this here circus," he added with a wry grin.

"Look up there," he pointed to the inscription on the wall above. "The words were taken from the Bible. John 8.23 I'm told. They were on the wall of the original Agency headquarters, and transferred here when this building was finished."

Charlie squinted, then read aloud,

Ye shall know the truth, and the truth shall set you free.

"Impressive," he ventured, not knowing exactly what to say.

"Yes they are," Riordan replied. "It's just that sometimes it takes a hell of a lot of effort to discover what the truth really is.

"Actually Charlie old boy, that is exactly what I want to talk to you about," he added as the three men squeezed into an already packed elevator.

As the doors drew shut, Charlie caught a glimpse of the Agency's memorial on the lobby's north wall, and the stars carved into the sterile marble.

"Eighty-seven of them" Riordan whispered, referring to the number of fallen CIA agents represented by the individual stars.

Charlie wondered if Emmett's star would become the 88th, or would that be kept secret as well.

5.

Charlie Connelly looked around the office. He and Ray Riordan were alone. Brady had slipped silently into his own workplace, as the three men walked from the elevator. His boss had wanted it that way.

Riordan was thumbing through his "to call" list that had accumulated while he was gone. Charlie's gaze shifted around the office before settling on the bank of clocks decorating the far wall. Interesting he thought, but he really didn't give a damn what time it was in Tokyo, or any place other than Chicago right now. He was curious to find out what Riordan had in mind, but he really wanted to get out of the building and go home.

While Riordan placed a call, Charlie's attention focused on the group of flags stuck in a wooden frame centered on the desk in front of him. The man had really been around Charlie decided, trying to recall the national origin of each banner.

Riordan put down the phone. "Well Charlie, I am sure you are curious as to why I wanted to meet with you. I don't blame you. You certainly have every right to know. You were his close friend."

Charlie shook his head to reject the level of familiarity Riordan's comments suggested.

"No, no, I heard him speak of you often." Riordan offered ignoring the gesture. He cleared his throat and pressed on. "Before I begin, I want to show some of the pictures our people took, before they cleaned-up his place." Riordan took a thin manila file folder from the top drawer of his desk. He removed several of the photos, and spread them in front of Charlie. They were full color views of an old man shot in the back of his head, with blood covering the papers underneath him.

Charlie grimaced and turned away.

Riordan pushed the picture closer to regain his attention. "He didn't deserve to die this way. We think it was someone he knew."

Charlie's brow rose briefly in surprise.

"We believe that because," Riordan continued expecting a greater response, "the door was locked, there were no signs of forced entry, so the killer must have been someone he felt comfortable with."

Charlie began shuffling through the remaining photos, the initial shock fading away. There was nothing to see, just a tidy apartment with nothing seemingly out of place—except a dead man sprawled across his desk. He looked closer at the picture Riordan had thrust toward him. "What are the papers underneath his head?"

"We are trying to find out. They are with the wizards at the lab."

"Nothing else?"

"Nothing—we went back after we removed the body to see if we could find anything that would help us. When we had more time, we conducted a forensic investigation for evidence. We dusted everything for prints. Hell, we even swept the premises for chemical, nuclear, and biological traces that might be present."

"Why would you do that?" Charlie asked becoming even more puzzled.

Maybe you don't remember reading about it, but we have been doing that ever since the Russians knocked off one of their defectors by slipping radioactive plutonium into his tea at a hotel in London. It drove the Brits crazy trying to figure out what happened to him until the tests came back. We didn't have any indication of that here, but we had to be sure."

"Did you have an autopsy for Emmett?"

"Yes," Riordan nodded, "Though it was pretty evident how he died."

Having such a clinical discussion about the death of a friend was beginning to get to Charlie. He wasn't as used to this as Riordan. He shrugged his shoulders. "Look, this is a terrible thing that has happened. I am very sorry about it, I did like and respect the old man, but there is nothing I can do about it."

Apparently, this was the opening Riordan had been waiting for. "I think there is Charlie. That's the reason I wanted to talk to you. I—actually we need your help."

Charlie drew back. He had been around the circuit long enough to know that when someone—in such a sincere tone--asks for your help it invariably leads to trouble.

"No I mean it," Riordan forged ahead sensing Charlie's defensiveness. "Here's the deal. Emmett's death is a big problem for us. If it gets out that one of our people was murdered—let's call it what it is, murder sure as hell--then we look bad. Really bad—you understand?"

"So get someone to investigate and find the killer. You have plenty of people here to assign to the job."

"Not as many as you might think. You have heard of the *war on terror,* it's all hands on deck—full speed ahead."

"So, we don't have anyone we can take off their current assignments to track down a shadow right now. And if we did, everyone would know about it. But, you can do that for us," Riordan offered, steepling his hands and peering over them with a most sincere and engaging expression. "You owe it to the old man."

"You are asking me to find a murderer who is possibly a mole within this organization? You're crazy, that's not my job. Never was. Nothing like it." Charlie was beginning to feel as if he was caught in a fast moving current that was swiftly taking him to a place he really didn't want to go, and he didn't like it. "In the first place," he added angrily, "I don't know why anyone would kill Emmett. Secondly, why would you ask me to find out, and even more importantly, why should I agree to help you?"

Riordan sat back in his chair. He was having more difficulty than he imagined. He had recruited assets during his entire career, and was damned good at it, he thought. But, this was turning out to be different. Charlie had previous experience with the Agency. Maybe knew them better than he did himself. Observing them from the outside might have given the man a better perspective than Riordan anticipated. However, he had to convince Connelly to do a job for him, and it wasn't going all that well.

Finally, he spoke, choosing his words carefully and smiling inclusively. "*Why* is very overrated in our business. *What* and *when* are far more important, and *who* is the absolute imperative of any intelligence operation. Find out *who* and usually everything else will fall into place, but you may never ever find out *why* something happens.

"Let me start over. I-we-need you to help us with the investigation. I know that you haven't been doing this type of thing. You are a corporate guy who analyzes stuff and plans things, and you look like someone who does that. What we need is someone who is analytical, but can get things done, and that is your specialty. Best of all, no one would take you for a spy guy. You provide us with a walking, talking case of plausible deniability.

"I will make sure that you have access to any information you need, and anyone you want to see, and you can go anywhere you like. Just don't take too long doing it. I've got a lid on it now, but I don't know how long I can keep it that way.

"Besides Charlie, it will give you a brief break from what you are doing. You will be helping your country by doing something important. We need you, and your country needs you." Riordan finished, he had given it his best shot, and he thought he could sense Charlie softening a little.

"I would be working here?" Charlie asked after a moment of consideration.

Got him! Riordan realized.

"Yes here. At first, I thought we might put you up in some out of the way office building with a fake name on the door to make it look like you sold real estate or prepared taxes or something like that. Or maybe stick you in a storefront at some nearby shopping center with funny lettering on the window that no one would understand. But I talked it over with the Admiral....

"The Admiral?"

"We have an admiral running the agency now. Actually, he is pretty good. Knows how to run big things, and he came from the NSA so he knows a lot about how secret things work. I checked with him about what I wanted to do, and he agreed to put you here so you have clear sailing."

Charlie recalled reading about the appointment of an Admiral as head of the CIA, and was amused by the nautical terminology that had unconsciously crept into Riordan's speech.

"You know Ray I really don't want to do this; I'm not the right guy for this sort of thing."

Uh-oh, buyer's remorse, Riordan realized, he had seen it before--often actually.

"Sure you are Charlie. You are just the right guy." Riordan leaned forward to appear more sincere. Actually, he *was* being sincere, so it was easier than usual. He really needed Connolly. The man was outside of the Agency, but he had some feel for it, and he had no one to contact other than Riordan. If anyone upstairs learned about Valentine, they would have their own team running around investigating every little thing and pointing fingers in every direction. No one could afford that type of scrutiny.

"Look, take a shot at it for a little while, and then if you want to back-out ok, no harm no foul."

The door opened and Barbara Richards peeked in. "Sorry, I thought you were alone. Your secretary was away from her desk," she blurted, her face flushed. "Sorry," she repeated.

"That's all right, come in." Actually, Riordan was glad to see her. Bringing someone else in now would seal the deal. He sensed an immediate affinity between the two of them. Approximately the same age Riordan guessed, and he knew that both of them took an analytical approach to problem solving.

Introductions and brief explanations were made by Riordan and, after receiving a nod from her boss, Barbara took the seat next to Charlie.

"Barbara knows the Agency; she can give you advice when I'm not available. She's been part of my organization for some time, and I am confident that she is aware of the need to keep your presence just to ourselves," Riordan assured him.

The fact that he could back out if he didn't like what he saw convinced Charlie to give it a try. Riordan was right that he felt a level of commitment to the old man, as well as a need within himself for something to personally commit to, other than passing time in a rose garden. Having someone to turn to within the Agency, other than Riordan, would also be a help.

"How would I even begin finding the killer?" Charlie asked, still uncertain.

Riordan thought for a moment, he wasn't entirely sure himself. "They taught us at The Farm," he began, "that when you are looking for a mole, or a murderer I guess, try to find who had the motivation. To find him,.. or her," he added, "you first need to apply what they called the MICE test."

"The what?" Charlie blurted, Not sure he had heard correctly.

"I know it sounds a little weird," Barbara added in support of her boss, "but listen."

"To find the perpetrator you need to first determine if he did it simply for Money, or because of his Ideology, or if someone is applying Coercion, or if it is simply to support his Ego," Riordan explained. "The hell of it is, there might be a combination of all the factors, and you are back where you started," he admitted.

The meeting apparently over, Riordan rose from his desk and stretched. "I'll drop you off at your hotel, and we will see you tomorrow." Charlie paused briefly before getting up, then rose and followed Riordan out of the office.

Chapter 6.

Charlie sat in an empty office, staring at a bare desk. Abruptly he pounded his fists in frustration. The previous evening had gone badly, and the morning had come suddenly. The night before he had called his wife to tell her he would be staying in Washington longer than expected, and tried to explain his reasoning.

He knew Beth would expect the call, but she was unsympathetic to his cause. When he had left their house, he told her he would be retuning soon. But, his assurance did not make his explanation any more acceptable. He understood that she had heard it all before. The call had not gone at all well.

Shortly after Charlie had fallen asleep, a loud knock awakened him. Going to the door, he was greeted by an angular, seriously bespectacled young man extending an official looking envelope. It was Ken Madden. Earlier in the day, he had been summoned from his familiar cyber world by Ray Riordan with orders to prepare the necessary documentation that would enable Charlie to enter CIA Headquarters. The package Madden offered contained detailed information on which elevator Charlie should take, directions to his new office, how to operate the retina scan, and other necessary details far too numerous to be absorbed that late at night.

Their meeting was brief, but the combination of his conversation with Beth, followed by the young man's presence, enforced the bleak reality of his earlier decision to become involved with the Agency. Charlie now realized the full extent of his decision and fully understood, as a consequence, he was abandoning his former world of clarity and re-entering a new realm of ambiguity. The result was a restless and sleepless night.

The dawn heralded a hot clammy Washington morning. Charlie decided to come to work early—before the rush hit. After nervously showing his new credentials, he was relieved to gain entry to the building without a problem. He seemed to fit in well with the others in the lobby. He had the same sincere and dedicated look that most of them unconsciously exhibited. The dark circles underneath his eyes also contributed to an appearance that was consistent with the drained appearance of his fellow civil servants.

Entering the Agency headquarters was much the same as any large organization he had been a part of. The retina scan was something else. He wasn't exactly sure how to approach it, and he felt self-conscious and a little foolish staring into a small digital peephole. He was glad the corridor was empty. No one saw him having to attempt it twice before the damned thing worked, and his door finally clicked open.

Now that he was inside the office, he had to decide how to proceed. The desk was clean. Only an old worn abacus, lying in the center, gave any sign it was ever occupied. He ran his fingers idly over the rows of beads, but he had no idea what they were intended to produce.

He swiveled to the table behind him. It held an antiquated black metal stereo set. He ran his hand over the sleek top, and pressed the first button available to him. The old black box came to life exhibiting a number of small lights. Immediately the room pulsated with an aria from Puccini's *Madama Butterfly*.

Charlie was startled at the depth of the sound, but smiled at the accompanying recollection of Emmett

Valentine who, he recalled, was sometimes referred to as the *Maestro*.

The cryptonym referred not only to the old man's love of music, but also to his innate ability to orchestrate the complicated activities of his foreign agents. It was like anything else, Charlie mused, some have it and some don't, and Emmett obviously had *it*. Now, Charlie realized, he was the man responsible for finding the person or persons who had ended the Maestro's life. It was a sobering thought that only increased his sense of frustration.

He began to look through the desk. Most of the drawers were empty. The center drawer held a small book with a series of numbers that to him seemed meaningless. It was like a highly abbreviated directory, with numbers arranged in a sequence that was unintelligible.

The bottom drawer held a folder with an assortment of newspaper clippings, each seemingly unrelated to the other. Once he finished searching through the drawers, he opened them all again — individually — carefully — to see if there was anything that Emmett might have taped underneath. There was nothing — not a dammed thing.

As he was attempting to bring some semblance of continuity to files that he had found, he was surprised to see a black skirted, white bloused Barbara Richards entering through a door on the opposite side of the office.

"Just came to see if there was anything you needed," she explained with a smile."Like your music," she added "but, isn't it a little loud?"

Charlie fumbled with the controls, and dialed down the volume. "He liked classical. I'm more of a country western fan," he grinned.

"Did you know him well?"

"Emmett? No, not well but, over the years, we did become better acquainted. I was outside his realm, and he mine, but we eventually developed a degree of familiarity. I recall on one occasion I heard *Madama Butterfly* playing on the other end of long distance telephone line, and asked him if he liked that particular opera. I was surprised at the frankness of his reply."

Charlie leaned back, relaxing in his chair. "He told me Puccini was one of his favorite composers. Then the old man added that he felt very sorry for poor Butterfly. Emmett believed Lieutenant Pinkerton took advantage of her and, after Cho-Cho San renounced her religion and her Asian Culture, the callow Lieutenant, as he referred to him, left her alone and returned to his own country."

"It is very sad, and this is the saddest part of all," Barbara observed as the female vocalist's voice soared above her instrumental accompaniment, "but, I always liked it anyway."

Charlie agreed. "It is a touching story, but I was struck by what Emmett said next. It was late at night, and our overseas connection was good. He seemed to feel like talking. Perhaps he was lonely. Anyway, Emmett told me he often thought this is what the CIA does with its agents. It turns them loose when they have served their purpose, and then coldly proceeds along its merry way.

"Do you agree with him Barbara?" Charlie asked. "Does the CIA throw away their agents when it no longer has any use for them?"

"Sometimes, I guess, but often it can't be helped. Can it?" she added defensively.

"That was Emmett's excuse. He told me that we are constantly at war with a ruthless enemy who wants to destroy our way of life. As soon as we think we have done away with one enemy, another arises. And, the only way we can survive is by being as cold hearted as they are.

"Do you think we are finished with the Cold War, Barbara?"

"We seem to think so here. The Administration believes that we have *reset* it, but I am not sure Putin agrees with that. He seems to be actively opposing us in the Middle East, and quietly undermining us in Eastern Europe. The result could be devastating if we are the only one who is disengaging.

"At least Riordan seems worried that Russia remains a threat," Barbara added. "He believes we are battling a new old enemy, on top of our other problems. That's why he convinced the Admiral to keep Emmett in the fold; he thought he had the capacity to view the world through a different prism than the rest of us.

"Why did you ask me that Charlie?"

"Well I found this in the back of Emmett's desk," Charlie replied, holding-up the list he had found.

"What is it?"

"Read it."

"It's headed **Moscow Rules**," she began, clearing her throat.

Assume nothing

Everyone is potentially under opposition control

Never go against your gut; it is your operational antenna.

Don't look back, you are never completely alone.

Charlie looked at her appraisingly as she read. She was definitely an attractive woman he decided, perhaps a little younger than he was. The white blouse made her tan more pronounced. Made her look quite athletic actually. And, the blond hair (with a tinge of gray) tied in a bun, gave her a scholarly appearance. Practical he thought. Reliable.

Vary your pattern and stay within your cover.

Any operation can be aborted. If it feels wrong, it is wrong.

Barbara cleared her throat again, and looked at Charlie. She may have realized that he was studying her as she read.

Lull them into a sense of complacency.

Once is an accident. Twice is coincidence. Three times is enemy action.

Pick the time and place for action.

There is no limit to a human being's ability to rationalize the truth.

"They sound familiar," Barbara observed when she finished. "The Agency kept pounding those rules, or something like them, into us years ago when I was in training."

"Where did the list come from? Who originated them?"

"They told us they came from a Russian defector who had been with the KGB in Ukraine."

"No wonder the old man had them in his desk," Charlie told her. "I guess he didn't want to forget who his real enemy was.

"But, that was pretty much everything he had there. Just those numbers, some clippings and the damned Rules," Charlie exclaimed in frustration. "I had expected files or something. Anything, anything at all."

"He was very security conscious. That's a certainty."

Barbara thought for a minute. "If you haven't been able to find anything here, why don't you try the file room?"

7.

Barbara led Charlie to the twelfth floor, her high-heels clipping noisily down the deserted corridor. She stopped abruptly at an unmarked door and scanned her card through the tiny reader. Once inside, a vast labyrinth of massive gunmetal gray filing cabinets confronted them. A pixie of a man immediately glided across the tiled floor blocking their further progress. Walter Thorndike, as Barbara introduced him to Charlie, gave the appearance of someone who had spent his life categorizing and organizing documents, and was greatly impressed with his own importance. His pale face was deeply lined, his hair wispy and unmanageable.

Walter shot an admiring glance at Charlie, as Barbara explained that they were there to look through some old files.

"Not possible my dear," he advised condescendingly, "without written permission from a Deputy Director."

"Are you really sure you want to bother him?" she asked reaching for the phone on the cluttered desk.

Her cold stare caused the little man to hesitate. She knew Riordan would not care, but it was a test of her authority, and she was not going to have it questioned by a file clerk.

Barbara had dealt with Walter before, and found him to be an insufferable but necessary little man. Still, he was a gatekeeper who had been there forever and had to be dealt with accordingly. Usually to be cajoled, but she didn't feel in a cajoling mood today. She had too many things to do. Being accepted by Walter Thorndike as an equal did not lead her list.

"Just sign the register then," he demurred, glancing again at Charlie.

"Emmett Valentine's," Barbara directed, as they entered their signatures on Walter's document.

"Valentine?" Walter giggled, punching the name into a massive keyboard. A floor diagram filled with arrows and indecipherable numbers slowly developed on a giant overhanging screen

"Follow me," Walter ordered, walking off at an unexpectedly rapid pace.

"Wait a minute Walter," Barbara ordered.

"Charlie, I have to get back, you don't need me. You are in good hands with Walter," she assured him, flashing an impish grin. "I have the list of numbers you found in the desk. I'll give them to Madden and see if he can make any sense of them. He's never met a number he didn't like," she added, leaving the two men alone.

With Walter leading the way, the two men weaved their way through a forest of filing cabinets. Walter's rubber soled sneakers squealed their progress over the highly polished file-room floors.

Charlie wondered if he would be able to find his way back, and licked his lips nervously. The air was desert dry, and a low moan of the dehumidifiers, straining at their task, filled the room.

"Try this cabinet," Walter advised, pointing to the one labeled V. "Be sure to call me if you need help" he smiled, punching a short series of numbers into the digital cabinet lock. "There is a desk at the end of the next row," he whispered as he disappeared around the corner.

Charlie was alone in a massive alcove filled with secrets, the extent of which he could only imagine. Would those he wanted be here? He was desperate for a lead, a hint, anything that would provide a place to start. Charlie knew the folders could span decades filled with wars--some of them declared, others not. Some of them known, others unknown to people like him. His task could be endless, but his time was not.

He hoped that the most current files would be first—filed chronologically, rather than alphabetically, instead of some more opaque system devised by the intelligence wizards that would further complicate his search. Could that be why Walter was smiling so broadly as he left?

Charlie decided to concentrate only on the first group of folders, which did turn out to be the most recent. If they failed to provide a lead, then to hell with it he concluded, he would have to try something somewhere else.

He extracted the first two bulging folders from the cabinet's top drawer. That was all he could handle without spilling papers all over the floor. The thought of a secret agent scattering secrets as he walked amused him, but he held the files more tightly as he continued.

He stacked the folders on the narrow table Walter had pointed out. The surface had a thin coat of dust. Apparently, the cleaners had missed this area—for some time. The overhead lights provided only weak illumination of the tabletop. The entire file room was cast in gray tones and faint shadows. He fumbled with the switch on an antiquated desk lamp. The bulb, shielded by a green shade, strained to provide a bare minimum of light on the loosely bound pages.

The first documents produced nothing that Charlie could understand or recognize. Paging through the folder it appeared that much of the contents were still encrypted. There were other reports of distant and unrelated covert operations, combined with emails, faxes, and handwritten notes not appropriate for computer retention. Still others were routine budgets, requisitions, meaningless expense reports, and receipts that any organization, even a clandestine one, requires to maintain a record of their basic functions and responsibilities. Such documents were obviously significant to someone, but nothing that he found helpful. Charlie yawned and shook his head to retain a modicum of concentration.

Other sections of the file related to actions a particular agent had taken, or contemplated, in the country where he was assigned. Initially, he was looking for the anomalous individual who might be seeking revenge. As he proceeded through the bound pages, Charlie began to realize what he was examining instead was the documentation of actions taken by shadow soldiers, battling in shadow wars never really declared, and never fully won. He felt intimidated by the level of valor and dedication described in the old manila folder.

The pages began to take on a degree of similarity regardless of the contents or chronology, but nothing that might provide a rational reason for Emmett's death.

Damn, he could use a cup of coffee. Fat chance finding one in Walter Thorndike's document crypt.

Putting the first manila folder aside, Charlie stretched, and began searching through the next file. He was suddenly surprised to come across his own name in the details of a report on Kazakhstan. He began to read Emmett's handwritten notes based on telephone conversations between the two of them. They occurred while Charlie was on a consulting assignment for the Vienna-based Global Bank, after he retired from Apex Electronics. He had almost forgotten about it—tried to anyway.

Charlie settled back in his chair as he once again recalled the details.

The assignment had begun innocently enough. He had sent the Bank a resume in response to an advertisement in the *Financial Times*. Considerable time passed until the bank management got in touch with him, requesting a list of references relating to previous similar assignments. A phone interview followed, and he subsequently received his job description, a contract, and airplane tickets to Almaty.

Once he arrived at the site of the mining project in the Tien Shan Mountains, Emmett contacted him. It was the first time they had talked in many months. Apparently, one of the old man's agents had been killed, throat cut actually, while he worked undercover in the Caspian oil fields belonging to the Kazakh Republic.

The old man believed it was the Russians who killed his agent, and called to warn him that he might also be in danger. It was never clear exactly how Emmett knew where he was, or how to get hold of him. Over the years of his random association with the Agency he had given up wondering about things like that and conceded, if they wished and it was to their benefit, they could contact him wherever in the world he might be.

At first, the project was much like the other consulting assignments he had worked on since retiring. There were other advisors involved, from other places, with other specialties than his own. The lead and zinc mine turned out to be a former gulag under control of the Russians prior to Kazakhstan becoming independent from the Soviet Union. Most of the personnel working the mine remained Russian. The consultant's assignment was to determine, for the new Kazakh Government, if the operation was worth the investment required to continue operations, or if it would be better to sell it to a private company.

To their surprise, the consultants found that the mine had potential for producing strategically critical rare- earth minerals. After that, the men suddenly began to disappear.

52

Charlie, working with the CIA field officer in Almaty, and Emmett in Washington, was eventually able to locate the Chinese operative involved in their deaths. Once he confronted the man with the evidence they fought, and Charlie shot the son-of a bitch. Killed him as a matter of fact.

It was not the first time he had killed someone, but that was Nam. Still, this agent had murdered his friends and deserved to die. He never regretted what he did, but sometimes he experienced flashbacks about the fight. Usually in the middle of the night. He shook his head to rid it of a bad memory.

After he returned from Central Asia, he promised Beth never again. And he meant it. Then.

It was getting late, and Charlie returned the two folders to the filing cabinet before removing others. He rubbed his eyes, and stretched his shoulders before beginning to page through the older documents. Nothing he had found could provide a lead to Emmett's death. The pages contained primarily routine reports of field operations spanning many months, and countless conflicts.

Now, Charlie was more frustrated than before he started. Were there any names that kept recurring he wondered? He rose from the table once more, and began pacing back and forth in the cramped study area. Nothing. Not a damn thing, he answered his own question.

Was there some connection between reports or documents that he had failed to find – a thread not connected to another thread – or one left dangling? Not that he knew. Disappointed, he replaced the folder in the file drawer.

He returned to his chair to reflect on what he had seen in the files. There was only one faint invisible thread stitching all of the documents together. That thread was a red one. He suddenly realized, all of the operations and documents related in one way or another to Soviet Russia.

He sat back and tried to organize his thoughts. Charlie had the distinct feeling he had become trapped in a time warp. The entire Central Intelligence Agency was in mortal combat with al Qaeda. These agents were all out in the real world, wearing Bedouin Robes, burqas, and hijabs while he was sitting in a dusty, dimly lit file room, wearing a Brooks Brothers blazer and Allen Edmunds loafers, assigned to locate a ghost from yesterday's Cold War.

Beth had been right, he should never have come out here. He missed her, but he hated it when she was right.

On the other hand, he knew he needed a challenge — craved it sometimes he reluctantly admitted. He had that now — in spades. At the same time, he readily conceded, his retired corporate contemporaries were playing out their retirement on the golf course at their local country clubs while he, at least, had a stimulating personal challenge to confront.

He returned to the filing cabinet. As he was about to close the drawer, he noticed for the first time every folder had the same three letters in the corner of each cover. His curiosity aroused, Charlie took the pen from his pocket, and searched for a piece of notepaper. Unable to find anything, he looked around to make sure he was alone before tearing a shred from the bottom of an old report. He quickly copied the letters before returning the files to their appropriate cabinet and the note to his pocket.

Afterward, Charlie tried to find his way out through a baffling and seemingly endless maze of identically sized cabinets. The study area was poorly lighted, but the passageways through the files were considerably darker. As he continued searching for an exit, he had the feeling he had become lost in an impenetrable forest, haunted by the ghosts of former agents and past operations. He moistened his lips and continued his search.

Stumbling through the stacks, and about to call out for assistance, Charlie suddenly found himself in the center of a large area bathed in bright fluorescent light. In the center, seated behind a massive desk, was a smiling Walter Thorndike, the king of his file folder realm.

"Can I be of service?" he smiled benevolently, rising quickly to greet his guest.

"Yes you can," Charlie replied, fumbling for the note in his pocket. "These three letters were in the upper right corner of each of Valentine's files. Do you know their significance?"

"Of course I do," Walter replied, pleased at the opportunity to display his knowledge. "They were placed there by the little woman who brought me each folder to be put away. A most fastidious woman. Very pleasant as well. Most of them who come here are not," he sniffed. "She made sure her initials were on each folder before she allowed me to have them."

"Emmett Valentine's secretary?" Charlie asked.

"If you say so, Mr. Connelly," replied the hopefully supportive keeper of the files.

"If those were her initials, what was her name? "

Walter's face fell. "I really don't know. I never asked, It was of no interest to me."

Charlie hoped he had correctly remembered Barbara Richard's floor number as he strode along the seventh floor hallway, attempting to appear as if he belonged there. He was aware that the floor, if it was the correct one, contained the offices of several deputy directors, their support staffs, and a variety of other top Agency officials. It was the epicenter of American intelligence. Windows were coated with material intended to prevent external eavesdropping. Each office was equipped with retina scan or digitally secure locks providing limited personal access. The hallways themselves were constantly monitored with concealed cameras and digitized motion sensors.

Some of the office doors were cracked open, and he could occasionally hear hushed voices coming from inside. He was afraid to ask directions for fear of unnecessarily identifying himself as an Agency interloper, even though his new identification papers made him an official Agency interloper.

It was late in the day, and many of the offices were already dark. Their occupants on the way home to waiting families, or however else they might choose to occupy their off-hours. Charlie feared that Barbara might be one of them.

Other offices were fully illuminated with powerful fluorescent lights. He was relieved to find that she was still at her desk, staring intently at her computer screen.

"Hi there Charlie," Barbara greeted him cheerily, looking up to find him standing awkwardly in her doorway. "Was Walter able to help you?"

"Well he did lead me to Emmett's files. But, I never found anything I thought would help. It's difficult when you don't know what you are looking for, but I didn't come across anything that might seem threatening. The only thing that might be helpful are these initials. They appeared on every file folder. Your friend Walter told me they belong to Emmett's secretary, and I would like to talk to her. She might be able to provide a lead, or have some idea why he was killed."

Barbara tilted her glasses from the tip of her nose and perched them on top of her head. "I recognize the letters.

They belong to Marissa Dolan. She was Emmett's assistant for many years, retired only a month ago. They were always very close," she confided.

It was another disappointment for Charlie. "Do you know where she can be found? I'd like to talk to her if she is still around."

"That's a good idea. I should have thought of that, but around here once you are gone you are immediately forgotten." Barbara picked up the phone and dialed HR. After a brief conversation, she wrote out an address and handed it to Charlie. "She wasn't supposed to give out this information, but she is a friend. We often work-out together."

"And friendship counts?"

"Everywhere, even here at the Company," Barbara smiled, returning her attention to the flickering blue computer screen.

Charlie turned to leave, chuckling at her reference to the CIA as "the Company." He had heard this before, and it always amused him. After spending a career in large corporations, he knew company and the Agency was definitely not like any company he had ever known. In his experience the CIA's principal role was to kill people and break things. A corporation's major objectives were to hire people and make things. He was becoming more aware of the differences with each passing day.

8.

Tysons Corner, Va.

Thunderheads rumbled across the Virginia sky, announcing the approach of another storm. Charlie paid little attention, preferring to focus on his rented Ford's GPS display. The traffic on his side of the freeway was light, with the majority of the cars on the other--the going to work-- side. This provided him a better opportunity to relax, and to think about what he wanted to say to Marissa Dolan.

He was not sure if she knew that her former boss was dead. He should have checked with Riordan before leaving Langley. If she didn't know, it could be a problem. He had drawn a blank going through the files. Since none of the data was computerized, he was unable to cross-reference anything that he found. Now, he had to depend on whatever information Emmett's secretary might be able to tell him. HUMINT, as the spooks like to refer to human intelligence, he recalled wryly.

Hell, he wasn't even certain she would be willing to talk to him at all.

None of Riordan's people seemed to be able to provide a clue—a lead, any damn thing that would help. The more time he spent in Washington the better life in Chicago seemed.

The digitized female voice on the GPS, suddenly warning him of his approaching exit, drowned out Waylon Jennings nasally intoning on the car radio that he was *a Rambling Man.*

Charlie began to pay more attention to what he was doing. Soon, he headed the Ford down the exit ramp, and on a two-lane road leading to Marissa Dolan's small town. The GPS voice continued her clipped directions. "Stop here." "Turn right." "Turn left at the next stop sign." "You are now at your final destination."

Charlie ignored her last command, and wheeled his car around the corner to get a better look at the street. It contained a row of small houses with stately trees shading neat lawns. The same developer had apparently built them all, providing each house with some small distinguishing feature to keep it from looking exactly like its neighbor. The area appeared to be a quiet and peaceful place for an older woman to retire after spending her life with the CIA.

He spent a few more minutes studying the street. There was little traffic, and no walkers. Only a lone mail carrier making daily deliveries, before moving on to the next block.

Charlie switched off the ignition, and got out of the car. It was a half block to the house, and he strolled nonchalantly, as if he belonged there. At Marissa's house, he searched for a doorbell, but found none. There was a heavy bronze knocker, shaped like an oak leaf, and he grasped it and dropped it against the white door, first softly, then more loudly.

When there was no response, he regretted not calling in advance. Still it was early in the morning and she should be home. He looked around quickly to see if anyone could see him before trying again. He waited, expecting the door to surely open. It did not.

There was a slender window beside the entranceway, and he peeked in, but saw no movement. He had come a long way, and he was reluctant to leave without seeing her. On the other hand, what were his choices? Get a cup a coffee and come back again? He considered that, but instead decided to try the backyard, and the back door. Possibly Marissa had not heard him. She was retired, and her hearing might not be as good as it once was.

Charlie skirted around the corner of the house. There was no way he could do it subtly, so he tried to do it quickly. The backyard was empty, but a large bay window next to the door provided a clear view of the kitchen.

He peered into the house before attempting the door. There was a woman seated at the table, bent over as if asleep. He knocked tentatively, afraid of frightening her. There was no response. He thought, perhaps, the back door might be unlocked. He jiggled the latch, but it did not give, and the woman did not stir.

Charlie was perplexed, frustrated, and beginning to become alarmed. He looked around once more before returning to the front entrance. There was the traditional floor mat, but nothing tucked underneath. He ran his hand over the cornice above the door. Nothing there either. Where would a woman who worked for the CIA hide a key?

On each side of the front porch was a large earthenware pot which contained a planting of red geraniums. He ran his fingers through the damp soil of the one nearest him, and quickly withdrew clutching a key. Not too original after all, he chuckled.

The key fit the door lock, and in an instant he was inside the house, closing the door behind him. Standing in the entranceway, he called Marissa's name, first softly, then more loudly. Still no answer. An ominous silence filled the house.

Oh please dear God not her too, he prayed, walking toward the kitchen. His prayer was too late; he was sure of that when he saw Marissa. Her back was to him, her shoulders slumped, and her head rested face forward on the kitchen table.

Drawing closer, he could see that one of the lenses of her glasses had shattered when her head fell forward, and a few tiny shards glistened in the light. Her gray hair fell over her eyes, but he could still see that they were open and glazed. The woman's mouth gaped, making what might have been an attractive face appear grotesque.

Her right arm rested on the table, and her hand clutched the handle of a patterned teacup. Charlie drew back in surprise, recognizing Marissa as the gray-clad older woman he had seen standing alone at Emmett's funeral.

Charlie felt for a pulse on the outstretched wrist, but found none. He tried again, placing a finger on her throat, but he could detect no sign of life there either. He reached for the nearby phone to place a call to 911, but hesitated. Something didn't look right---didn't feel right. First Emmett, and now his secretary. It was too damn coincidental.

What had the Moscow Rules said about coincidences? He couldn't remember. It probably would not have helped anyway. It was also obvious that it was far too late for the emergency responders to assist the very dead Marissa Dolan.

Charlie replaced the phone, wiping off any prints he might have left behind. It suddenly occurred to him that he might not be alone in the house. The body was warm, and the woman's cheeks retained a level of color. He should have thought of this earlier, but he had not. Just another mark of the amateur he thought.

Looking around the small living room it was obvious that Marissa was a good housekeeper. Everything was in its proper place. He could not detect signs of any previous search for documents, or other types of information she might have hidden there. Each book in the bookcase seemed to be where it should be, with all the back covers rigidly aligned. The magazines were stacked carefully on the coffee table, apparently undisturbed by any stranger rummaging through them.

He went over to the mantle above the empty fireplace. There were two pale figurines. One on each end. One of them was a young woman in a frilly dress and bonnet. On the opposite end was a young man in britches and Sheppard's jacket holding a staff. They were both facing each other but were separated by the length of the mantelpiece. Charlie ran his fingers underneath the mantle in case there might be something hidden there.

Charlie crept up the narrow stairway to the second floor as quietly as he could. Even so, halfway up, one of the stairs creaked. He paused to see if anyone had heard. Apparently, they had not. His breath came heavily as he neared the top, and his shirt felt plastered to his back. He wished he had brought a gun, but it was a relief to find no one hiding on the second floor.

The beds in the two bedroom house were neatly made. The drawers in the cabinets were tightly closed, and the clothes in the closet were on their hangers arranged in neat rows. He checked the contents of each drawer but found nothing unusual. The shelves in the closet contained extra bedding, neatly folded. Nothing was hidden underneath the layers.

The cabinet in the bathroom was filled with bottles of medicine, and an assortment of make-up. He closed the door, and moved on. He felt that he was wasting valuable time, but he had to make sure he was not overlooking something that a more experienced person might find valuable.

Apparently, Marissa remained active as the second bedroom contained an assortment of exercise equipment crammed into the limited space.

Returning to the kitchen, he forced himself to look once more at the body. The death seemed too sudden to be normal. How many people die drinking a cup of tea? He whirled the smoky liquid in the cup before sniffing it. He set the cup down quickly. The tea had a distinctive odor to it, and he blew his nose to clear the offensive smell.

Charlie fished in his wallet for the list of contact numbers Barbara had given him the day before. The first one belonged to Ray Riordan, and he punched it into his cell. A secretary answered, and immediately patched him through to her boss.

"You're right," Riordan agreed, after listening to Charlie describe what he had found. "It's not right. Not right at all. I'll get the housekeepers down there to see what they think. Even if it was a natural death, we will want to make sure there is nothing around that might link her to us, and to Emmett. If it was not a normal death we damn sure want to find any evidence that would lead us to whoever is doing this before the local police come plodding through."

Before hanging up, Riordan also asked Charlie to see if he could he find something that would contain a sample of the tea. "We'll want to make sure that our people have a chance to analyze it, before it is accidently thrown out. Then get the hell out of there before someone notices you, and come back here."

Charlie did as Riordan advised, carefully relocking the door and replacing the key in the flowerpot as he left. After that, he attempted to stroll to his car without looking out of place on the still peaceful residential street.

Charlie turned on the ignition, and then sat for a moment reviewing what he had found. He felt bad for Marissa. She had spent her life dealing with secrets for the CIA. Then, when she left the organization, and had safely retired, someone killed her for whatever secrets she knew. Perhaps, for something she never realized she knew.

It began to rain heavily, and Charlie turned on the car's windshield wipers as he pulled away from the curb. He retraced his route through the streets of the small suburb, before picking up speed on the connecting road to the freeway. As he drove, mulling over what he had found, Charlie noticed a car behind him that he had first seen as he was leaving Marissa's neighborhood. The gray Lexus, with its halogen lights cutting through the darkening sky, was now traveling the same route he was taking. Initially, he thought nothing of it, but then the car seemed to be drawing closer-- certainly closer than he cared for.

Charlie punched the accelerator, and the Ford responded immediately. The Lexus also increased its speed. As the two automobiles approached the on-ramp, the trailing driver pulled alongside as if to pass, but instead cut sharply in front. Charlie stomped on the brake, and spun the steering wheel. His Ford swerved and careened off the road, stopping with its front wheels hanging over the shoulder.

The Lexus sped up the ramp, and quickly out of sight. Charlie's breath came in quick bursts. It was over too fast for him to have thought about getting a plate number, and much too dark to have seen it clearly if he had.

Was it just an overanxious driver, Charlie wondered, pulling too close on the damp pavement? Someone eager to get home perhaps—or late for an appointment. Probably just another coincidence he decided, spinning his tires on the tall wet grass before getting his car back on the concrete.

Then he remembered the Moscow Rule about coincidence he had tried to recall earlier. *Once is an accident. Twice is coincidence. Three times is enemy action.*

Glancing down, Charlie noticed that the small bottle holding a sample of tea he had painstakingly collected was now open, and spilled over the car's floor mat. He pounded his fist on the steering wheel and floored the gas pedal, furious with himself for once again being the novice that he was. The road was clear in front of him; the Lex well out of sight.

9

Langley, Va.

Ray Riordan slowly put down the phone. Another death—good God poor Marissa. First Emmett and now Emmett's secretary. He had tried to put a lid on the old man's death to protect the Agency---and his own career. He knew the Ivy Leaguers at Langley would love to get rid of a man like him. He was considered a roughneck—a no class guy. This could provide them with their chance. That was why he brought in Connelly who had no discernible connection to him or the CIA. He had thought he had it handled, zipped up tight, but now he was not so damned sure.

He had learned long ago, when you are dealing with a bureaucracy it's not possible to play a simple tune and expect people to dance to your melody. Bureaucracies need complex arrangements, involving many musicians or your song will never be heard. That was why he had Connelly. He didn't want to draw attention to his own organization— being heard was the last thing he wanted. Maybe he had handled it poorly at the outset, but it was too damn late to change now. He was committed, whether he liked it or not.

"Linda," he shouted, "get me Frank." Frank Hawkins was the head of the Housekeepers. They were the ones who tidied-up bad things for Langley. They had two major qualities. They were neat—damn careful actually, and more importantly, they could keep their mouths shut. They also had very bad memories-- some said convenient memories. They forgot what they did immediately after they did it.

Linda placed the call then, like all good secretaries, she listened in:

"Frank? Thanks so much for picking-up so quickly." It never hurt to keep these guys in good favor. Riordan proceeded to relate what Charlie had told him about finding Marissa Dolan.

"She sure looked dead," he informed his friend on the other end of the line. "Could be natural—and pigs could fly. You know after what you saw at Emmett Valentine's office—well this woman was his long-time secretary. Worked for him for years. And, you knew they were close—very close. She knows—knew—practically everything he did. If someone killed him for what he knew, it makes sense that the same person would have to kill her as well.

"Linda get me Marissa's address," he hollered, holding a beefy hand over the phone and listening to Frank Hawkins at the same time. "And another thing, Connelly told me she was holding a cup of tea when she died. Yeah—yeah tea, that's what I said tea. Should you wear your whities? What? Oh yeah the hazmat suits. Good idea. Could be anything in the tea. Just like what got that poor bastard Litvinenko in London.

"You have never heard of a man called Litvinenko? Well it has been a few years ago. He was a former KGB agent. Got in trouble with Putin for speaking out against him. Did hard time in Russia and fled to Britain and eventually became a British citizen. Against their advice, he continued to criticize the Kremlin up until he had a meeting with a couple of Russians in a London hotel. He had a cup of tea with them, then went home and collapsed. The Brit doctors finally decided that he had been slipped a tiny amount of thallium. It destroyed his immune system, and he eventually died. Good-bye defector.

"Anyway Frank, do me a favor would you? See if you can wait to put the suits on inside the house. I understand that it is a quiet suburban neighborhood. Try to slip in and out of there in the night, would you please?

"Yeah, yeah, night. I know, overtime. I'll authorize the old OT, just try to do it discreetely.

"And Frank, don't forget to bring back a sample of the tea. When you get it back here, have the doc's check for everything that could have killed her, and let us know what they find out. I'll remember this old pal. And keep it quiet for us like always."

Riordan put down the phone, and looked around the office. "Linda get me Ralph Gross. He is out of the office? Leaving tonight for Cairo. Then get me Brady." He should probably have called Brady first anyway, but somehow when things go sideways he always relied on the man with the muscle. Always did. Always would.

He was still upset that Emmett was dead. It shouldn't have happened like that. The old man was a warrior and warriors should die in battle not at a desk. The old man was a different type. Most of the spymasters he had known were self-absorbed bastards. They had the ability to manipulate people without feeling any empathy for them—ends justify the means type of people—but Emmett cared. He cared for his people, and he cared for his country, and now he was gone. Riordan decided, once again, that he would do everything he could to get the old man's killer. It was the right thing to do.

Brady came into the office quicker than Riordan expected. That was good, he thought. That was what an assistant should do. Quick, he liked quick. Brady sat down, and Riordan filled him in on what Charlie Connelly had found, and then brought him up to date on sending the housekeepers in to clean up the Marissa Dolan *situation*.

"Unless Connelly comes up with something new, I don't know where we go from here," Riordan complained. He looked at Brady, hoping for a suggestion.

Brady stared blankly at his Boss. "Well you might talk to Madden and see if he has anything," he finally offered. "Connelly found some numbers in Valentine's desk and gave them to Barbara who then, since they were numbers, gave them to Madden. Maybe he has come up with something."

"Linda find Ken Madden," Riordan yelled, glad to have an avenue to explore.

The two men sat silently, trying not to look at each other while they waited for their numbers man to appear. It was unusual for them not to have the answers, and they presently had none.

They didn't have to wait long before Madden's slim frame slipped through the doorway.

"Hello there my boy." Riordan greeted him with strained joviality, "I understand you have some numbers that Connelly found. Have you had a chance to run them through your computer yet?"

Riordan knew that the young man was not used to being summoned to the boss' office on such short notice. Usually Riordan had as little to do with him as possible. It wasn't that there was any animosity between the two of them; it was just that Riordan didn't care for—didn't understand really—the service he had to offer.

"No I haven't," Madden stammered.

Riordan's face fell. Brady rose from his chair and went over to the window.

"I didn't have to use the computer." Madden added quickly, "I just looked at the numbers for a few minutes, and understood what they were."

"And?"

Not getting an immediate reply Riordan roared, "what in the hell were they?...Or are they?" he added less forcefully.

"They are actually octal numbers," Madden replied with a nervous smile.

Both Riordan and Brady greeted this information with blank stares. Brady had returned from the window to his chair. Perhaps too soon.

It was not as if Riordan actively disliked Madden, but it was because of times like this when you had to work to get an answer explained. He didn't want answers that you had to take a college course to understand. Anyway, he had always been suspicious of men who rode bicycles to work...wearing rubber suits.

"Oh yes octal numbers," Riordan cleared his throat...."so what are octal numbers? I seemed to have forgotten their significance."

"As you know, "Madden began.

Riordan knew damned well when someone — anyone — his wife even, began an explanation with 'as you know' you were in for trouble. Or at best being bored to death.

Madden substantiated the point by repeating his opening line. "As you know, binary, hexadecimal, and octal are all different ways to represent a number. A number can be perfectly converted between the various systems without any loss of numeric value. We are most familiar with the decimal system because it is based on the power of ten. That is," Madden was warming to the subject, a beatific smile on his face, unaware he was riding this horse alone, "the numbers 0,1,2,3,4,5,6,7,8,9. With these ten numerical symbols, we can represent any quantity we want. When we run out of symbols we combine them, for example 1 with 0 for 10, 1 with 1 for 11, etcetera and etcetera."

He looked around the room for understanding, or at least acceptance. Failing both, he continued. "The binary system which depends only on 0 and 1 was useful for the early digital computers because one represented an electrical impulse, and zero the lack of one. You first converted decimal to octal and then octal to binary.

"The octal system?" Brady interrupted, attempting to get the train back on the track.

Madden now realized he had lost his limited audience, and made a last stab at recapturing them.

"You remember the film *Avatar*," he stated, attempting to rely on pop-culture. "Well the language of the extraterrestrial race that the film is based on utilizes an octal numbering system, probably because of the fact that the people of the Na'vi race, featured in the film, have only four fingers on each hand. And, in contrast, we the people of the human race have five fingers and ten on both hands."

He looked at his audience with satisfaction, hoping for a semblance of understanding.

"So what are the frigging numbers," Brady shouted, unable to take the lecture any longer.

"They are telephone numbers," Madden blurted, attempting to raise his voice to the same level as Brady's without appearing overly hostile.

"Telephone numbers?" Riordan asked in astonishment. "Why in the hell would Valentine write telephone numbers in octal?"

"I don't know," Madden conceded. "Probably because he could convert them easily, and they wouldn't be readily understood by anyone who would casually come across them."

"Well I guess we are proof of that," Brady agreed.

"Whose telephone numbers are they?" Riordan asked, relieved they were finally getting somewhere.

"Once I had converted them, I ran them through the listeners at the NSA. They could come up with most of them. They didn't seem to be anything particularly interesting with those — family and stuff like that."

Riordan kicked the leg of the table in disgust. It startled both Madden and Brady.

"There were a couple however — overseas numbers-- that the buggers couldn't identify," Madden quickly added, then hesitated as he turned to see Charlie Connolly entering the room.

Riordan rose from his desk, motioning toward an empty chair at the table. "Glad you dropped by. That was a hell of thing about Dolan. Any idea what happened?" he asked, glad for any excuse to change the subject.

Madden and Brady were unaware of what their boss was referring to, until Charlie quickly filled them in on what he had found

Riordan once again took command of the meeting. "Did you know that the numbers that were in Valentine's desk were telephone numbers converted from the decimal system to octal?" he asked, handing Charlie the list that Madden had prepared.

Charlie looked at Riordan and laughed. "Hell no! Of course I didn't." It had been a long day, and he had no idea what the man was talking about.

"Wait a minute; I do recognize the first number." It was the one most frequently called, and one the NSA couldn't peg. "It belongs to Vincent St. Claire.

"Get me a plane ticket to Vienna," Charlie ordered. "Business Class," he added quickly.

As charlie Connelly made preparations to leave for Vienna, Ken Madden slipped quietly out of the office, returning to his pale gray world of zeroes and ones.

10

The Austrian Air Triple 7 dipped and then regained altitude before circling Dulles and heading east. Charlie reclined his seat, and tried to situate his long legs in a more comfortable position. He had been surprised to recognize Vincent St. Claire's telephone number topping Emmett's special list. He should not have been, he supposed. He knew the two men had shared a similar background, and were as close friends as two men ever get in a world where whispers are treated as shouts.

Now, he wondered if he should have mentioned to Riordan about his run-in with the Lexus. But what would it have gained? Nothing, he concluded. He would have ended-up looking like a chump. No marks on the rented Ford, and no identification of the driver, so what was there to tell? If it was meant as a warning, he had failed to get the message. To hell with it, he decided deferring the incident to an ancient memory.

He ordered a Bombay martini and, after a few sips he began thinking once again about his own situation. What was that quote from the *Godfather*, he tried to recall? Then it came to him. "Just when I thought I was out they pull me back in again." That was it. That sums it up. That was how he felt about the CIA. Just when he thought he was done with them, they brought him back in again.

He was sure Beth would agree. She was angry when he called to tell her he was going to Vienna for a quick trip. She knew damned well what that meant. He was chasing shadows again. She didn't understand. How could she? She didn't' feel the sense of responsibility to the Agency he did. She did feel, however, a similar if not greater responsibility to her family. The two had always presented a conflict.

Charlie's mind raced back to his first active role with the Agency. It was in Lima. Up to that time, his association with them had been limited to providing advice — answers to questions that some unknown faceless person in Washington had dreamed up, and sent out to the Chicago office for follow-up. Actually, he was somewhat flattered by their attention, and always tried to provide a different and authoritative perspective.

These meetings had been going off and on for over a year-- more off than on actually. Then it changed when Washington came directly to him in the form of a young woman operative by the name of Karen Kincaid.

He smiled recalling their first meeting. *Tall and tan and young and lovely,* the opening line from Carlos Jobin's "Girl from Ipanema" ran through his mind as she entered his office and showed her identification. Washington had called earlier to tell him that someone would be coming, but he had not expected someone quite like her.

She was a willowy woman, wearing a tailored dark blue suit, white blouse and a small but, he guessed, expensive string of pearls. Attractive as she was though, there was an air of aloofness about her as she sat down, straightened her skirt, and stared directly at him. She was sizing him up for herself. He fully understood that, and didn't mind at all. As a matter of fact, he liked it. It was the professional thing to do.

She was not that young he found later, probably around the age of Barbara Richards, he suspected. The Agency must have had one hell of a recruiting class around that time to bring in that quality of female agents.

The CIA knew he had been traveling to Peru frequently. They tracked those things then — and probably still do. The South American country wasn't the bucolic home of the Incas that you see in the travel photos. Not even close. At that time, the Sendero Luminoso, a radical group run by a man named Abie Guzman, paralyzed Peru. Their intent was to take over the country, and turn it into a Communist *paradise* like Mao had done for China. It seemed ironic; at the time China was becoming more capitalistic—*capitalism with a smiling face* they called it-- Guzman was trying to take Peru backwards in both time and philosophy. It was more than bad timing; it was ludicrous. That didn't stop the radicals, however, from blowing up anything they could find in Lima.

The Agency had made contact with a group that was actively opposed to the radicals. It was an underground organization they believed they could trust, more than the Peruvian Police. As Karen had explained it, they needed someone not connected to the American Government to get a sizable amount of cash to their friends. A NOC, someone traveling under non-official cover—not going in and out of the American Embassy as their own operatives did. Most importantly, she convinced him that he would enable them to maintain an aura of *plausible deniability.* Just a little favor, next time he went down, Karen explained. She apparently knew he was leaving for there in a couple of days.

Charlie agreed. Somehow he always did. What harm could it do? Just a little errand. She gave him two envelopes. The large one-held the money, and the small one contained his instructions.

The park was directly across from the Palcio de Gobierno, the official home of El Presidente. As he sat on the park bench, he watched the red and black uniformed guards, with their gleaming gold Roman style helmets and glistening silver swords, begin the slow goose-stepping ritual that marked the daily changing of the guards.

With his attention diverted by the ceremony, he was surprised to feel a slight brush against his hand. Instinctively he recoiled clutching more tightly the cash filled envelope wrapped, as they had directed him to do, in a copy of the Wall Street Journal. Turning, he saw a nun cloaked in a full-length black habit and white scapular collar. After whispering the words he was told to expect, she casually picked up the paper and rose to leave. He watched in astonishment as the tiny woman glided away on hidden feet, the paper already magically concealed somewhere within her long flowing robes.

Later in the day, still on the Agency's dime, he hailed a cab and directed the driver to take him to the *La Rosa Nautica*. It was a favorite ocean front restaurant of his that he had suggested to the Agency to use as a meeting place.

It was early in the evening, but the place was already beginning to fill with the important makers and takers of Peruvian society.

He found a place at the crowded bar, ordered a Pisco Sour, and watched the sun begin its daily dive below the coastline. Suddenly he felt a tap on his shoulder and turned to see a small attractive brunette, fashionably dressed, with flashing dark eyes. There were no words exchanged. Nothing said, as she brushed against him and slipped a note into his pocket. Before he realized what had happened she turned and made her way toward the restaurant's door.

Many eyes followed her exit, but he focused his attention on the note he had just received. It was a signed receipt for the money he had delivered earlier in the day. Was this the woman who received the money he wondered? Or perhaps someone else? He never found out, but always remained curious.

The flight attendant delivered his dinner, distracting from his reverie, and returning him to the present world 27,000 feet above the Atlantic.

The Austrian Airline's tray provided a too small filet, too well done, accompanied by an over-baked potato. The

Austrian Riesling, however, was excellent as was the tiny chocolate torte.

There was a time when a cigarette would have been in order at the end of a meal. But that was long ago, even though it would still be welcome.

He had already seen the in-flight movie--a year ago. It was still too early to try to sleep.

He recalled the file folder Brady had given him as he was about to leave Riordan's office. It had surprised him at the time that the assistant had not mentioned it earlier during the meeting. It was done so casually he had forgotten about it until now.

Charlie glanced around the cabin. Most of his fellow passengers were engrossed in the movie, or had fallen asleep. The flight attendants had finished clearing the dinner trays, and were directing their activities toward cleaning up the galley, while chatting amiably with each other. He was the only person in his row, so he felt confident that no one else could see what the folder contained.

There was a handwritten note, with William Brady's name printed at the top, paper-clipped to the two following pages. Charlie shifted position to take better advantage of the plane's small overhead light. It was still hard to determine what the document contained. Part of the problem was the poor quality of the image, and the gray tone of the paper. Brady's note informed him that he was looking at the results of the scientist's effort to resurrect the blood soaked papers found underneath poor old Emmett's head.

Charlie rotated the paper toward the light. The first sheet contained a picture of an extremely well-endowed young woman, in a daringly low cut gown, smiling coquettishly into the camera lens, while holding a pistol suggestively alongside her pouty cheek. He could not stop staring at the image. The woman was beautiful all right, but why would Emmett find her so intriguing?

While he had been able to determine what the first sheet contained, he was still unable to make any sense of the second. He rose from his seat, he had wanted to stretch anyway, and headed for the rear of the plane.

The light was much better inside the lavatory. Placing the two sheets of paper side by side on the counter, he could see that there was a picture of the same young woman, standing alongside Dmitry Medvedev, the former President of Russia who had been bookended by Putin. Dmitry was smiling broadly while awarding her one of the country's most important medals for her espionage activities in the West.

It was now clear to him why Emmett was studying the picture of the young woman, but what did it mean? With a jolt, he recalled the furor at the time of the woman's arrest in the United States, but he was foggy on the details. Why, he wondered, would someone kill a man for possessing information that was widely known?

Charlie returned to his seat, and dimmed his overhead light. Now he had more questions than before he was given the reprocessed documents. Hopefully, he would be able to find the answers in Vienna.

11

Vienna

The Austrian Air flight made a bumpy landing at the Vienna's Schwechat *Flughafen*. It had turned out to be more turbulent over the Atlantic than Charlie expected, and he was glad to be on the ground. After finishing the cognac the night before, he had dropped off to sleep. It still proved to be a restless night, and he felt tired.

Soon Charlie joined the other deplaning passengers squeezed tightly together on the airport bus that was transporting them across the asphalt tarmac to the waiting terminal. The Vienna airport was smaller than most in Europe, and he had been there often in the past, using it as a convenient transfer point for ongoing flights to the Mideast and Africa. Inside the terminal, a variety of odors filled the stale air, and he looked around for a familiar marker.

The Vienna airport had become one of the crossroads of the new global economy. The waiting lounge area was filled with tired, sprawling passengers wearing kaftans from Kuwait, dashikis from Africa, saris from India, with an occasional Englishman in tweed suit and regimental tie sprinkled among the mix.

Charlie soon found the luggage area, and claimed his bag. The customs zone was nearby, and he passed through it easily with his newly minted passport. It seemed that Ken Madden had been very thorough in providing all the necessary documents for his revised identity.

The air outside was crisp, bearing a forewarning of approaching fall. Some of the people strolling along the early morning streets were already wearing sweaters and coats as they went about their daily business.

Austria, the land of Strauss, strudel, and spy craft Charlie reflected, as the taxi sped toward his appointment with Vincent St. Claire at the Global Bank. The former center of the Hapsburg Empire had traditionally been a neutral island at the center of conflict and, as a result, functioned as the hub of European espionage activity for generations.

During World War II, the German Army made a relatively effortless occupation of the country that was once Hitler's birthplace. After the war, the Allies divided Vienna into four zones, with intelligence operations of the United States, France, Russia and Great Britain actively competing for an unfair advantage. Their covert activities continued during the Cold War, and intensified more recently with the additions of Asian and Mid Eastern services. Now the stealing of secrets had become more involved, focusing on commercial and technical intelligence rather than merely political.

This result has been the development of a different type of agent exchanging secrets with their more sophisticated controls in the elegant coffee houses scattered along Vienna's Graben Strasse. While the direction of intelligence activities has changed, the level of activity had not, and most believe that Vienna continues to remain the legendary bridge between East and West and the center of western intelligence activities.

Charlie was well aware of the city's history as his cab entered the Ring Road, and shortly deposited him in front of the imposing Global Bank Building. It was a commanding structure, with a marble-sided facade meant to instill confidence in anyone who might enter through its elegant revolving doors.

The empty elevator sped him to the fifth floor where a stylishly dressed older woman greeted him. She smiled, and rose stiffly from her desk.

"Mr. Connelly?" she confirmed, leading him toward an imposing mahogany door. "Mr. St. Claire is expecting you."

"Ah my good man, so good to see you again." Vincent St. Claire greeted him warmly, motioning as he did toward a leather chair facing his desk. "So sorry to hear about Emmett, but it was good of you to call."

Making himself comfortable, Charlie could see the spires of several of Vienna's centuries' old churches framed in the large office window. A consortium of Western countries had established The Global Bank at the end of the Cold War to aid in the transition of former Soviet countries from a command economy to a more market-oriented structure. The directors placed Vincent St. Claire in charge of the Bank's activities to guide it through the transitory period. He had remained ever since.

It had been some time since the two had met. Charlie studied the older man closely. Vincent was tall, thoroughly British in appearance and demeanor. He was viewing *old school* Charlie realized, very old school. Vincent was a distinguished looking man, dressed in a starched white shirt, striped tie, a crisp gray pinstriped suit with creases that could draw blood, topped off with a silk handkerchief casually hanging from the breast pocket.

The years had been kind to Vincent. He had acquired a few more wrinkles since they last met, and his hair had turned a distinctive white. He remained, as he had always been however, a distinguished gentleman. He was the type of man who would generate confidence in anyone he met. As Charlie studied the man across from him, it was apparent that Vincent was beginning to move about in the restricted manner older men sometimes do, but his speech remained quick and decisive, lacking the brittleness that people his age sometimes exhibit.

Vincent didn't inquire why Charlie was there. He knew. Once he learned that Emmett had been murdered he knew someone would come looking—wanting to talk to him to get a lead on who it might be. When Charlie called to set up a meeting, he understood he was the one who was chosen—and he knew why.

"Emmett was the one who suggested I send you on that Kazakh assignment," he began their discussion. Charlie stiffened with surprise. Before he could reply, Vincent continued. "He had this problem out there; someone had killed one of his agents working in the Caspian Region. He couldn't afford to send anyone else to look into it, and he knew the Bank was involved in this mining project there. You had worked on that Ukrainian thing for us so we agreed you would be the perfect person to go. It worked out well for all of us. You got a job, the Bank got the project finished, and Emmett found out who had killed his man. By the way, I was never sure exactly how that turned out?"

Charlie filled in the blanks for Vincent. "Once we found who was trying to sabotage the mine, we were able to make a connection through the man's wife in Almaty to someone in the Russian Embassy. After that, we could figure out who had scrubbed Emmett's guy. So it worked out, as you say, well for all of us."

"You and he go back a long ways don't you Vincent?" Charlie thought he had better get more control of the direction their conversation was taking.

"Back to the beginning, I guess." The older man leaned back in his chair and gazed out the window to better focus his thoughts. "Emmett had been with the OSS during the war, running agents in France. Immediately after the war ended the Cold War began. The OSS became the CIA, and they assigned Emmett to London to work as liaison with our far more experienced MI6. We worked closely together for several years. He, at that time, was the rash American, and I tried to provide the pensive counterpart."

A shadow of a smile crossed the old man's face.

"Tea?" Vincent interrupted his own monologue. Charlie nodded his agreement. "Gerta tea, please," Vincent spoke softly into the large intercom on his desk.

"Where was I? Oh, yes. One thing Emmett excelled at, even then, was recruiting and running agents. He had a knack for people. Instilled confidence in them. Disillusionment and dollars are the two principal factors that cause a person to betray his country. He knew that, and he used his knowledge superbly.

"His talents were honed further as the Cold War progressed. We worked at a time when the two nuclear powers — there were only two then you recall-- operated in an environment referred to as one of Mutually Assured Destruction or MAD as they liked to call it euphemistically. Emmett since has told me that we were the original Mad Men." A thin smile again creased Vincent's lips. "Long before it became a popular television show."

The old man cleared his throat. "As the years passed, we kept in touch. Exchanged information — that type of thing. Until my wife finally convinced me that it was time to hang up my cloak, sheath my dagger, and leave MI6 behind." The old man chuckled at his turn of phrase. "I used the contacts I had made working in global intelligence to become an investment banker, finally ending up here in Vienna as director of this institution."

Vincent grew silent as Gerta entered the office and deposited a large silver tray in the center of his desk. In addition to the tea service, she had added several slices of *Sacher tortes*. After she left, Vincent passed the plate of chocolate covered orange cake to Charlie, and resumed his narrative.

"Time passed. Both of our wives passed with it I'm afraid. Our mutual loneliness drew us closer together. I maintained a fascination with the intricacies of the *black science* of foreign intrigue and Emmett was still mucking around in the shadows, running spies in the more god-forsaken areas of the world. My position here allowed me to—so to speak—keep my hand in the game. We helped each other when we could."

Charlie could not contain his curiosity any longer. "Did Emmett give you any idea what he was working on when he was killed?"

Vincent stared out his window once again. It was a beautiful view. "Nooo" he exclaimed through pursed lips. Turning back to stare at Charlie he replied. "Nothing I can put a finger on."

"Take a look at these papers," Charlie asked, pushing the folder across the desk. "These were found where he was shot."

"Why is the paper so distorted? It looks strange."

Charlie had not intended to open this subject if he could avoid it. "They were soaked in blood," he replied softly. "The wizards at Langley worked with them to recover the images."

Vincent let the pages flutter to his desk. "I recognize that woman." He pursed his lips in a low whistle, "and I remember the incident. We spoke about it at the time. Emmett thought there was more to it than met the eye. You Americans have some rare references," he smiled condescendingly.

"As a matter of fact, Charlie my friend, I have a file I built on the situation. It tells quite a story. You can have it; I no longer have any need for it."

Charlie nodded his gratitude, while Vincent worked the intercom. Soon Gerta entered the room with a large file folder. Vincent pointed to Charlie and she deposited it on the desk in front of him. "Keep the damn thing; I don't want to see it again."

Charlie glanced through the folder quickly, and put it in his briefcase.

"Why was the NSA unable to peg the telephone number that Emmett had for you? The one I used to get in touch when I was working in Kazakhstan?" Charlie asked Vincent, shutting the clasps on his briefcase. "If I knew, why didn't they? That's what they do."

Vincent did not answer immediately. Instead, he swung his chair around so he could better look at Charlie. Study him better. The old man was beginning to show signs of fatigue.

"You have that number because I gave it to you when you were going to Central Asia. I feared that you would be unable to reach me over a regular line."

"I don't understand," Charlie frowned.

"You probably don't," Vincent smiled. "That is the way it is supposed to be.

"The world is not the way it used to be. You are younger. You may not recognize it, but let me assure you that it is drastically and dramatically changed. The English have not been the same since we lost Suez. Our empire has been growing smaller ever since--along with our ambitions. We have had to depend on you, and as you might expect we resented that dependency.

"Now your country is beginning to show the signs of strain. No longer willing to assume your normal role of ascendency. You are more tentative now, and it leaves a vacuum.

"Concurrently we have the rise of Islam, and the Russian bear is providing a new old enemy with strategic objectives that are ominous if not overly apparent. They seem to be tilling the fields in Syria and Iran in order to gain control over the entire Middle East. "As far as both our intelligence systems are concerned," Vincent continued, "the two of them have become leaky boats. We have had our Cambridge Communists, and you--why just look at the Wiki-leak debacle and now the revelations of your PRISM program at NSA. In addition, the Chinese have stolen all of your defense secrets as easily as if they bought them at— what is the name?" Vincent paused for a moment then burst out, "Costco, as easily as if they had bought them at Costco." He smiled broadly at his clever analogy.

Charlie was surprised to hear Vincent speak at such length, and so candidly. Normally he was more reserved, but the subject seemed to be an extreme irritant to him.

"Well, some of the old hands have had enough. We got together and used our resources to establish an alternate algorithmic communications grid. We formed the new grid to communicate just among ourselves."

"Who is on your grid?" Charlie asked, astonished at what he was learning.

"There are a limited number from the CIA, some active and some ostensibly inactive. There are a few of us with MI6 backgrounds, some with the German BND, the Vatican, and a very select few with the Mossad."

"The Vatican?" Charlie repeated, shocked.

"Oh yes, they are not very active now, but they were instrumental in fighting the Communists in Eastern Europe during the Cold War. You must know that the Papists were gathering global intelligence long before any of the rest of us."

"And Emmett was...?" Charlie's voice trailed off.

"Oh yes. Emmett very definitely was on the grid."

"There was this other number on his list that the NSA couldn't find."

"It was?"

Charlie searched in his pocket for his note. "The second one," he told Vincent handing him the folded piece of paper.

"Oh yes, I recognize that number. She is certainly on the grid." Vincent smiled broadly. "She would love to hear from you, I am sure. She could be of immeasurable assistance I believe. She is very active with the Mossad. You must, by all means, give her a call."

As Charlie was getting up to leave he heard Vincent say, "Just a minute old friend, I have another file that I prepared for you. It is just a brief description of some of those within our organizations who have betrayed our trust in the past. It may give you a better idea of what you might be looking for now."

Charlie took the file and put it in his briefcase, along with the other information Vincent had provided. As he was about to go through the office door he heard Vincent's final remarks. "Emmett always told me find the mole, and you will find your answer."

12

Fading rays of sunlight bathed Vienna's historic buildings in a half-light. Charlie stared distractedly out his hotel room window, thinking about his earlier meeting with Vincent St. Claire. Papers from the old man's file on the American spies were scattered carelessly across his hotel room's desk. The file had the title *Operation Ghost Story*, a term, he learned later, originated with the FBI. In it, the spies were referred to as Illegals because they had assumed stolen identities of Americans. They worked under the direction of SVR headquarters, known in the West as *Moscow Center*.

He had begun to page through the contents immediately after his return from the meeting with Vincent, but he had become discouraged. He was impatient, hoping to find an immediate answer, and it had not presented itself on a cursory reading of the clippings. Charlie had spent most of his life in a highly controlled corporate environment, and he was not used to the poorly choreographed chaos that his life had suddenly become.

He turned away from the window and returned grudgingly to the articles on his desk. They painted an interesting caricature of an established Russian sleeper cell, deeply embedded — deep cover agents they were termed-- in American society over a period of many years. The most prominent of these operatives was Anna Chapman, the glamorous young woman whose picture Emmett Valentine was studying when he died.

It had to be more than coincidence, and the shooter had to be someone Emmett trusted to allow him into his apartment, and later take a position that would permit a shot to the back of the old man's head. Someone as experienced as Emmett, schooled and skilled in tradecraft, would never allow a person he feared get around to his back.

On the other hand, Vincent would not have accumulated the file just for the fun of it. He was an important man with many responsibilities. This type of person did not spend time collecting irrelevant newspaper articles unless he believed they might later provide some valuable purpose.

As he thought more about their meeting, Charlie became increasingly convinced that Vincent had not told him everything he knew — or if not *knew*, certainly thought-- about the circumstances surrounding the murder of his old friend. A person like Vincent, who had spent his career in the realm of intelligence, is not quick to volunteer information. Over time, they become intuitively protective of their sources and methods. Secrets have a way of ingraining themselves into a person's character, until they become all consuming. Vincent, in all likelihood, was not immune to this.

There had to be something in the file Vincent thought would provide a possible lead, and Charlie began combing through the contents once more, with even greater care. There were 10 of them, he recalled, trained from childhood in the art of espionage.

Over the years of the Cold War, there had been continuing speculation that Russia had established, and actively operated, a Potemkin-like village expressly for the training of future agents and their eventual assimilation into American culture. The Russian village, so it was said, was constructed to appear like an average American town. Operatives who were intimately familiar with the varying American idioms, accents, colloquialisms, and gestures trained the prospective agents. The trainees read American papers and magazines, listened to the Voice of America for news as well as pronunciation; and were eventually expected to fit in to American society as if they originated there. It was likely that members of this sleeper cell trained under comparable circumstances.

Anna Chapman first surfaced in England as an economics student with a Russian accent who subsequently married an aspiring British artist. The *UK News of the World* quotes her husband regarding their marriage, and innovative sex life, as exceptional. The article went into considerable detail regarding whips and other methods of bondage, including their entry to the *mile-high club*. She eventually left him, and traveled to the United States where she made contact with other Illegal's, as they were referred to by the SVR because of their stolen identities.

Several of these operatives were *coupled* by Moscow Center, prior to their departure to the United States, and encouraged to have children together to enhance their deep-cover status. These Russian agents had established their false identities with the intent of becoming Americanized in order to build long term relationships with important sources, and gather classified information without raising suspicion. When they were arrested, the spies had seven children ranging in age from one to twenty years old. Most of them were born in the United States.

The Russian agents attempted to obtain military secrets, as well as political and economic information. One of the members worked for several years as the in-house computer technician at an American consulting firm, which advised clients on how government decisions might affect global markets. Company managers at the firm included an important Democratic fundraiser, and a former Federal Reserve vice chairman.

Another one of them was able to get close to a scientist who was working on bunker-buster nuclear bombs. He unknowingly provided information on small yield high penetration nuclear warheads recently authorized by Congress. The members also sought out information on other aspects of pentagon planning, as well as the U.S. policy toward Central Asia, and the possibility of terrorists gaining access to the Internet.

They communicated among themselves through false identities, invisible writing, secret rendezvous sites, and even set up a special communication system, using a private wireless network through linked laptop computers, to report back to Moscow Center.

Charlie wondered if it could be similar to Vincent's analogous communications grid. He was impressed at the extent of the information that the old man had assembled regarding the Russian operatives. It was obviously important to him he decided, looking out his hotel window once again. On the opposite side of the street, a vendor with a wheeled cart was busy serving a rowing line of customers.

Charlie locked his room, and rushed down the hotel stairs hoping to get to the vendor before he moved his cart to another location. Dodging through traffic, he reached the hawker just as he was beginning to close up shop. Charlie selected a huge Vienna sausage stuffed inside a dripping bakery bun, then sprinted back through the heavy late afternoon traffic to his hotel.

Back in his room, he finished the sausage and washed his hands, before continuing to search through Vincent's file.

The deep-cover spies were under surveillance by the FBI before they were suddenly picked-up in their operation *Ghost Story*. Another suspect, the article said, was apprehended in Cyprus, but skipped bail the day after his arrest.

Moscow's court records also indicated that two other Russian agents managed to flee the U.S. before they were charged. One of these was a long-term SVR agent believed to be the American *control* for the group.

The captured Illegals pleaded guilty as charged, and were flown to Vienna just twelve days after being arrested. Many of the American agents involved in the arrest reflected surprise they were released as rapidly as they were. Charlie wondered about that as well. The spies had been working undercover in the U.S. for many years but, when they were uncovered, they were exchanged almost immediately.

Charlie rubbed his eyes. It had been a long day and he was getting tired, but the unlikely chain of events continued to intrigue him. Once the agents arrived in Vienna, they were immediately exchanged for four Russian nationals who were previously convicted in their home courts, and imprisoned on charges of espionage and high treason.

The exchange was carefully synchronized. Two special planes, one from New York and the other from Moscow, landed at Vienna's airport within minutes of each other. They were parked nose to tail on a remote section of the tarmac. The individual groups were shuttled between the two planes, passing each other on the way. Once the spy swap was completed, the planes took off, returning to their respective points of origin.

Once again, Charlie thought, pulling his chair from the table, Vienna had taken center stage in an exchange reminiscent of an old Cold War movie. Instead of an exchange on a bridge in Berlin, this took place in a remote section of an airport. The difference was that the Cold War was now presumably over. In Charlie's mind, Emmitt Valentine was correct once again in his lingering suspicion of Putin's *new* Russia. It appeared that they were acting in the same way they did before.

His bewilderment intensified, Charlie shoved the papers aside, and rose from the table to stretch and peer again out the window. What he had read seemed to make no sense as it went around in his mind.

The sun had set, and the lights of the city were starting to show through the increasing darkness. In the distance, he could make out the lights of the Prater amusement park shining brightly; outlining the Park's fabled Ferris wheel.

As he watched, it almost seemed to Charlie that he could hear the sound of zither music rising from the street below. Perhaps? No, of course not that would be impossible Never the less, he strained to see Hollie Martins and Harry Lime, the infamous third man, discussing their association in one of the small compartments of the Ferris wheel, as it revolved around---and around in the growing darkness.

13

Charlie lay down on the bed and stared at the ceiling. It had been a long day it and had taken its toll. He had come to view the continued rotation of the Ferris wheel as a metaphor for his investigation into Emmett's death; rapidly going in circles and getting nowhere.

Glancing at his watch, he was surprised to see how late it was. By now, he had hoped to hear from Karen Kincaid. Leaving Vincent's office, he had asked the secretary to place a call for him to the second number on Emmett's list. When no one answered, he left the phone number of his hotel room on her recorder. He could have left the number for the encrypted cell phone they gave him at Langley, but he was reluctant to use it for his conversations with Karen for fear they might be screened by unseen listeners.

Closing his eyes, his mind drifted back to how, in the past, their paths had continued to cross and then separate. When he returned from Peru, he had called Karen to setup a meeting in his office at Apex Electronics. She was on time, a trait he always admired, but she seemed more reserved than during their previous meetings. There were deep circles beneath her eyes, and she appeared tired. He hadn't thought much of it at the time. Many people were tired then. The economy was in decline, and everyone was working harder than before. He imagined that there was a similar affect, even in Washington.

Karen was eager to learn the operational details of what had taken place in Lima. Afterwards, she asked him for the receipt he had received for the transfer of cash that had taken place. Karen thanked him for his service, formed a weak smile, and said they would be in touch. That was the last he heard from her, or from the Agency, for many months. He was too busy to think much about at the time.

He found later through Emmett, shortly after the incident in Peru, a political cloud of criticism had engulfed her at the Agency. Questions arose about the operational wisdom of transferring large sums of money through a man with non-official cover to a group of Peruvian dissidents with a questionable history. The radical Sendero Luminoso had become entrenched in many parts of Peru and was threatening to gain control over the economic center of the country. The American government was unwilling to take overt action to displace them, and Karen's plan of feeding funds to an alternate operation was the best that anyone could suggest.

At the time, the CIA itself was under a cloud. A red plague was spreading rapidly across South America. The Agency, concentrating its activities in Eastern Europe, was poorly equipped to counter it. Congressional investigations and criticisms were focusing on the rumor of Agency sponsored assassinations in Chile, to assist President Pinochet retain power. The *Dirty War* in Argentina was becoming increasingly violent as the military government attempted to crackdown on a well-financed group of radicals. In Colombia, the Contras were threatening to take over that government; and there was a legitimate fear that all of Latin America could become Communist.

In Washington, the management mullahs at the CIA were searching for a way to mount covert actions without overt commitment. They welcomed Karen's approach. She had used a carrier (Charlie) who had no connection to the CIA---someone non-traceable — a thoroughly deniable source who had made a successful transfer of funds to an organization willing to actively combat the radicals. In doing so, this was established as a *modus operandi* that could serve as a model for future covert activity.

At first, at least, this was the official view. However, the Intelligence Agency, like most government agencies, is not without its political undercurrents. Karen's success, particularly as a woman, drew considerable management attention...and envy in some quarters.

There had always been a clash of cultures at Langley that grew more divisive as the Agency grew larger. Since its inception, the organization relied on individuals who were able to operate independently and decisively. In order to maintain the organization's bureaucratic demands it also required people who were adept at moving the monstrous administrative details that a growing organization demands. Karen had found herself at odds with the administrators, and the paper pushers were gaining more power because they were more evident on a daily basis.

Soon there were rumors floating around the corridors that some of the funds for Peru had possibly found their way into a Bermudian bank account. Never proven, but often repeated. Eventually, her former staunch supporters abandoned Karen. She had become an organizational liability. Afterward, there was a warrant for her arrest, and Karen turned up missing.

Emmett was sad to relate these events to Charlie. They had occurred when he was inactive—out of the loop as he described it. The rest of the story Charlie got from Karen herself.

Emmett had been sidelined, and several managers were vying for his vacant position. One of them, she believed, saw her success as a possible threat. Documents, from an unnamed source, began to appear accusing her of receiving a kickback from the group in Peru. She saw what was happening, and decided there was no viable alternative than disappearing until it all blew over. She thought she was good at that. She had been trained for it, hadn't she?

Someone at the CIA tipped off someone else at the FBI regarding where she might be found—and they found her--hiding in a cheap motel in Tucson. Something about phone records she thought. Anyway, they sent an agent to pick her up. It turned out the young man was just out of training and the only person who was readily available. He made the arrest, but first had to call Washington for further orders on where he should take her.

It was hot that day in Tucson—no big surprise. While they were waiting, she asked if she could take a shower. He agreed. He could lock her in the bathroom, what could go wrong?

Before she went in to shower, she took off her blouse and asked the young agent if he could unsnap her brassiere. He laid down his gun, and she chopped him in the neck, just as they had trained her to do.

Karen was out of there, on her way to Mexico, and the young agent was handcuffed to the bed. Try explaining that to your boss.

The phone rang jarring Charlie awake. He must have dozed off. The room was pitch black, and he had difficulty adjusting to where he was. He stumbled toward the sound of the ring, knocking papers off the desk, along with the remnants of his sandwich. Fumbling for the receiver, he heard a muffled voice that was at first fuzzy and indistinguishable. A faint whirring noise rose, then quickly faded away as the line cleared.

"Charlie—Charlie Connelly?

"Where are you Karen?"

"I can't tell you that right now, but after I left Odessa for Tel Aviv I was taken in by the Mossad. They knew my background, my training, *and my problems*; they thought I would be perfect for them."

"Have you heard that Emmett was murdered?"

There was a pause, and Charlie thought he heard a sharp intake of breath. "Karen?"

"Yes Charlie, I just heard. We have a contact in Washington and they let us know. But, I still have difficulty believing it."

"The people at the Agency don't want it known."

"It isn't."

"The people there want me to see if I can find who killed him."

"I know," Karen told him.

"I-- they believe it was someone with the FSB."

"We do too. Charlie we need to talk."

The line began fading in and out. First stronger than weaker, Charlie was worried they would lose the connection.

"You mean talk, talk?"

"Yes old friend, I mean talk, talk."

"Where Karen?" Where should we meet?"

"Where we used to. Do you still remember?"

"In Kiev?"

"Tomorrow--can you make it tomorrow? Late afternoon, all right?

"I remember where," Charlie confirmed. "I will try to catch a flight out of here early tomorrow. Can I reach you on this number?"

Karen paused. The silence provided his answer.

"We will use the old protocol. If you are not there tomorrow, I will try the next day, same time, same place. If you or I don't make it the second time, everything is off. Ok?"

"Ok Karen." The line went dead.

Charlie hung up the receiver. His heart was racing. Her voice had sounded as strong as ever, and just as appealing.

By now, his eyes had grown accustomed to the dark. Only the blinking neon lights outside his window illuminated the interior of his room. He found the mini-bar and looked inside. The small fridge was well stocked with Swiss chocolates, small sausages, a large assortment of European liquors, and German beers. Charlie soon found what he was searching for, the bright blue bottles of Bombay Sapphire gin. He poured the contents of two of them into an ice-filled glass; as Queen Victoria smiled approvingly from the label.

In the distance, an ambulance raced through Vienna's now empty streets with its claxon caroling the eerie two-tone warning familiar to Europeans, but unnerving to a lonely American in a darkened distant hotel room.

Gazing out his window, he could see the vague outline of the Ferris wheel that had closed down for the night. Only a few faint warning lights flickered in the distance. He raised his glass in a silent toast to old times and old friends, and contemplated what might lie ahead.

14

Langley, Va.

"Do you understand this crap?" Ray Riordan asked, looking up from a report he had just been handed by his assistant. "It says here, 'the toxicity of certain elements depends very heavily on their physico-chemical form.'" He rolled his eyes and cleared his throat before continuing. "'Speciation of arsenic compounds is achieved by separating the compounds using HPLC and measuring the individual species with the PS Analytical Millennium Excalibur.'" It was the first of several pages he had been given by the CIA's chemistry lab after they analyzed the contents of Marissa Dolan's teacup.

Disgustedly, he wadded the report into a tight ball, and tossed it at Bill Brady.

Brady caught it with his left hand, deftly transferred it to the right, and in a continuation of motion drilled the wastebasket near the door with the remnants of the chemistry department's detailed report. A self-satisfied smile crossed Brady's face, while his boss grinned his approval.

"It means" Brady responded, "that the gnomes down in the chem lab believe that Marissa Dolan was killed by someone who was able to sneak arsenic into her tea."

"That's pretty unsophisticated. I was expecting something more exotic like plutonium or a rare type of South American poison."

"Apparently this does the trick. The result is a coma leading to death. It's sometimes called the 'housewife's revenge' because the lovely little ladies often use it to do away with their straying husbands without his knowing it.

"Another name for stuff is *inheritance powder*," Brady continued, "since that's the way some of the royal families of Europe did away with their parents who were hanging on to the throne too long. More recently, King Faisal the 1st of Iraq was thought to have been led down that last lonely road by someone in his entourage who was slipping him arsenic."

"How do you know all this stuff?"

"Stuff?"

"It's a technical term," his boss assured him with a wry grin.

"Actually I don't, or didn't, that is. To be truthful, the little man in the big white coat who gave me the report told me. He was pleased with himself that he was able to come up with your answer so quickly, and wanted to provide me with the Cliff Notes.

"So now that we know it was arsenic, what does that tell us?" Riordan asked, impatiently drumming his fingers on the desk.

"Well it tells us what we already expected, that it wasn't a random heart attack. Marissa was murdered. Who, or why, is still a question. That's what you have Connelly for. Speaking of Connelly" Brady added, "I forgot to tell you, I got a call from him. He was in the Vienna airport on his way to Kiev."

Riordan looked puzzled. "Kiev, why was he going to Kiev? For that matter, why the hell world anyone want to go to Kiev?"

"Beats me. He was in a hurry, had to catch his flight. Said he had a lead that he was following, and wanted to know who we had there."

"I already know. Same guy we have had there for a couple of years. He keeps asking for a transfer. His wife says there is no social life and she's bored, and he's frustrated."

"And he is?" Brady asked.

"Barry Durand. He is a good man, but his official cover is Commercial Attaché, and all he does is make arrangements for visiting dignitaries, touring advisory groups, advising visiting business men where the best restaurants are, and a lot of other jobs that he thinks are a consummate pain in the ass.

"But, I don't get it," Riordan looked perplexed, "the political situation there has been a caldron ready to boil over. The Russians thought it was their prize colony, and they have been trying to regain control ever since the country became independent. Durand should have plenty to do trying to keep track of that."

Brady shook his head. "You're right he should have, but State has clamped down on any covert or overt activity for that matter, for fear of antagonizing the Russians. We are still trying to get their cooperation with Iran and Syria and don't want to get them upset in Ukraine. As a result, Durand is strictly a Commercial Attaché like his title says. If someone should walk in off the street with information he might be obliged to take it, otherwise he is just a glorified tour guide---with a frustrated wife."

After his assistant left to see if he could pass Durand's name on to Connelly, Riordan was alone with his thoughts. He knew Charlie was doing his best, but there was a feeling that time was running out. Nothing specific exactly, but sometimes in the executive dining room he felt that eyes were watching him more closely than before. If there was even an inkling that someone on his watch was murdered, and he hadn't reported it to the cousins at the FBI to investigate, he would be out the door without a pension.

The key word in government recently was *stove-piping.* If you didn't share your information, but instead held it to yourself, you were *stove-piping,* and that was being a bad bureaucrat--a very bad bureaucrat indeed.

Riordan forced himself to get back to work by picking up the report he just received from Ralph Gross. It described the information he had been able to accumulate in Cairo. The country had regained a level of calm, compared with the turmoil confronting the rest of the Middle East. Gross was trying to establish assets from there that would provide an insight to the Muslim Brotherhood's activities in Syria, and Libya. Those countries were on fire, and Gross preferred the luxuries that Cairo provided rather than getting shot at somewhere else.

Riordan couldn't blame him. He recalled his time there, living at the Hilton overlooking the Nile, with a long bar frequented by men in spotless white robes and black and white kaffiyehs on their heads, drinking vintage bourbon that was unavailable in their own countries. If you had to be somewhere in the area, Cairo was preferable to other places with their more stringent moral constraints.

Sometimes Riordan wondered if this was really the best way. Things were not progressing very rapidly for Gross, and the information he was providing was no better than what was available through normal press accounts. But Gross had told him that the Agency believed they needed a physical presence in the area in order to maintain a position in the intelligence community

There were times, since joining the Agency, that Riordan regretted it. And, the times seemed to be occurring more rapidly since he had risen to his present position. It was the overpowering bureaucracy that he had to contend with in order to get anything done.

A government agency, he reflected, is like a person. In the beginning, as it was in the formation of the CIA, it is like a young man. Vigorous, optimistic, eager to get something accomplished and somewhat idealistic as well. The young man grows more jaded as he grows older, and becomes more set in his ways, while at the same time growing heavier around the middle. Riordan smiled at his analogy. When he — it--becomes older the instinct to survive becomes dominant and the idealism fades. Was it the Agency he was thinking about, or was it more personal?

To hell with it he concluded. A man's gotta do what a man's gotta do.

His mind drifted back to his present problems. Perhaps he should send Brady over to check on Gross. It wouldn't be unusual. Maybe even Barbara Richards. He would have to think about that he decided, stuffing Gross's report into an already crammed desk-drawer.

15

Charlie was fortunate to find a cab waiting outside the hotel. The early morning haze was just beginning to lift, as they sped toward the airport. On the way, he watched as rugged street cleaning equipment competed with small delivery vans for control of the busy thoroughfares. Austria's economy, along with their neighbor Germany, had avoided the economic malaise that was gripping the remainder of Europe, and the early morning activity was evidence of the country's continuing prosperity.

He awkwardly folded himself into the narrow seat of the Ukrainian Airlines 737. His sole consolation for the cramped quarters was that it was only a three-hour flight from Vienna to Kiev. He had tried to book on Austrian Air, but the carrier didn't have an early flight. It was important for him to arrive in the morning to meet with Karen that afternoon.

Brady had called as he was about to board. It was just a name, Barry Durand, but he knew what it meant. Durand would be the CIA's man at the American Embassy in Kiev. He had asked Riordan for a contact in their earlier conversation. He knew from previous experience that his Agency contact would be operating under official cover, either as a cultural or commercial attaché, at the Embassy. This would enable him to claim official immunity if he was caught doing something he shouldn't be doing inside Ukraine. There was no plan to use the name, but he wanted to know who the man was in case he did.

Charlie looked out his window at the panorama of open fields, sliced by the Danube and bounded by snow-capped mountains, rapidly passing beneath him. It was difficult to realize that the vast amount of land he was viewing had, until only recently, been part of the massive Soviet Union that emerged from the Second World War. The citizenry of the conquered countries had become Russian, regardless of their centuries' old ancestry or national inclination. The end of the cold war had changed that and now, new old countries were attempting to reclaim their role in an unfamiliar economic environment. Ukraine had been part of that rebirth, and was still experiencing nationalistic growing pains.

The seatbelt sign had been off for some time, and Charlie adjusted his seatback. The final words of Vincent St. Claire, *find the mole and you will find your answer*, echoed in his head. He reached under his seat and found his briefcase. He hoped Vincent's file would provide a clue to Emmett's killer.

Charlie was surprised to find the first person referred to was James Jesus Angleton. It was a familiar name. He had read about the man many times in the press. JJ, as he was sometimes referred to, was not a spy in the strictest sense. He was instead the man the CIA had appointed to head up Counter Intelligence. He was in effect a spy catcher—a whack-a-mole if you will. Charlie smiled to himself at his own lame witticism.

Angleton had started his career at about the same time as Vincent and Emmett. He was born in the United States and grew-up in Europe, the son of an American executive with the old National Cash Register Company. He attended Yale University and subsequently graduated from Harvard Law School, before joining the society conscious Office of Strategic Services during WWII. Also, like Emmett and Vincent, he had learned his spy craft under the tutelage of the more experienced British MI6.

Later, after serving in several capacities in Europe for the CIA, Allen Dulles brought him back to Washington at the height of the Cold War. It was also during this period when there was growing fear that Communist sympathizers had become embedded in the political structure of the United States Government. Dulles had decided that Angleton was the man to dig them out.

The Agency gave Angleton considerable power, which he unhesitatingly exercised. He became universally feared, and often hated around Langley. Unconstrained, the spy catcher was responsible for the premature demise of many careers — many based on only conjecture and dubious circumstances.

Angleton's own career ended because of what he hadn't found. During his years working with Britain's MI6, he had become friends with the former Cambridge socialite Kim Philby. Philby had risen steadily within his own organization at a rate similar to Angleton's rise at Langley. He was believed to be slated eventually to head-up England's own intelligence agency. In preparation for his expanded responsibilities, he was assigned to a liaison role with Washington. The two men became even more close than they had before.

During Philby's absence from Britain, information came to light regarding his own clandestine connection to the KGB, and he was forced to flee to Moscow. He spent the remaining years of his life as a hero of the Soviet Union, and his previous contacts within the two intelligence agencies immediately fell under suspicion.

Although there was never a connection found between the two, Angleton's career ended without ever uncovering an imbedded mole at Langley. It was also thought, by some, that the zealousness displayed by him, failed to produce tangible results, and allowed subsequent moles such as Aldrich Ames and Robert Hansen to go undetected.

While Charlie was studying the file, a slender blond flight attendant, in her Ukrainian blue uniform, passed through the plane serving coffee and rolls. The limited breakfast was enough for him as he thought about what had befallen the Agency's premier mole catcher. Could a similar destiny await his own efforts? He wondered if this had been Vincent's way of cautioning him.

Charlie shook off the thought, finished the sweet roll and drained his cup. He could have used a refill, but the young attendant was back in the plane's galley, chatting with the copilot.

He looked around the plane at his fellow passengers. Most of them appeared to be European business people and minor government officials willing to endure the early morning flight in hopes of establishing or renewing their Ukrainian contacts.

The next name in the file belonged to Robert Philip Hanssen. Hanssen was associated with the FBI rather than the CIA, but still had access to a treasure trove of highly classified information. He provided his Russian handlers with sensitive security information for over twenty years. He was so trusted at the Bureau they never gave him a lie-detector test, when it was their policy to do so as a matter of routine. The FBI eventually was able to uncover his identity by using fake information as a trap, and tracing it back to him as the source.

Then there was Aldrich Ames. Charlie extracted his information from the file and studied it closely. Looking back at these people, their actions seemed to be so obvious it was astonishing they were not discovered earlier than they were. Ames was a counter intelligence official who, along with his Latin wife Rosario, passed the names and covert identities of at least nine U. S. agents, and their techniques, to Moscow over an extended period from 1985 to 1994. Ames was a high spending alcoholic who the Agency never expected to be betraying them.

How could they not catch on to such an obviously flawed person, Charlie wondered. Were there equally obvious signals being sent by the murderer of Emmett? Where would he look? Was it an agent in place, or some other long forgotten adversary who had come back seeking revenge?

He was sure that whoever did it was not sharing his flight to Kiev, and Charlie wondered if he was doing the right thing. He wasn't sure, all he knew was Karen told him that he should meet her in Kiev, and since he had no better idea that was what he was doing.

He looked at another profile of a man who had been trusted and who ultimately betrayed that trust. This time it was not to Russia, as Charlie had initially expected, but to America's most trusted friend- Israel.

Jonathan Pollard, born in Texas, worked as a civilian analyst in naval intelligence. He was always sympathetic to the Israeli cause. He eventually made contact with an Israeli Air Force Colonel who was studying in the United States, Pollard informed his contact of instances where the United States was withholding information from Israel and offered himself up as a spy. Pollard's espionage efforts were eventually uncovered, and he was sentenced to life imprisonment. The conviction has proven a to be a point of contention between Israel and the United States, and frequent efforts have been made to have him paroled—so far to no effect.

There were others in Vincent's file, many others, from all branches of the U.S. government. Charlie once again felt overwhelmed by the enormity of his task. If so many people who were willing to betray their country had been uncovered and punished, how many had not. Were many of them still providing valuable information to the enemy, and was one of them the one who had killed Emmett?

Or perhaps Vincent was wrong, perhaps his death was for another reason entirely.

In the past, counter espionage efforts had centered on people within the government who were willing to provide this country's military secrets or human intelligence. HUMINT, as he recalled, was one of the Agency's favorite acronyms.

Now, there was a new role for enemies of the United States. They were people without a perceived foreign connection who were willingly using their technical knowledge to obtain and reveal how their country managed to intercept and analyze international and domestic communications. Their stolen hard disks were able to contain more U.S. secrets than could have previously been stolen by a regiment of spies.

This new species of homegrown mole was even more difficult to find, and even more difficult to punish since their motives were more ethereal. Could this type of internal enemy be the type he was searching for? Possibly. Who knew? It only made his task more difficult.

Charlie stared out the plane's window in despair. Below him were the steppes of Ukraine, bounded by a great expanse of mountains shielding the rich farmland that formed Russia's breadbasket, as the country traditionally had been referred to in the past.

The flight attendant had left the galley, and her copilot had returned to the cockpit. The seat belt sign was flashing the ancient 737's impending approach to Kiev's Boryspil Airport.

Charlie turned away from the window to secure his seatbelt, and adjust the back of his seat to the obligatory upright position. He had reached a decision. After he met Karen Kincaid, he was certainly obliged to do that, he would call Riordan and tell him he was giving up and coming home. He was not accustomed to failure, but he knew it when it confronted him. There was no possible chance that he was going to find the person he was looking for in Ukraine, or any other damned place for the matter. This was the end of the line.

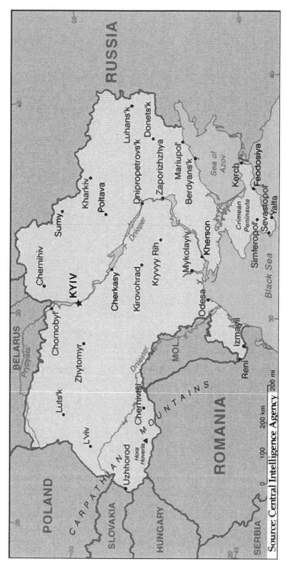

16

Kiev

The Ukrainian Air flight bounced on the tarmac, its wheels screeching in protest on the damp concrete. Charlie checked his watch—an old habit on landing. It was 10:30 am, providing ample time to make his afternoon appointment with Karen.

As the plane taxied slowly toward the terminal, passengers began gathering their overhead luggage, ignoring the attendant's instructions. By the time the plane's engine whined to a full stop the attendant was already standing at the exit door, and the passenger line was in full formation. The heavy fuselage door gaped open and the people filed out, hurriedly heading toward Customs.

The airport was old and rundown, and undergoing a much needed renovation. Bag in hand, Charlie joined the line moving sluggishly forward. Suddenly he was being nudged by the man behind him. "You're next he whispered." Jolted out of his reverie, Charlie slid his new passport under the bulletproof glass partition. A square-jawed woman in a leftover Russian Uniform glanced at his photo, then frowned at him from beneath her pie-plate hat. She stared directly at him attempting to match his face with the document photo. From there she glanced at the wide mirror strategically placed above and behind him that provided a view of his feet, enabling her to determine if he was attempting to appear shorter or taller than the height specified in his passport description.

Regardless of how many times he had gone through an entry process, his palms invariably grew moist when he was under the scrutiny of a uniformed agent. The glowering uncivil servant vigorously stamped his passport, exhaling her bureaucratic frustration, before wordlessly handing the passport back and nodding for him to move on. The next nervous traveler immediately took his place.

Outside the terminal, Charlie flagged the first cab idling in the waiting line. "Dnipro Hotel," he ordered the driver, settling back in the worn seat. The old Lada automobile jerked away from the curb, farting a gray stream of exhaust behind. After getting on the Karkhiv highway, the driver lighted a foul-smelling cigarette, and headed toward the city center as fast as the ancient engine would permit.

As he rode, Charlie thought about calling Beth when he got to the hotel to tell her of his decision to give up the search for Emmett's killer and return to Chicago. Not now, he decided. Sometime later, after he met Karen. For now, he walled off any thoughts of home or family. There was just his assignment to think about now. He knew from his past experience that was the way it had to be. He had to give up the reality of a retired businessman working for the CIA, and effectively assume the guise of someone else. Someone that could not be tracked back to the Agency. Plausible deniability as the Agency people were so fond of saying. That was what he needed--plausible deniability.

Charlie gazed out the window at the stream of traffic, wondering who he was to be in Kiev. The last time he was here, it was as an international consultant. That seemed to provide an acceptable legend. Perhaps this time he should assume the role of a corporate executive on a business trip, hoping to expand the market for his nebulous products. Or an employee of some alphabet-laced government agency. That might work. There were plenty of them wandering around Eastern Europe.

On the other hand, perhaps a lone traveler on vacation. Charlie recalled that the travel writer Paul Theroux, in his recent book *Ghost Train to the Eastern Star,* wrote of 'Being invisible — the usual condition of the older traveler is much more useful than being obvious.' Maybe that would be a reasonable role to assume.

Certainly not the truth. That would not be acceptable in espionage shy post-Soviet Ukraine. He smiled to himself. The truth never works in situations like this. He would just have to make it up as he went along, and see what best fits the mold.

He knew, however that it was important to assume a role of some sort, and then tailor his characteristics to fit the perceived mold. The business executive would move with confidence, real or assumed. The government employee, on the other hand, would exude caution, hoping not to antagonize, but just get along and get out. Whatever character he chose, Charlie realized that he would not be able to pass as a native Ukrainian--at least not for very long.

He tentatively decided on the wandering international consultant who was affiliated with an important sounding organization. Preferably one with the inference of money in the title. Everyone wants to accommodate a man who is close to money. It suddenly came to him. He was with the Global Bank. Why not? He was sure that Vincent would not object to having a new employee in Ukraine.

The driver tried to strike up a conversation — in Russian, and quickly gave-up when Charlie attempted a response in English. After that, the two men rode in silence.

As they drew closer to the city, the traffic increased proportionally. The driver concentrated on the traffic, while Charlie became lost in thought.

It had been several years since he had been in Ukraine, and he recalled the country's depressing history. The Ukrainian Republic was, after Russia, the most important economic component of the former Soviet Union. The country's fertile soul and extensive resources also contributed to its sad history of failed sovereignty. From the time of the Mongol hordes, up until recently, the country had only a brief association with independence; and at least a part of Ukraine, at one time or another, had experienced control by Lithuania, Poland, Austria, Hungary, Romania, Czechoslovakia, Germany, and often under the boots of an invading Russian Army.

None of these occupying forces were ever timid about dispersing their genes among the conquered population. The evidence of their questionable generosity was evident, to varying degrees, in the features of today's Ukrainian population they were passing on the road.

This lack of experience with independence had made the transition from Soviet control more difficult for the Ukrainian people than for perhaps those in Poland, Hungary, or East Germany who had a more defined history of self-governance.

Charlie recalled that his previous exposure to the country had been as an advisor to a producer of military electronics in a former *closed city*. The company, Karpaty, was attempting to adapt their defense equipment to products more fitting for an independent consumer market. The company, like the rest of the country, was having considerable difficulty making the transition.

The loud blare of the taxi's horn, warning a pedestrian who had unconsciously ventured off the cross walk, brought Charlie back to the present and, along with it, the present's pressing problems.

He looked around him, and began to recognize some of the landmarks that had once been familiar to him. "St. Sophia," the driver said making the sign of the cross. They were passing a golden-domed cathedral with a wedding-cake baroque style bell tower.

116

The cab continued down the now crowded Stalinist style main boulevard. Passing the city's Independence Square the driver continued his newly assumed role as tour guide. "Maidan Nezalezhnosti," he informed his passenger pointing toward a tree-lined park with a tall statue of Winged Victory dominating its center.

Charlie glanced in the direction the driver was pointing and the memories came flooding back. The chestnut trees that lined the avenue were beginning to lose their leaves, just as before when he was in Kiev. The newly abandoned leaves swirled in the air as the taxi sped past the park.

One thing notably missing was the protestors that had occupied the Maidan when he was here before. It was the days when the "Orange Revolution" was at its height. Most of the more vocal protestors were students who carried rolled up mattresses and had pitched tents. Many of them, he recalled, would stand on empty egg cartons to protect their thinly soled athletic shoes from the hard cold concrete walkways. The color orange was everywhere then; in their clothes, their balloons and particularly in their bright orange banners the students waved so vigorously.

Their efforts had eventually brought down the government. A new government was put in place, along with much needed reforms. Improvements were made — for awhile. The new government was replaced by many members of the former regime. Some of the reformers were put in prison, the old scandals remained hidden, and the economy had stalled.

As Charlie neared the hotel, the recession that had overtaken Ukraine was clearly in evidence. Many of the shops appeared vacant, and the numbers of people walking the gritty city streets were more than would normally be the case at this time of day. The old babushkas, with their long black coats and well-worn headscarves, were back operating their tiny stalls along the sidewalk. People looked as sad as they did when he was in Kiev before, but perhaps that was only his imagination.

Once inside the hotel, he signed the register as one Charles Connelly representing the Global Bank. The clerk, smiled (that was different from when he was here before) and held out his hand. Charlie guardedly relinquished his passport. This always made him nervous. With any luck, however, he knew he would have it back, after the local police had checked it, and before it was time for him to leave the country.

Walking through the lobby towards the elevator it was obvious that, since the hotel had passed into private hands, considerable effort had been made to make the reception area more customer acceptable. The area was well lighted, and the formerly gray walls were now covered in walnut wood paneling. Before, most of the hotel's guests were Europeans, or from neighboring Soviet states. Now, the lobby was filled with groups of Chinese tourists waiting to be picked up by their bus, and smoking impatiently until it arrived.

As he exited the elevator at his floor, Charlie immediately noticed the absence of the former ever present and ever watchful "floor lady." They were the eyes and ears of the former Soviet regime who kept close track of the comings and goings of the hotel's guests for the local authorities.

After unpacking, he thought again about calling Beth to let her know of his decision to return to Chicago. He looked at his watch, thought better of it, and instead unpacked his bag. He wanted to make sure that he was on time for his meeting with Karen. He had been surprised to learn from Vincent that one of Emmett's principal coded telephone numbers belonged to a person who had not been part of the Agency or, as far as he knew, the intelligence community for several years.

Why Karen and Emmett had continued their contact with each other was just one of the many questions he hoped his meeting with her would answer.

17

Walking along Khreschatyk Street, headed toward his rendezvous with Karen, Charlie felt the old Ukrainian malaise setting in again. It felt as if there were two eyes burrowing into his back, following him wherever he went. He paused suddenly in front of a store whose entrance had a large angled window. He knew that it would provide the perfect opportunity to get a reflected glimpse of anyone who might be tailing him. He saw nothing alarming. What was it about Kiev that always made him feel this way? Was it Kiev — or just a bad case of personal paranoia?

He stopped at the electronics store he had been looking for. One he remembered from before. Then, it was stocked with shelves of bulky Russian built television sets. Now the sets remained, but additional shelves of imported cell phones supplemented them. A young woman stepped behind the counter ready to assist him. Fortunately, she spoke English. The store personnel had become used to dealing with foreign customers staying at the hotel.

Charlie found what he wanted, and the price was right. He was glad he thought to exchange money before he left the hotel. Actually, the price was the main thing. He didn't know one brand from another, and didn't care. What he was looking for was a cheap phone. A throwaway — *a burner,* as they are known in the intelligence trade.

He needed something that could not be traced, but would enable him to communicate with Karen while he was in Kiev. A set that would be off the grid, to use Vincent's term, then thrown away after a few days use.

The phone he bought was plain vanilla--no whistles and few bells. Hopefully, it could send and receive, and that was all that was important to him now.

Back on the street, his new phone in his pocket, Charlie walked along the winding bank of the Dnieper River. He wanted to appear, if indeed someone was watching, as a person with time on his hands. Someone who was going nowhere. Certainly, not a man on his way to meeting with a fellow member of the intelligence community.

The river had a toxic odor to it. Indeed, Charlie thought, the entire city of Kiev used to be toxic. Chernobyl was well within a 60-mile radius of the town's center. Close enough for the city to be contaminated after the nuclear plant exploded. Now it was better they said, the contamination subsided. But, when he was here before, the State Department was still rotating its people in and out every few months for safety's sake. Perhaps they still were.

Now, he had heard that the country was running sightseeing tours into the dead zone, even though an inordinately high cancer rate remained among the people of Ukraine.

He passed a large church, and paused to glance casually around and behind him. Something an idle tourist might do who was unsure where he was. He was startled then, when the ornate church door burst open, framing a young couple in all their wedding finery. Happy friends, throwing rice and wishing them well, quickly surrounded the bride and groom. The young couple seemed full of promise. It reminded Charlie of his own wedding day.

He quickly walked on, it was important for him to be on time.

The ticket booth to the city's ancient funicular was on his right, and he purchased a ticket. He waited only a few seconds before a fully loaded car appeared. A small group of passengers spilled out onto the platform. Charlie quickly took their place before the car began its motion once more, in the opposite direction from which it had just arrived.

He grasped the car's window ledge as the chain slipped a cog then caught itself, and the antiquated funicular began its jerky decent. Charlie squinted as he peered through the dirty windowpane at the scene below. In the distance, he could see the outline of the tour boats lined-up along the banks of the Dnieper, waiting for their next scheduled departure before their brief season drew to an end.

It was on one of those boats he remembered that He and Karen had escaped Kiev. He had never expected that he would have to flee the city when he arrived for his consulting assignment with the IESC. Then, he never thought that he was going to run into Karen either. It was just a coincidence. But, his life had been full of coincidences. It if it were not for coincidences, he thought, he would have had no life at all.

She was in a restaurant, having dinner with several men from the Ukrainian Government. He didn't recognize her at first. She had dyed her hair. Women can alter their appearance that way easier than a man. She saw him staring at her, but turned away. The group she was with finished first and left the restaurant. As she passed his table he didn't look up, instead concentrating his attention on his order of chicken kiev. He thought it appropriate when he ordered it, but then he wasn't so sure.

After she passed, he was certain it was her, same height, same assured way of walking. But, what in the hell was she doing in Kiev?

In a few minutes Karen had returned, and sat down beside him. She went on to explain that when she fled the United States she went to Mexico City and from there to Kiev. She was originally from Ukrainian parents and spoke the language. It seemed to be a good place to hide from the FBI, the CIA, and whoever else might be trying to find her.

She had taken a job with the Ukrainian Government. They needed people who spoke English, and were familiar with a capitalist form of economy. The job provided a place to hide, in addition to making a living, and she felt relatively safe until she bumped into him eating his chicken Kiev.

Now, here he was inside a funicular on his way to meet her once again, just as they used to do so very long ago. He hoped that the clanking jerking chain dragging his car downward toward the river wasn't providing a mechanical metaphor for what was happening to his life. For awhile, after he had left Apex Electronics and put aside his association with the Agency, his life moved along at a predictable rhythm. Now, it was filled with frustration and uncertainty, and he had a feeling that it might be spiraling out of control.

But, he was damned curious why Emmett had kept in contact with Karen, and Vincent too. He was even more curious about what she might know about Emmett's death, and why she wanted to meet him.

Enough of this soul-searching bullshit Charlie decided as his cable car passed through the now leafless trees, and then came to an abrupt stop. The doors opened automatically, and he stepped out on the station platform. He paused briefly to see if anyone exited the cars behind him, but he was alone. All alone.

He hoped he remembered the way. He stood for a minute to orient himself, then started down the flight of stairs to the street below. Kiev possesses a schizophrenic architectural appearance. Much of the city is composed of unattractive neo-Soviet cracker-box buildings. The Podil district, where he was walking, is primarily made up of old buildings that have managed to retain a reasonable level of charm. Mainly students from the nearby university and tourists frequent the district.

Recalling Karen's directions, Charlie trudged along Andriyivsky Uzviz. Art galleries and small shops lined the old street, mixed in with a variety of inexpensive restaurants. The area was undergoing some renovation he noticed, and there was a hotel under construction that was not there before.

He was relieved to see ahead of him the bright blue and green spires and round domes of St. Andrews. They served as a beacon for him. The church was his destination.

Charlie entered through the heavy wooden doors, and peered around the dark interior. It was early afternoon, and only a few women in their gaudy headscarves were scattered sparingly among the wooden pews. For such an ornate exterior, the inside of the church was starkly plain. The principal decoration was a large painting of the church's namesake hanging above a large unadorned alter.

Under Russian control of Ukraine, St Andrews had been converted into a museum of architecture as part of their attempt to eliminate any semblance of religious influence in the country. The scars resulting from their effort were still evident throughout the ancient interior.

Charlie peered through the gloom, and thought he recognized someone who might be Karen. She was seated in one of the rear pews, back to him, facing the alter. She could have passed as a cleric in repose or meditation. Instead of a headscarf, Charlie saw the dark headpiece of an anorak. It was something she might wear, he recalled. He took a seat in the row behind her. His hand gently brushed her shoulder. It could have been an accident if it turned out to be someone else. Someone he didn't know.

It was not. She turned toward him, smiling. "How is my favorite spy?" she asked grinning.

"Better now that I have found you," he replied.

Her headpiece slipped off, revealing recently darkened hair, tied Ukrainian style in a tight braid. "It's been a long time old friend," she told him gently patting his cheek.

He could see that circles had formed around her gray green eyes, and there were faint creases on her forehead that had not been there before. Charlie was struck by how vulnerable his old friend now appeared. Never the less, she was still an astonishingly attractive woman.

"What are you...?" He stopped at the soft sound of footsteps approaching. They both turned to see an old man shuffling down the adjoining isle. He stopped before the row of votive candles, inserted a coin, and lighted a match. The old man blessed himself then watched intently as a small flame flickered before him. A slender column of smoke rose toward heaven, presumably carrying his intentions along with it.

"Let's leave now," Karen suggested, rising from the pew and heading toward the entrance.

Charlie followed obediently. She knew where they were going: he did not. He watched admiringly as she moved along the aisle with supple grace. He was now depending on her to provide the answer to his own prayers.

18

The street was crowded, and Charlie and Karen walked in silence. Soon she motioned, with a nod of her head, toward the doorway of a coffeehouse they were passing.

Once inside, the two of them found a table that was isolated from the others. Karen sat facing the doorway, while Charlie sat across from her and to one side in order to watch what was going on behind her. They both assumed basic tradecraft routines without thinking.

"Well..." he began, then hesitated. There were so many questions he wanted to ask, now that he had the opportunity, he didn't know where to begin.

Karen took the initiative. "I know you are curious where I have been the last few years."

"You could say that," he replied with a slight grin.

"You remember the last time we saw each other, it was in Odessa."

Charlie nodded, but said nothing. He remembered it very well. He had thought of that moment often in his sleep, and sometimes when he was awake.

"You were catching a flight back to the United States," she continued, "but I had nowhere to go. I couldn't leave with you, the FBI was still looking for me there. I have heard they really don't care for someone who ties up one of their agents, and then runs off to Mexico. Particularly when that someone turns out to be a woman. A woman who worked for the CIA," she added emphatically.

"I couldn't go back to Kiev. Not then, they were still looking for me because of what we had done. I couldn't stay in Odessa very long, they would start looking there too. There was a freighter that would be leaving soon for Tel Aviv. I contacted the Israeli consulate and asked for a visa. My mother was Jewish, a Jewish Ukrainian who had fled to the United States, so I claimed asylum."

"Asylum?" Charlie asked puzzled.

"You have heard of *Babyn Yar*?" Not waiting for his answer, Karen continued. "Over 33,000 Jews were massacred in Kiev in a single operation during the war. The killing was ordered by the Nazi military governor of the city, and conducted by the SS as part of their campaign against the Russians. The dead bodies were dumped in a mass grave, and covered up. The Germans claimed that it was in retaliation for Ukrainian guerilla attacks on their troops.

"A giant ten-foot-high bronze menorah had recently been erected to commemorate the anniversary of the event, and officials from Israel had come to Kiev for the occasion. They joined the Ukrainian President in leading a procession to the site. Hundreds of people, many from different countries, also attended the ceremony carrying red and white flowers. It was very emotional, and because of that the Israeli consulate officials were particularly receptive to my request."

Watching Karen describe her discussions at the consulate, she seemed to be very fragile, and Charlie could easily understand how she might have persuaded the officials.

The coffeehouse was beginning to fill, and he noticed that Karen's eyes would furtively follow each new arrival until they were seated.

"When I got to Tel Aviv," she continued, "I recalled the name of a man with the Mossad I had met when I was still with the Agency. He had been part of the Israeli-American group that worked on the Stuxnet computer malware that sideswiped Iran's nuclear centrifuges.

"With things getting worse in their area of the world, the Mossad needed all of the experienced help they could get. Particularly someone who was as familiar with U. S. intelligence practices as I was. The man heard my story and was very sympathetic, knowing how things like that happen at the Agency. He turned my name over to the Shin Bet to check me out further."

"Just like the FBI would do for the CIA in the United States."

"Exactly Charlie, just like that," Karen confirmed.

A waitress brought cups of very strong black coffee, and set them down on the table before them. To the waitress, or anyone else who might have been watching, Charlie and Karen would appear like any couple enjoying a rare moment of relaxation between them.

"So now you are working with the Mossad?"

Karen nodded her agreement.

"How did Emmett have your telephone number?" Charlie asked, deciding to change the subject.

She took a deep breath before continuing. "Emmett and I had kept in touch. He had always been concerned, knowing how the Agency had abandoned me, and he deeply regretted their actions. He was out of the loop at the time but... well we kept in touch. He had always been like a mentor to me."

As Charlie listened to Karen describe the circumstances leading up to joining the Mossad, her shoulders sagged and a sad expression crossed her face. Watching her now, the melody from *Madama Butterfly* raced through his mind, and he was reminded of Emmett's earlier observation regarding the way the Agency sometimes abandons its agents. He messaged his temples to erase the thought, and the damned melody.

"Why do you think Emmett kept coming back?" Charlie asked. "The Agency just didn't seem to have time to be bothered with Cold War hangers-on. They kept kicking him out when they didn't need him. Then things would change in the world, and they would give him a call to come back and do what he did best, and he would always return."

Karen thought for a minute. "I really don't know, but I think that he missed the thrill of the game. Matching wits with the enemy, that sort of thing. You know it gets to all of us. At least those of us who care.

"Actually, it was Emmett who gave me a reference to the Shin Bet. The man from the Mossad knew Emmett from way back. They had worked together on the Jonathan Pollard debacle."

"How did you find out that Emmett was dead?" Charlie asked.

At that inappropriate time, a group of English tourists, seated by the door, burst out in loud laughter. All eyes in the coffee house were drawn to their table.

The Brits sheepishly looked away.

"His secretary, Marissa Dolan, told me. She knew Emmett had been in touch with me over the years, and thought that I would want to know."

Charlie was afraid to ask, but forced himself. "You knew Marissa was dead...killed, as well didn't you?"

Karen's face turned pale. "No...how...what happened? My God, not Marissa too.

"She was a very nice woman," she added sadly. "Why, why would they do that?"

Charlie told her about how he had found Marissa. Afterward they both fell silent, concentrating their gaze on their coffee cups rather than looking at each other.

Finally, Charlie broke the silence. "And you have also been in touch with Vincent St. Claire all this time?"

Karen nodded, and took another sip of her coffee. "Yes Charlie, all of this time."

The way she replied, he fully realized just how deeply she felt that it had, indeed, been a very long time.

Suddenly, he felt very sorry for Karen. It seemed life had dealt her a very poor hand in creating problems she had done nothing to deserve. But she was a survivor, and he had a great deal of admiration for survivors.

"So they brought you in to find out who had killed Emmett." It was half statement, half question.

"Yes, Karen that is exactly what they did," he admitted. "You know Ray Riordan?"

She shrugged, and shook her head. "I think I recall hearing the name, but I really don't know him."

"He asked me to see if I could find out what happened. Find who killed Emmett. He needed someone with no connections to the Agency. I didn't want to, but he talked me into it.

"Actually, I thought a great deal of the old man, and I wanted to find out what happened to him. But now I realize I am in over my head."

Karen studied him as they spoke. "You asked me about Emmett, Charlie, but I wonder why do *you* keep coming back? You seem to be a good family man, a good husband, a good father—what keeps bringing you back to the dark side of the world?"

"I wonder about that sometimes myself," he told her rubbing his eyes. "Perhaps it's the challenge, the travel…I don't know. I guess I am a Catholic with a Protestant work ethic. I could probably sit here suffering from morbid introspection, but the truth is…at least I think it is…that work has been good in my life.

"I like being productive." His voice sounded hollow even to him, but he pressed on. "If I don't work it's unhealthy. I feel useless. It is very therapeutic for me to get up every morning and know that I have something to accomplish—a problem to confront---a puzzle to solve. Even after I retired, I found that I needed a challenge—even if sometimes like now—the challenge seems to be bigger than I am. So, I guess in an odd way I get a sense of satisfaction out of this. It is my form of basket weaving."

Charlie looked away briefly, then reached into his coat pocket and withdrew the papers that Emmett was looking at when he died. He glanced around before spreading them out in front of Karen.

"This is all I have," he admitted ruefully, pointing with his forefinger to the articles.

Karen glanced at them briefly, and nodded her acknowledgment. "I am familiar with the story about the Illegals. We were following it all very closely in Tel Aviv. None of us could figure out how they managed to operate so long—so many of them, without being detected. Even more, once they were discovered, no one could understand why your country was so willing to exchange them---just a matter of a few days after you rolled them up."

Charlie immediately noted Karen's reference to *your country*, but said nothing. Apparently, she had mentally made the full transition from America to Israel and from the CIA to the Mossad.

"I wondered the same thing," he replied. "It seemed that we got so very little in return."

"Karen nodded her agreement. "That is the reason I thought we should talk," she told him pointing to the picture of the spy that fled the country before the FBI made the arrest. "He's the one they said fled to Cyprus and then disappeared. We think he is here--here in Ukraine---in Kiev actually. That is why I am here, and why I thought we should meet."

"Who is he?" Charlie asked, folding up the articles and returning them to his jacket pocket.

"The name we know him by in Israel is Colonel Markoff—Dmitri Markoff. He was stationed here in Ukraine after the war, and became a favorite of Stalin. Later he transferred from the army to the KGB. They find people of his type particularly appealing. He was sent to the Andropov Institute—the KGB Training Academy in Moscow.

"After that..."

"Wouldn't he be very old—too old by now?" Charlie interrupted.

"About the same age as Emmett—or Vincent for that matter," she shrugged.

"Anyway, over the years, he developed a specialty. He became very good at planting false defectors. KGB or GRU officers who, on the surface, say they are disillusioned with communism or, more recently with Putin's Russian Federation. They say they want to build a new life in the West, and are willing to provide state secrets or false agents in return. Often when I was at the Agency we would bring them in---in from the cold, as the saying goes. But, we rarely trusted them. Practically never as a matter of fact.

132

"The theory was then—and probably still is, that Soviet leadership would never take the chance of letting any of their citizens with knowledge of state secrets, come under outside control for any length of time. But then you never know.

"Sometimes these false flags would defect to other countries. Great Britain, Germany... who the hell knows. We couldn't keep track of them all."

"False flags?" Charlie interrupted.

"False flags," Karen explained patiently, "is a term that intelligence services use for operations they might establish that could cause embarrassment if they were discovered and traced back to them. So, they make the operation look as if it was done by someone else. Some other country. A false flag.

"Anyway, that was why the Mossad found it strange when Markoff turned up in America. We kept track of him the best we could. Then the FBI rolled up the ten Illegals that had been operating in the U.S. for God knows how long. Once they were arrested your FBI kept them for a couple of days, and sent them back to Russia. The US knew exactly where they came from and immediately shipped them back.. Nothing false about them at all.

"At the same time, Dmitri takes off for Cyprus, and then here.

"It was all very strange." Karen concluded. "It just didn't smell right."

"Do you believe that Dmitri was the one who killed Emmett?"

"Yes Charlie I do. So do my people. He had the opportunity. Emmett might have known him from the old days, and would have been interested enough in what he had to say to let him into his apartment. Then bang," she whispered, pointing her forefinger at Charlie and making a wry face.

"But how do we find him in Kiev?" Charlie asked. "Do your people know where he is?"

"Not yet. The people at the consulate and the synagogues have feelers out, but nothing yet. They would like to find him as much as you would."

They looked at each other. "Check at your embassy," Karen finally suggested. "If you do it discretely, they might be able to help. I know they have set-up an undercover network here, and they may be able to pick up something."

That seemed to be the best plan for the moment. The only plan actually. The two of them exchanged their phone numbers in order to maintain contact. Charlie punched Karen's into his new burner, and she provided him with a numbered list of meeting places, and associated fallback locations.

Karen left first. Charlie watched to see if anyone would follow her. No one did, so he figured out the exchange rate on their bill, and what he hoped was an appropriate tip. By the time he left the restaurant Karen had already disappeared.

Classes at the nearby university had apparently concluded for the day. Young people filled the streets, usually in groups, heading for wherever students go at the end of the day. Charlie envied them. They seemed to not have a care in the world. It was a black and white world for them, while his was largely gray.

The funicular stained glass terminal building was cloaked in evening shadows. As soon as Charlie opened the door to his compartment, the cable caught and the tram began to jerk forward. He stumbled inside, quickly sliding the door shut. As he began to ascend, he looked backward towards the Dnieper, which was now hidden in fog.

As his car moved haltingly toward Kiev's upper city, he felt much better than he had before. At least now he had a name. A clue. A lead finally. Something to act on.

One thing he knew, he could not leave Kiev as soon as he believed he might, earlier in the day.

19

Last night's call to Beth had gone better than expected. She understood, and accepted his commitment to Emmett, and to the Agency. Things were going well with her. She was planning to spend some time with their daughter, and was looking forward to that. His wife learned years ago, when he was busy traveling the world, to be an independent and resourceful woman.

It was good talking to her, he missed their visits, and he was looking forward to finishing his assignment and returning to Chicago. Now, Charlie needed to see if he could recall how to get to the U.S. Embassy, and then see what type of assistance they might be able to provide in locating Colonel Markoff.

It was still early, and there were only a few people in the lobby. It was much different the night before when he had returned from meeting with Karen. Then, the lobby was filled with groups of men, and a few women, milling around, pacing back and forth, smoking heavily and looking sheepishly at one another; apparently waiting to be picked up and taken somewhere.

When Charlie had approached the desk to get his key, he asked the bespectacled night clerk about them. The little man smiled slyly, paused briefly and then replied. "They are all here to get introduced to our country's principal resource or..uh..ah.. economic asset you might say." His smile grew broader at the sight of the puzzled look on Charlie's face.

"Asset?" Charlie asked. "What...which....?"

The clerk couldn't wait for the question to form fully. "It is women... mostly blond haired, but not necessarily...

as long as they have…" He interrupted himself, and his eyes darted around the lobby before making the international gesture, known instinctively to all men, signifying large female breasts.

"They are here on *Romance Tours*, as they are euphemistically called, all of them looking for Ukrainian brides. We are a poor country with little opportunity, and they bring in much needed foreign exchange.

"We do have, however, an unusually large number of attractive women who would rather be somewhere else, almost anywhere else. Ukrainian women are no fools. After years of Communist Party control, they place great emphasis on financial stability. Often they feel that this is not available at home.

"Men from all over the world, but mostly America, come here to find a bride and provide that…ah stability", he smirked.

"You can find our women all over the internet. The men correspond with them, and can't wait to come here to meet them. They come by the planeload. They go to the dating bureau---take them out, and sometimes take them home to Cleveland, or somewhere."

Charlie had turned away to return to his room, but hesitated and returned to the desk. "Ok, I get it—I think, but what are the foreign women doing among the groups?"

The Clerk just shrugged. "It's a brave new world mister Connelly."

Charlie put last night's conversation behind him, concentrating instead on trying to recall the way to Sikorsky Street and the American Embassy.

Outside the hotel, the air had become crisp, and he turned-up the collar on his jacket. Looking around he was unable to recall which direction to take, and decided to hail one of the cabs waiting at the curb.

Staring out the window, as the taxi headed toward the embassy, Charlie saw people congregating around corner kiosks or ambling leisurely from store window to store window. Before, when he was in Kiev, there was considerable unemployment and the streets were more crowded with people who had no place to go. The situation had gradually improved, but Ukraine remained one of the poorest economies of all the ex-Soviet Republics. Now there were fewer people at this time of day, and those that were evident seemed to be more directed in their movement.

One thing that appeared the same was the elderly *babushkas'* in their long skirts, heavy sweaters, and bright headscarves. Charlie watched the old women setting up their crude stands to sell an assortment of candy, chewing gum, and cigarettes to the people passing by.

In many places of the world, cigarette smoking had been substantially reduced. This did not appear to be the case in Ukraine. Perhaps, Charlie decided, a nearness to the Chernobyl exclusionary zone had reduced people's concern for the effect of nicotine on their health. Besides, he grinned, it was a well-known fact in Russian countries that sufficient amounts of vodka could offset the detrimental effects of practically anything.

A tall iron fence separated the embassy from the street. Charlie paid the driver and approached the gate. A young marine carefully examined the outstretched passport, and then nodded him through.

The embassy was housed in an old multi-storied Russian-style box building. Inside, a marine sergeant, wearing a shirt lined with rows of ribbons, stood behind a glass-enclosed desk. The enclosure was centered under an official portrait of President Obama.

138

Charlie handed his passport over the counter. "Charlie Connelly for Mr. Durand," he advised. The marine checked a list, found the correct number, picked up a phone, and pointed toward a small waiting area across the lobby.

Charlie had just finished paging through a glossy brochure describing the commercial benefits of sugar cane production in Alabama when he heard his name. Looking up, he saw a tall young woman walking toward him, wearing a short silk skirt, and a tight sweater that strained every one of its polyester fibers. "Nadia Kitson," the slender blonde woman smiled. "Mr. Durand's administrative assistant. He is looking forward to meeting you."

Charlie followed the young woman as she led the way down a poorly lighted corridor. Her greeting had surprised him. He hadn't called in advance, and he had not decided to visit the embassy until yesterday. Was it just a form of greeting, or had Durand *actually* been expecting him? Curious he thought, quickening his stride to catch up, as his guide opened an office door and stood aside waiting for him to enter.

On his way to the embassy, Charlie had prepared a cover story for the Commercial Attaché. He was to be, once again, the international executive from Apex Electronics who was visiting Kiev prospecting for business. The story evaporated immediately as Durand rose from his desk extending his hand. "Charlie Connelly, good to see you, Ray Riordan told me to expect you, and provide any service that I can." He motioned toward a chair in front of his desk.

"What had Riordan told you I was doing here?" Charlie asked as he sat down. Nothing was as he had expected, and he wanted to see how much Durand knew, while revealing as little as possible.

"Said you were on a search for someone. Working under non-official cover. Doing a job for him, and I should help. Provide any assistance I can."

So much for secret Charlie thought, looking around the office. It was larger than most he had visited in his corporate travels involving embassy visits. It was also more sparsely decorated. A large walnut desk of course, but very little on the walls. Only one painting depicting General Custer at the Little Big Horn. Charlie hoped that the picture would not be prophetic.

Durand continued. "Of course I was happy to help, that was a hell of a job you did for us last time you were here."

"What do you know....what I.. what happened....how," Charlie stammered. Surprised the information about his previous trip remained so readily available.

"The file," Durand tapped his forefinger on the brown manila folder on his desk. "I looked it up in the file when they told me you were coming."

"God-damn it," Charlie exploded pounding his fist on the desk.

Durand recoiled in surprise.

More calmly, Charlie attempted an apology. "They told me there would never be a record of what was done here," Charlie explained.

"Sorry about that old chap. Didn't know it was to be a secret. You should know by now that the Agency is good at stealing secrets, but it's not worth a damn at keeping them. I'll be sure to burn the damn thing, after you leave. You can be assured of that, but what did actually happen?"

Nadia entered the office unannounced, causing a pause in the conversation. She carried a tray with cups and a carafe of coffee, which she placed on the desk between them. She smiled at Charlie, and left

Charlie accepted the gestured offer of a cup of coffee, and declined the extended sugar and cream.

Somewhat calmer now, he wondered how much to tell before deciding what the hell, the information apparently had been safe so far, and he needed Durand's assistance. It might be better if he knew the truth rather than speculation.

"I was here on a consulting assignment," he began. "A real one," he added to distinguish it from the lie he had been prepared to tell.

"I met someone that I had known before, who was working in the Ukrainian Government. At that time it had only recently become independent and was still staffed with Russian sympathizers."

"Not so different now." Durand interjected reaching into a desk drawer and withdrawing a bottle of Johnny Walker Black. He waved it back and forth enticingly in pendulum fashion.

Charlie shrugged his rejection, and continued. "She was an American who was concerned that some of the leftover Soviet missiles would get into the wrong hands.

"The Kh55's" Durand offered, setting down his cup, and putting Johnny Walker back in the drawer

"That's right eighteen Kh55 cruise missiles." Charlie confirmed. The Russians had left them here when they suddenly had to pull out of Ukraine.

As he began to recount the story, his mind was still backing and filling attempting to filter out the details that might be harmful to him, or more importantly to Karen. "The sale to the Iranians was going down quickly. They were close to taking possession of the hardware, along with all of the support and training documents they would need.

"It was scary stuff. I had a contact at Langley that I had dealt with in the past and decided to give him a call."

"The Maestro," Durand offered. "It's in the file," he added apologetically.

"Yes that's right. Did you know him?" Charlie asked.

"Heard of him, never met him. How is he doing?"

Charlie studied the man across the desk from him, and decided that he must not know everything about what he was doing in Kiev. "He has retired," Charlie lied. "Well deserved," he added as an afterthought to increase his credibility.

"Valentine—the Maestro," Charlie continued, "told me that he wanted the transfer stopped. At the same time, he didn't want anything done that might cause a problem for State."

"I recognize that tune," Durand offered shaking his head. "It hasn't changed a hell of lot since. That's all I hear from the mandarins at Langley---don't do anything to upset the pinstripes at State."

Charlie tried to appear sympathetic, but he had enough problems of his own.

"The Ukrainian Government was desperate for money. Their old customer, their only customer, had been the Soviet Government and the Russians were no longer willing to buy from their former satellite country.

"That left only the missiles that were of any value to anyone else, and the Iranians were the only ones who wanted them. Missiles aren't exactly like a used car. You just can't get in and drive them away. You need

142

documentation describing how to install them, maintain them, and of course shoot them if you need to.

"The missiles had already been crated, and the boxes were camouflaged and waiting on top of their railcars for shipment to Iran. There was only a single Ukrainian expert left that knew what it all meant, and he and the documents were to accompany the missiles."

Before Charlie could continue, the door opened and Nadia came into the office, removed the tray, smiled and left.

Both men watched in fascination at the young woman's rhythmic exit.

Durand shook his head and returned his attention to his guest. "So what happened to him?"

"He had an accident."

"Bad?"

"Fatal."

"So that was why you and your friend needed the embassy here to help get you out?"

"Exactly," Charlie confirmed. "The missile expert had an eye for my friend, and wanted to meet her at his dacha in the dead zone before he left for Iran."

"The dead zone? Around Chernobyl?"

"What can I tell you," Charlie replied. The property was cheap. So was the Ukrainian Government that got it for him. Apparently, he didn't care. Technical people are a little opaque sometimes.

"Anyway, my friend wanted me to drive her there. I did. We didn't know exactly what we were going to do when we got there, but we knew we had to do something. When we arrived it was evening. He saw the lights of the car approaching, and ran out to greet her. Visions of sugar plums dancing in his head I imagine. As he approached he saw there were two of us, and he got scared. He pulled a gun and took a shot at me.

"I drove over the son of a bitch."

"Wow," Durand exhaled, viewing his guest with new found admiration. "Fatal?"

"Fatal," Charlie confirmed.

"Afterward, we went inside the dacha. The room was filled, floor to ceiling, with operating manuals, diagrams, and stacks of papers. We had no idea what they were, but we could tell that they were all labeled Kh55."

"So then what?"

"So then we did the only thing that we could do."

"Yes — Yes," Durand added expectantly.

"We dragged the expert back into his dacha, poured vodka-- which there was plenty of –"

"Leave it to the damned Russians," Durand exclaimed.

"--all over the documents. After that we set them on fire, and the whole place went up like a Viking funeral."

"It must have been beautiful," Durand exclaimed. "A bright night fire blazing in the deserted woods of a nuclear dead zone, What could be a better way to destroy the mullah's missile capability."

"It was effective," Charlie assured him. "But then, we had to get the hell out of Dodge. Your people here were as eager to get rid of us, as we were to go. The airports and train stations were being watched around the clock. So they, rather ingeniously, I thought, booked us on a tour boat going down the Dnieper to Odessa. It was slow, but effective."

144

"Sometimes slow is good," Durand grinned, reaching once more into his drawer and extricating his friend Jack Black.

This time both men had a drink.

.

20

Durand put his friend Johnny Walker back in the drawer. Using the colloquial *mister* he asked. "So *Mister* Connelly, what can your humble civil servant do to help?"

It was the moment of truth once again for Charlie. He had to determine just how much information to provide. He recognized he would never be able to locate a Russian colonel in Kiev without the help of the Embassy, so he decided to provide as much information as necessary to gain Durand's assistance.

He took the papers describing the Illegals from his pocket and spread them on the desk. "I am looking specifically for this one," he pointed to the faded picture of the man he now knew as Colonel Dmitri Markoff. "I have reason to believe that, after he left Washington, he first went to Cyprus and from there to Kiev."

Durand scanned the documents. Pausing at the picture of Anna Chapman, he pursed his lips in a silent whistle. "And why are you looking for Markoff specifically?" the commercial attaché inquired, eventually moving his glance to the second page lying on his desk.

Charlie shrugged.

Durand had not expected an answer, but he had hoped to receive one never the less.

"Look Charlie, I want to help in any way I can, but you have to understand what we are up against here. As you know, I am listed on the Embassy roster as Commercial Attaché, and I do try to perform that function. Host Congressional junkets. Entertain visiting business executives. All that happy crap.

"The Consul General knows what it is that I really do, but never wants to hear of it from anyone else. He wants to preserve his precious plausible deniability." As he spoke the words plausible deniability Durand emphasized his point by writing them in the air with his forefinger.

"For everyone else here it is supposed to be a secret that I am with the CIA. But, I don't know how secret it is.

"Actually I do. It is not very secret at all. Most members of our staff are Ukrainian—like Nadia. The State Department calls them "foreign service nationals." Often, either because of patriotism or coercion, they report on the activities of their employers. Because she works for me she has been cleared, but who the hell knows.

"All of our Embassy personnel are tailed; their offices and apartments are bugged. My cover, in all likelihood, was blown the day after I arrived--if not the day before. It is a common slot for intelligence agents. We know that, and most of the local services know that as well. It's one thing if it is in Guatemala or London, for example, because no one really gives a damn.

"It is considerably different here. Ukraine is a semi-hostile environment. Not too long ago it was Russian, and the government is still mostly Russian bred if not born. The real Russians and half the Ukrainians would like to get the country back under the Soviet sphere. Putin referred to the Soviet collapse a *the greatest geopolitical catastrophe of the 20th century.*

"You know one thing that hasn't changed here since independence?" Durand asked, warming to his subject.

"No," Charlie answered cautiously, but still curious what the station chief was going to say next.

"Its corruption. That's what makes it so hard to operate here. The economy has all the characteristics of a damned matryoshka doll. You know what they are don't you?"

Durand didn't wait for an answer. "Well you know, ya got this big damned wooden doll filled with other dolls that at first you can't see. Then, when you take it apart, each doll gets smaller and smaller. Well, in this country when you finally get to the center, there is nothing there but corruption and you can't build a nation on that."

"I get the picture," Charlie replied, trying to get back to why he was there. "Life is tough, but you are still better equipped than I am to find a colonel in a Russian haystack."

Durand smiled at the reference. "Clever. Very clever. But, I want to make damn sure you understand just what the hell we are up against here. Everyone knows that Ukraine is philosophically, and practically the crown jewel of Russia's lost empire. Kiev was the birthplace of Russian culture and Putin believes that it remains an integral part of Russia's geopolitical center. He would do anything to get it back."

Charlie was set back by the seriousness of Durand's tone. He began to reconsider his chances of getting help from the Embassy, and he felt a nervous tightening in his stomach.

"I want to help you, and I will," Durand assured him. "Still you have to understand the situation here. In addition to all of our political problems, we have now been *Snowdened* like everywhere else in the intelligence community. After the super-secret NSA let him walk out with their god-damned secrets, all of our networks in Ukraine are hiding in their storm cellars shaking in their boots. We had spent years setting up secret cells within the Ukrainian Government, and around the country. Now they all want to come crawling back behind the wire.

"And you know what Connelly, I don't blame them. I am a little frightened myself and I spend most of my time tucked safely away behind Marine protection."

Charlie stared at Durand. He knew he was exaggerating, but he got the picture. The commercial attaché looked like he could have been a marine at one time himself. He had big hands resting on his desk, and a thick neck and broad shoulders. But, time had taken its toll. He now had a big gut straining against his tightly buttoned shirt.

"This doesn't mean I can't help you find the Colonel. I still have some resources that might be helpful..."

Charlie's mind drifted as Durand continued to dwell on his problems. He had seen him before. Not Durand exactly, but other men like him—in government, and in corporate life. Time had passed them by, and they were stuck in a job with a dwindling future. Their wives were still hopeful for another assignment with an advancement, but people like the men knew better. If a transfer did come, it would mean a change of scene rather than substantially enhanced responsibilities.

"You have to understand the political situation here....."

Some, in Durand's position, get tired of the game. They grow stale and disengaged, waiting out their pension. Others reach a point in their life and feel a compelling need to leave. To eventually get the chance to become a consultant perhaps. Charlie knew some of these. At least a few of them. But he didn't think that Durand was a quitter. He appeared to be a lifer who was still dedicated to his task, with considerable energy left.

Charlie had spent much of his career appraising the capabilities of men he might be working with, and he believed that he was good at it. You had to be to succeed.

Charlie decided that the man seated across the desk was still a player, and that was what he needed.

"So I am more than willing to help," Durand concluded, I do have a contact in the SZRU that might…

"The?" Charlie interrupted.

"SZRU is the Ukrainian's Foreign Intelligence Service. Something like the CIA, but more like the KGB since that is where most of them trained. I am a little hesitant about asking them to help us find a renegade Russian Colonel."

Charlie nodded in agreement. He felt like he was drowning in bureaucratic babble.

"To further complicate the situation, there are people on our side who don't want to think about the Cold War warming up all over again. It would only deflect attention away from the War on Terror, and they are afraid the government is unable to walk and chew gum at the same time."

"Multi-tasking they refer to it now." Charlie offered.

Durand looked at him suspiciously. "Exactly," he said tentatively. "Anyway it's very sensitive here, and I need to get authorization before I commit any resources for anything. You understand I am sure."

Charlie understood. "I need to bring Riordan up to date anyway. Perhaps you can get your authorization at the same time. So how do we do that?"

"Contact him you mean?"

"Yeah that's what I mean. Contact him without alerting the rest of Eastern Europe."

Durand rose from his chair and motioned for Charlie to follow.

He faced the blank wall behind his desk and pounded his fist against it, then paused momentarily before doing it a second time. A large door slid silently open, and Durand gestured, mimicking a head waiter leading a customer to a prized table.

Charlie started down a steep, poorly lighted series of stairs. It reminded him of going down to his grandmother's cellar many years ago.

He tried to adjust his sight to the faint light. Just as he had managed to do so, Durand flipped a switch at the bottom and bright lights engulfed a large equipment filled room.

"Welcome to the bubble," Durand grinned, as the door above the stairs slid shut with a pneumatic hissing noise.

Like most American embassies, the one in Kiev contained a secretly constructed secure room that could be used primarily as a classified communications hub; and in abnormal times, God forbid, as a refuge for Embassy personnel should the need arise. This one, like most, was lead-lined and windowless. The tightly sealed room was air-conditioned, but the faint hum Charlie heard was the white noise generator meant to foil any possibility of enemy eavesdropping.

The two men occupied two of a large bank of heavily padded office chairs, and positioned themselves side by side in front of a row of communications equipment and screens. As soon as Charlie sat down, he felt jets of air going up his pant legs. Startled he turned to Durand.

"Oxygen," Durand offered. As he was searching in one of the drawers beside him. An air-tight plastic dome descended from the ceiling engulfing them, and the communications console in air-tight security.

Charlie stared in consternation at his surroundings.

Apparently finding what he wanted, Durand extracted a heavy loose-leaf notebook, with pages separated by alphabetical tags. "I can never remember the damn codes," he apologized, rapidly flipping through the pages.

"Here it is, Ray Riordan," he told Charlie with a self-satisfied grin. Turning back to the communications console Durand removed the plastic identification tag from around his neck and swiped it through the digital scanner near his arm. The console came alive with a flashing green light, and he rapidly keyed in a series of numbers.

"We wait now," he told Charlie, "while the codes get cleared and routed through NSA to Langley."

The signals raced out of Kiev, over Greenland, and eventually into CIA Headquarters.

"Riordan here," the gruff voice on the other end of the line filled the small communications office.

"Connelly," Charlie replied. "I am with your guy in Kiev, and wanted to fill you in on what has happened here." With that introduction Charlie went on to describe in some detail, while omitting others having to do with Karen Kincaid, how he believed that Colonel Markoff may have been responsible for Emmett Valentine's death and was now in Ukraine after fleeing Washington.

"Could be," Riordan agreed. "So now what? You know that you have free reign to do what has to be done, as far as I am concerned—and no one learns about it later."

At that point, Durand intervened. "I have limited resources here, both physically and politically. Connelly has asked me to assist him in finding the Colonel, which I am willing to do, but I need your authorization before I proceed." With that as an introduction, Durand went into some length describing his situation at the Embassy, and into greater detail describing his limitations.

"Whatever it takes from both of you," Riordan interrupted, fearing that the connection might be lost if it lasted much longer. "If Connelly thinks that Markoff is his man, I want the bastard *clipped*, out of the way. Understood?"

Charlie objected, "I have never done *wet work* before. Can't you send someone else?"

"No," Riordan roared. His voice faded and then grew stronger. "There is not enough time to bring someone up to speed, and get him over there. If it is the Colonel, he may not stay long. You lose him then what do you have?" Riordan quickly answered his own question. "Nothing—not a damned thing."

The instructions were clear enough. Connelly had stated his case, and Durand had described his own limitations in providing assistance in locating Markoff.

"Before we end this," Riordan added brusquely. "I assume that you still have *one time pads* at the Embassy. Bring Connelly up to speed on them," he ordered just as the signal was lost.

The conversation with Washington ended abruptly. Durand flipped a switch and the plastic dome receded into the ceiling.

Charlie Connelly, the retired corporate executive, sat in dazed silence. He had never expected this. Probably should have, but didn't. Somehow, he had never thought that it would be left up to him to eliminate whoever had murdered Emmett Valentine. He had always believed, innocently he now knew, that if he did find the killer the person would be turned over to the Agency to be dealt with in whatever manner they decided.

Now what the hell had he got himself into? *Clipped--wet work,* he was only barely familiar with the terms.

At the same time, Durand stared at the console wondering how he could use his limited resources to uncover Colonel Markoff.

Finally, Charlie broke the silence. "One time pads—what in the hell are those?"

Durand led the way up the stairs. "They are an antiquated method of secure communications that are unexpectedly coming back into use. I'll show you how to use them when we are back in my office."

At the top of the stairs, Durand again applied pressure to the door's appropriate sweet spot. It responded by gliding silently open. As the access grew larger, both men glimpsed Nadia standing by Durand's desk. She was intently examining the newspaper article Charlie had left during the earlier conversations.

Nadia turned toward the two of them with a broad smile on her face. "I know this man," she told them, pointing to the picture of Colonel Dimitri Markoff.

Both men stared at each other in astonishment.

21

Durand didn't seem surprised to see his secretary in his office reading the material on his desk. She, on the other hand, seemed to find her boss walking through the office wall an everyday occurrence. Charlie found the entire scene unsettling.

"What—who—how do *you* know a Russian Colonel?" Durand stammered.

"Do you know where he is?" Charlie added.

Nadia was surprised at the level of interest exhibited for what she had originally considered to be an innocent observation. Not knowing exactly how to respond she offered a muted "Yeeess, I didn't know that he was a Russian Colonel, but I have seen him before."

"Here?" Durand asked.

"Where?" Charlie added.

Still uncertain how to proceed, Nadia began her tentative answer. "Well...you see my cousin Elana...she--she came here from Ivano Frankivsk. Under the Soviet regime, it was a closed city. Not many eligible men, and she would like to find a husband. One who is rich, and who will take care of her. Better than what she might find here. Maybe move to America, or London or somewhere nice."

"I understand," Durand interrupted impatiently. "Lots of Ukrainian young women feel that way," he cleared his throat, "but what does that have to do with..."

"The colonel?" Nadia answered. "Well you see one way of doing that is to go to a place where they have a dating agency."

By now both men were completely confused, but willing to wait out Nadia's explanation, hoping it would eventually lead to a clue to the colonel's location, since they had none.

The men sat down at the desk. Nadia pulled up a third chair and sat down as well. She sat with knees tightly together, nervously tugging at the hem of her tiny skirt.

"A dating agency?" Durand prompted.

"Yes, yes a dating agency. At least that is what they call it. That's one of the names at least. You understand there are a lot of woman like Elana in Ukraine right now. So some of them sign up with the agencies in order to meet foreign men who are looking for a young woman to marry. The agency puts their pictures on their websites along with," Nadia hesitated searching for the right word in English—"their physical attri—attributes." She looked at the two men to see if they were understanding what she was trying to tell them.

Regaining confidence she continued. "Sometimes the agencies have parties for the men who have come to Ukraine to personally meet with the woman they have only seen on the internet.

"Romance Tours," Charlie injected his new found knowledge.

Nadia nodded in agreement. "Yes that's right Romance Tours."

Durand had no idea how in the hell this was leading to Colonel Markoff.

"And Colonel Markoff?" he prompted.

"Yes, yes. Colonel Markoff," Nadia picked up the offered thread. "Well you see these parties are held sometimes two or three times a week."

"Where?' Charlie asked.

"Well the ones that Elana attends are held at a place they call the *Catacombs*. It is in the Podil District."

"And you sometimes go with her?" Charlie asked, beginning to understand.

"Yes," Nadia giggled her assent. "But I don't belong to the Agency. I am happy here. I just go along to provide moral support. She, you understand, is a country girl, new to the city."

It was still not clear to Charlie exactly how this involved the colonel. "And the colonel?" he tried again. "The colonel goes to these parties?"

"Oh no, he lives there."

"He lives at the Catacombs?"

"They have rooms upstairs. Sometimes the couples go to one of the rooms for a little more privacy," Nadia blushed.

"And?" Charlie pressed.

"And your Colonel Markoff lives in one of those rooms on the second floor," Nadia replied. "I have seen him go up and down from there often."

Durand was immensely relieved. His concerns about mounting some type of extensive surveillance program apparently was no longer necessary; as well as his exposure to upper management criticism if his efforts went sour.

"Thank you Nadia, you have been very helpful, Durand told her. He looked at Charlie, who nodded his agreement they had found what they had been looking for.

"We may need you again Nadia, but that is all for now," Charlie added as the young woman quickly rose to leave.

"What do you want to do now," Durand asked after Nadia had left the room.

"Do you know anything about the Catacombs?" Charlie asked in reply.

"Not specifically. We have heard that the Russian Mafia runs a lot of these bridal agencies as a front for sex trafficking and it sounds like your colonel would fit in well with them. It is also possible that the KGB is involved. It is not entirely unheard of for spies to use attractive women as 'honey traps.' The practice is as old as the *art* of intelligence," Durand grinned.

"I'll have to think about it," Charlie told him, rising to leave as well. He had come to the Embassy to see if they could help him locate the colonel, and they had done that in an unexpected way.

Now he wanted to talk it over with Karen. He knew that she was somewhere in an Israeli safe house and he wanted to give her a call.

"By the way," Durand stopped him before he got to the door. "Riordan told me to provide you with some one- time cipher pads. Are you familiar with them," he asked reaching in his desk drawer.

"Not exactly. What in the hell are they?"

"They are an old technology that has recently become new again. Oddly enough, the old ways of communicating have become the least vulnerable. Some people feel that they provide better communications security than some of the high powered crap we are using now. In addition, they are more portable."

Charlie moved his chair closer to the desk and sat down.

Durand began, "They operate on the mathematical principal of matching sets of random numbers *once* between the sender and the receiver in small groups in a coded message...."

"Like texting?" Charlie asked.

Durand looked at him skeptically. "Not exactly."

"In small groups in a coded message," he repeated, "the matching set then becomes your source code."

"Sounds complicated," Charlie offered.

"Well not really, once you get used to it. And it is handy. Once the groups are in the message," Durand forged ahead "they can be translated into words by referring to a non-reusable key. But they can be used only *once*. That is the secret of them and, of course, that is the reason they are called one-time cipher pads," Durand concluded, staring at Charlie for some sign of comprehension.

"They used to be an integral part of any agents equipment when he went into the field, since it provided a convenient and secure means of communication. They can still do that."

Charlie had begun his career in the computer industry, and had some sense of random number generators and what could be done with them, but this might require some additional consideration.

"Thank you for the equipment and the explanation," Charlie offered, slipping the device into his jacket pocket.

He started to leave and turned to retrieve the articles he had left. "Need a copy?" he asked Durand.

No, I have Nadia," Durand grinned. "Stay in touch."

Out on the street, he could feel the one-time pad in the back pocket of his jacket. He had bought the Barbour Commander Jacket in Washington before he left for Vienna.

The light weight waxed-cotton exterior was water resistant, and the five pockets, including two in back, were perfect for storing a variety of devices.

He decided to walk back to the hotel. The days were already growing shorter, and he pulled the collar of his jacket higher on the back of his neck.

Kiev is an ancient city that just grew through the ages without the benefit any form of central planning. The streets resemble a crazy quilt of intersecting angles, wandering through the city without any recognizable pattern. In other words, it fit Charlie's mood perfectly.

He didn't remember the way as well as he thought he would. Fortunately, he could see the towering *Rodina Mat* statue towering over the city, and he used its sword as a directional beacon. The *Defense of the Motherland Monument* depicted a female warrior equipped with a giant sword and shield, and Charlie headed in its direction, recalling that it stood close to his hotel.

Walking along Khreshchatyk Street he once again passed the fountain-filled Independence Square, referred to as the Maidan. Earlier in the day, the park had been virtually empty but it was now filling rapidly with people preparing to form another demonstration similar to the old Orange Revolution days.

The current thuggish regime had imprisoned a political rival by the name of Yulia Tymoshenko who, with her blond braids and acerbic tongue, had been a leader of the previous uprising. She had, in turn, gone on a hunger strike. The demonstrators Charlie was watching were waving banners with her picture, and demanding her release. The protesters were not alone in their demands. The European Union was also pressing for her freedom by denying the country a coveted partnership in the EU.

Things had not changed as much as he had first thought Charlie realized as his hotel came into view.

By now, it was a lightless late afternoon in Kiev. He looked at his wristwatch. It was the previously agreed upon time to contact Karen. He thought it best to call her before he got to his room, in case the room was no longer secure.

Charlie found a small sheltered doorway close to his hotel. He glanced right and then left to make sure he was alone; then waited for an approaching bus to pass so that its rolling sound wouldn't interfere with their conversation. Hiding in the shadows, he felt like a pimp or a drug dealer. Then he remembered he was a spy, and hiding in the shadows is what spies are supposed to do.

The bus sped past, trailing its noise behind. Charlie checked the street again. The old man on the corner, selling ersatz Russian Army watches, was folding up his cardboard stand and moving away. When he was gone, Charlie punched Karen's number into his throw away phone, and waited anxiously for her reply.

22

Langley

Riordan switched off the scrambler, breaking the connection with Kiev. The call from Connelly and Durand had been unsettling. He looked around his office, considering what he had just learned. Perhaps Markoff had wiped Emmett, and it was possible, as Connelly thought, that he was hiding in Kiev. He was Russian, and Kiev was almost like Moscow.

Durand didn't seem particularly confident that he would be able to find the Colonel if he was there. He could sympathize with him. Being a CIA station chief in a politically sensitive city wasn't easy. Particularly now that there was a good chance that all of his conversations were being recorded, and could later embarrass him and the United States.

But what if Connelly could find Markoff. What then? What does he do then? What do I do then?

What if he doesn't find him, then where will I be? Riordan wondered. Up the creek without the proverbial paddle, he decided, providing an answer to his own question. The problem was he had too many questions and not enough answers.

Riordan got up from his desk and went to the window, where he stood staring downtown at the Federal District. He felt the need to do something. But what?

He turned away from the window and returned to his desk. "Linda, get me Barbara Richards," he bellowed. When in doubt give orders. That was what he had learned in the military, and sometimes it worked

By the time Barbara entered his office, Riordan had composed himself and was signing- off on a stack of papers that had accumulated on his desk.

"Barbara." Riordan began, I have just heard from Charlie Connelly. He believes that Colonel Dimitri Markoff is somewhere in Kiev."

Barbara had to search her memory. "The Russian that was the control for the Illegals the FBI recently picked up?"

"Exactly. Did we ever have much on him?"

"Not that I am aware of. I was never really involved," she replied, puzzled at the question. Riordan should be aware that she had nothing to do with that case. If someone in the department was involved, he should know who it was.

"I didn't think you were," Riordan assured her. "But you have such a good relationship with what's his name in the file room....?"

"Not really," she quickly injected. Barbara saw what was coming, and didn't want anything to do with it.

"What *is* his name?"

Barbara paused, "Thorndike—Walter Thorndike." She knew what was coming.

"Yes, yes Walter Thorndike. Could you trot down there and see what kind of a file we have on Colonel Dimitri Markoff."

"Of course," she replied. She had been around the Agency long enough to know that when an assistant director asks you to do something you smile and agree to anything. Well *almost* anything, she decided as she left Riordan's office.

Barbara was angry. Mad that she was asked to do what she considered to be a clerical task. After all, she *was* a staff analyst, and she had done tours overseas. Tours, as a matter of fact, that were damn dangerous. And by God, she did them well.

The angrier she got the faster she walked, and soon she was at the door to the file room. She swiped her card, and burst through the door.

"The AD wants to know what we have on a Colonel Dimitri Markoff," she asserted, facing the Agency's document gatekeeper. The insufferable little twerp.

Walter Thorndike sat majestically behind an oversized desk, underneath a large 24 hour clock.

What an obvious affectation she thought. It gave the appearance that the file-room was military, and he was the furthest anyone could be from a military man.

"Which AD?"

"Ray Riordan, do you want to call him?"

"Of course not," he smiled amiably. He knew Riordan and certainly didn't want to antagonize him.

"Markoff?" Dimitri Markoff?" he asked entering the name into a large keyboard on his desk.

An alphabet of names rapidly sequenced on the screen above him, finally settling on one and providing an alphanumeric floor location.

"Just a minute dear," Walter smiled, trotting-off in the direction the numbers had directed.

It was not a minute. As a matter of fact, it was a hell of a long time before Barbara saw him returning. This time his relaxed gate had turned into a controlled run.

164

"It's gone," he sobbed. "I don't know where. My records show that it was here, but it is not now."

"Where is it if it is not here?"

"I don't know—I don't know," Walter replied angrily.

"Has someone checked it out?" Barbara asked.

"They must have, but I don't know who." By now, the little man was approaching a state of panic. His system had failed him, and it was patently obvious to a woman. A woman who was staring furiously at him. A woman sent by one of the most influential assistant directors in the entire agency.

"I'll find out who. I'm sure I will. I will call you as soon as I find it. Don't worry," he assured her, wiping perspiration from his brow.

"Could the file be under another name," she suggested. "A cryptonym perhaps?"

"A code name for a Russian Colonel? Unlikely, but I couldn't find it if I didn't know what it was. I have a directory of them. I'll see what I can find, but it is unlikely," he confirmed.

Barbara returned to Riordan's office more slowly than before. One thing that Walter could do well was to keep track of the volumes of files the CIA routinely accumulated. That was the reason the little prig remained in charge as long as he had.

"Ray," Barbara paused in Riordan's doorway.

"What did you find?" he asked looking up from his work.

"Nothing. Not a damn thing. Walter had a file, but it's gone. The little ass was almost in tears. He assured me that he will find what happened to it and let me know, but right now it is a dead-end."

After Barbara left, Riordan resumed his position at the window. While she was gone to the file room, he recalled who from the Agency had been involved with the FBI. It was Ralph Gross who worked with the cousins rounding up the Illegals. Perhaps the file was in his office. He would have to see if he had a copy of the combination to his security safe. Perhaps it was there.

23

Kiev

The hotel lobby was beginning to fill with groups of people waiting to be gathered up for the evening's *Romance Tours*. There was little mingling among them as each person was seemingly only intent on finding the companion of their dreams. Some stared at pictures they brought, while others paced nervously waiting for the anticipated arrival of their guide.

The desk clerk pointed Charlie to the group waiting for transportation to the Catacombs. On his way to join them, he noticed Karen coming through the hotel's revolving door. She was dressed in black slacks, and the same dark blue anorak and gold colored turtleneck she had worn earlier in the day. Her hair was pulled back in a severe bun, and she wore little makeup. It was apparent to him, but unlikely to anyone else, that she had taken great pains to dress in a manner that would draw little attention or emphasize the attractive woman she actually was.

Charlie moved to join his designated group, and Karen followed at a distance. There was no sign of recognition between them. They had agreed, during their telephone conversation, to stay detached until they had an opportunity to better appraise the situation.

Some of the other groups had already departed when a young woman breezed through the doorway displaying a broad smile, and a large badge with *Catacombs* printed in bright red letters. Her group obediently fell in behind, as she led them to a waiting van.

Charlie entered first and went to the rear, while Karen took a seat near the driver. Inside, the stale air from earlier tours mingled with the strong scent of duty-free French cologne worn by the recent travelers.

Their vehicle pulled away from the curb with a grinding of gears, and headed immediately into the evening traffic flow. Picking up speed, the van careened through the narrow cobblestone streets before beginning its steep decent toward the Podil District. Discarded debris from previous excursions cascaded from the rear of the vehicle toward the front, and Charlie clutched the armrest to keep from falling forward. He could see Karen, several rows ahead of him, bracing herself against the back of the driver's seat.

They soon leveled-off, and the driver expertly slipped his vehicle to a stop in front of a large stone building. A garish flashing sign announced their arrival at the Catacombs. The vehicle's doors swung open, and their guide led her flock from the van to the buildings wide doorway.

Once inside, they obediently followed the young woman into a tunnel-like corridor. An occasional torch lighted their passage, casting flickering shadows along the hallway's solid rock walls. An attempt had been made, for reasons known only to the psychedelic Russian designer, to pattern the building's construction on the network of tunnels and tombs that formed the burial ground for the early Roman Christians. In a further attempt to emulate the original catacombs, rough paintings of doves and peacocks lined the otherwise bare stone walls. A web of smaller corridors fed off the main passage and lead to individual rooms available for private parties.

A burst of bright lights finally announced the group's arrival at their evening's destination. The guide led them into a cavernous chamber filled with empty tables of varying sizes. Along the opposite wall was an astonishing array of attractive, predominately young, Ukrainian women. Each one bearing highly visible name tags, seated on padded folding chairs, hopefully waiting for their pre-arranged or unarranged suitor.

Most of the women were tall, blond and slender, with high Slavic cheekbones, wearing tight leather pants and chunky earrings. A few of them were more elegantly dressed looking as if they had just returned from a sorority soiree. Others provided, in their facial structure, evidence of their early Asian ancestors.

Balalaika music filled the room, and all eyes turned toward the approaching visitors. The young ladies giggled nervously, and whispered together behind well-manicured hands as they appraised the foreign visitors entering the room. Each of them attempting to guess which of the men were the most prosperous and which might be interested in their favors.

Internet photos were brought-out, woman selected, and tables gradually filled. Charlie nodded toward Nadia seated among the rows of young woman. He had called the Embassy from the hotel and asked her if she could be there.

Karen joined Charlie at his table, while Nadia raised an inquiring eyebrow. The large room began to fill with waitresses dressed as Cossacks, wearing large fur hats, and bright red tunics adorned with gold epaulets and brass buttons. Below the tunic, instead of the traditional baggy riding britches of the wild Russian warriors, the young women wore skin-tight lace panties, and shiny black boots. They moved through the crowd balancing trays with slender shot glasses of Stolichnaya vodka, and bottles of Sovietsky champagne. Other young women circulated through the room offering an assortment of traditional kebabs, blinis, sour cream, and caviar.

As the evening progressed, Charlie and Karen continued to study the crowd, hoping to catch sight of Colonel Markoff. They were not the only ones making appraisals that evening in the Catacombs. There was a continuing flurry of activity between the individual tables, between the people at the tables and the dance floor, and between the dance floor and the rows of hopeful young women seated along the wall. The level of activity continued to increase as prospective suitors were accepted, rejected, or exchanged. An occasional couple would detach themselves from the rest and, somewhat furtively, climb a flight of stairs to the upper floor, and then disappear.

As they watched, Charlie was becoming increasingly concerned that there would be no sign of the Colonel, and underneath the table he would nervously wipe his sweaty palms along his trouser legs. Waiting made him nervous. He wasn't used to it. Charlie studied Karen more intently. Their current situation seemed like an old tune that kept coming back. They had been through all of this before. It was if they were both playing from an old script without knowing how the story ends.

Karen on the other hand was more used to waiting. She was a field agent and that's what field agents do—wait—and watch, and she was experienced at doing both.

Charlie once again removed the clippings from his jacket pocket. He wanted to make sure he would recognize Markoff if they did see him. He tried to convince himself that he could, but was still not sure. The Colonel might be nearby at one of the other tables and still go unrecognized as far as Charlie was concerned.

At the same time, he tried to keep a close eye on Nadia. She was presently dancing with a heavyset man who moved gracelessly to the music. She noticed him watching and smiled.

Turning toward Karen Charlie asked, "How did you ever became aware of the Illegals in the United States? I thought you were gone by then."

"That's right, I was. It was almost by accident. Remember when we first asked you to become an active player?"

"Of course, it was on my trip to Lima," he replied almost ruefully. "You wanted me to carry money down to a group you were funding in Peru. Right?"

"Right Charlie. That was the time. What we didn't know then was a connection had developed between a member of the group we were working with there and Guzman's radicals.

"I am sure you remember the woman who slipped you the receipt while you were at the *Rosa Nautica*. She was well educated, sophisticated, and a TV reporter. At that time, everyone at the Agency believed she was part of the opposition to the Peruvian radicals. That was why we became interested in working with her.

"Later we found she had once been kidnapped by Guzman's followers. They insisted that a video tape of their demands be aired on her television station in exchange for her release. When you were there, everyone believed she was a victim. It wasn't until much later we discovered she was, in fact, a willing participant."

While Karen was talking, Charlie would occasionally glance at Nadia, in case she spotted the Colonel.

"It was long after I left the Agency, and was in Tel Aviv," Karen continued. "My handler at the Mossad had a contact with the FBI. He was aware they had become suspicious of a group of undercover agents working for Russia's SVR. I identified one of their picture as the woman we had dealt with in Peru. She had married one of the suspected Illegals and was living in New York with him under an assumed name. My handler notified the FBI, without mentioning me of course, and the Bureau followed up on it."

Voices of the crowd swirled around them. The music had grown louder, the smoke thicker, and the activity more frenetic. Time was fleeting and, as the evening was drawing to its eventual close, the visiting princes were becoming more anxious to find their Ukrainian Cinderellas.

Nadia came spinning past in the arms of another man, more agile than the last.

As Karen finished her story, Charlie turned away and noticed Nadia vigorously motioning toward the stairway behind her partners back. A tall man with broad shoulders was coming down the steps. Charlie once again checked the pictures. It was Colonel Markoff, he was sure of it.

The man from Moscow Center was dressed in the same casual style as most of the other men in the room, but his carriage was more erect and purposeful. He weaved a serpentine path through the tables then, once clear of them, strode directly toward the corridor leading to the outside door.

Charlie looked inquiringly at Karen. She hesitated, and then nodded in agreement. They rose from the table, and headed toward the stairs. Karen attempted a shy giggle, for appearances sake, as Charlie gave her an affectionate hug. To anyone watching they were just another couple anticipating the romantic pleasures available on the second floor of the Catacombs.

24

The second floor hallway was long, narrow, and poorly lighted. A bare bulb, half way down the corridor, provided the only illumination. It was the type of place people walked hoping they would not be observed — or recognized.

Charlie noticed there were six doors on the right, and five on the left of the passageway. The first doorway on the left was twice the size as those on the opposite side. There was another noticeable difference. The large door had no knob or handle, while all the others did.

That had to be the Colonel's room, and the door was designed to be opened only with a special key. He pressed against it. There was no give. Charlie stepped back and removed the wallet from his back trouser pocket, selecting a credit card from the large group he had accumulated over his years of international travel. Karen kept watch on the stairway, while he tried to slide a card between the lock and the door jam.

He inserted the card once, then once again. Each time the lock failed to release. The card was too thick he decided, and nervously searched through his wallet for one that might be slimmer. Fingering nervously through them, he eventually selected his American Express card. On the second attempt, the lock released, and the door gaped open.

He began to enter, but hesitated when Karen placed her hand on his arm. Pointing two fingers towards her eyes, she went to the door across the passageway. It was unlocked, and the room vacant. She slipped inside to watch and warn him if she saw the Colonel returning.

Markoff's room was much like a thousand others that Charlie had stayed in during his travels. There was a large double bed, with a stand beside it. On the other side was a doorway leading to a small toilet and shower area. A tall armoire stood on the opposite side of the room. Next to it was a writing desk and lamp, along with a carafe and two empty glasses. Nearby, on top of a set of drawers, was a Korean television set and an oversized mirror.

Charlie hurriedly looked around the room, searching for where he might find some form of identification to confirm that it was the room of Colonel Dimitri Markoff. He was sweating, although the room's temperature was cool.

He started to open the door to the armoire when he heard the clicking of a latch. His first instinct was to try and hide inside the cabinet, but there was no time. The Colonel entered the room, and immediately saw Charlie's figure reflected in the mirror on the opposite wall.

Charlie's mind raced, trying to find an acceptable excuse. Of course there was none. He could only stand and stare at the Russian, who was reaching into his inside jacket pocket.

Charlie realized immediately what the Colonel was reaching for. It was something for which he had no match. Instead, out of desperation, Charlie grabbed the metal water decanter off the desk and flung it as hard as he could at the Colonel.

Luck sometimes accompanies the innocent, and the decanter struck Dimitri in the center of his forehead, opening a deep gash above the bridge of his nose. The decanter clattered on the bare hardwood floor. The Colonel staggered backwards clutching his nose; his small Makarov automatic pistol tumbling beside the decanter.

Dimitri was older than Charlie, but equally as tall, and schooled in martial arts by some of Russia's best instructors. He managed to maintain his balance, and reached for the gun that lay at his feet. Before he could recover it, Charlie lunged forward only to be staggered by a karate chop aimed for his neck, but glancing off his shoulder. Charlie caught the Russian with an elbow to the temple, staggering him backward.

Dimitri somehow regained his balance, and grasped a knife concealed behind his back. With his other arm, he seized Charlie and spun him around. Dimitri spread his legs, taking a stance that would allow him to drive the knife deeply into Charlie's chest.

Charlie could see it coming, but he was defenseless to stop it. Suddenly his hand grasped the stinging lobe of his ear, while hearing behind him the dull thump of a muffled Beretta.

A small hole opened in the center of the colonel's forehead that began spurting blood. He fell forward, arms flaying the air, grasping for Charlie's throat. His dagger, with the red star of the old Soviet Union on the handle, fell to the floor with Dimitri falling on top of it.

Karen rushed across the room, and kicked the knife from underneath the fallen Russian colonel.

"Oh my God, I'm terribly sorry Charlie," she apologized dabbing his bleeding ear with a tissue. "I was watching the street from the front window. I didn't believe he would come back so soon. He must have forgotten something, and I missed him. I heard the door open, but it was too late to warn you. I *am* sorry," she repeated patting his cheek.

Karen turned Markoff's body over, and picked up his gun with tissue covered fingers. Her hand was trembling, as she hurriedly formed the Russian's fingers around the handle. She knew that his fingers would soon tighten on the grip.

As she worked, she tried to steady herself. It was the first time she had actually killed a man, and she desperately needed to conceal her emotions.

"What are you doing?" Charlie was shocked at the blood dripping into Dimitri's sightless eyes. At the same time, he felt a flood of relief that it was now over. Emmett's murder was solved, his death revenged, and the search for his killer was ended.

"I'm going to try and make this look like a suicide," Karen replied. "We have to get out of here, but while I am doing this look around and see what you can find."

"Do you think it will work?" Charlie asked. "Do you think they will believe it was a suicide?"

"Probably not for long, but maybe it will take a little while for them to figure out what really happened," she replied searching through the Colonels pockets.

After Charlie finished going through the clothes in the armoire he started opening the desk draws.

"Charlie…"

He turned to see Karen paging through Dimitri's passport.

"..when exactly was Emmett killed?"

So much had happened he had to think. "I am not sure *exactly*. I remember when Riordan called me at home. I left the same day. When I arrived, he and Brady picked me up at the airport and took me directly to the funeral." His mind was racing trying to recall, and at the same time wondering why Karen was curious.

Charlie finally came up with a date. "Why are you asking?"

"That is what I thought I had heard. Markoff couldn't have killed Emmett then. He was already in Cyprus."

"Oh my God," Charlie swore. We've killed the wrong damned man."

"Don't feel bad," Karen told him. "Dimitri Markoff spent his life working for the Kremlin. He was one of Russia's greatest spymasters, and he was responsible for the killing of more innocent people than you and I will ever know.

"Finish what you were doing and let's get out of here before someone finds us," Karen whispered, looking behind the pictures on the wall.

"Nothing. Not a thing," she declared. "Let's get out of here before someone finds us."

Charlie finished looking through the bathroom cabinet, before heading for the doorway. In his haste, he stumbled against the desk. A Kiev telephone directory fell to the floor with a thud.

Karen turned around, and made a face.

Charlie stooped to replace the directory. As he did, a sheaf of papers tumbled to the floor.

"Jesus, what in the hell is all of this."

"Quickly Charlie, we don't have time to look through them now. Put them in your pocket, and let's get out of here."

As they were leaving, Charlie made sure the door locked securely. They both automatically checked the corridor on the way out. There was nothing, no activity at all. At the top of the stairs, they intertwined their arms around each other and swayed their way toward the first floor.

There were fewer people than before, but none of them paid the slightest attention to Charlie and Karen. They were all far too concerned with their own affairs to be interested in anyone else.

Charlie scanned the room, and was relieved to see that Nadia and her cousin Elana had already left. The two conspirators made their way directly to the corridor leading to the exit. It was empty, and they quickly left the Catacombs and the dead man from Moscow Center behind them.

25

When they were safely outside of the Catacombs, Karen first looked one way then the other to see if she could identify any type of surveillance that might place them at risk. Because the building had served as the *rezidentura* for one of Russia's most famous intelligence agents, it made sense that someone from either the Ukrainian Government or the Russian Federation might wish to keep track of who was entering or leaving. Karen had studied streetcraft, with the CIA and the Mossad, and she was confident of her ability to identify any hostile provocations.

It was a cool, but pleasant evening. The street was busy enough, filled mostly with students and tourists, and she couldn't recognize anything that might be threatening.

"What now?" Charlie asked pulling up the collar of his jacket to offset the weight of the documents he had stuffed in his pockets. As they walked, he tried shifting them around so it would be less obvious to anyone who might be watching. The two of them easily melted into the crowd. Just another couple out for an evening's entertainment in the Podil District.

"My place," Karen replied. "It will be more secure than your hotel."

They headed toward the funicular. Both of them felt shaken by their experience, and they wanted to leave the Podil District behind as quickly as possible.

At the Poshtova Square station, they waited impatiently for their car to arrive. Standing on the platform gave them another opportunity to see if someone was following them, but they were safely alone. There was little conversation between them. Both were thinking about what had occurred at the Catacombs. Their cable car arrived and the doors swung open. Once inside they remained silent, thinking about what might come next.

Charlie had been convinced that Dimitri was the man who had killed Emmett. Now he knew that was not the case. But if the Colonel was not the one, then who was? The trail for him had ended in the Catacombs; now his only alternative was to go home a failure. He was not used to failing at something he had set out to do, but he would be glad to get out of Kiev. He had enough of its political problems, and he didn't want to get embroiled in any of that.

The tram car gave a jolt, and the doors slid open. Karen and Charlie got out at the Upper City platform. There was a taxi stand outside the station, and Karen gave the driver the address of her safe house. As they pulled away, she turned to look out the cab's rear window to make sure there was nothing following behind them. They had just killed a Russian agent and it appeared, for the moment at least, they were getting away unnoticed.

The taxi stopped in front of a large two story house in a nondescript residential district. The place was set back from the street, partially hidden by large trees. Leaves covered the sidewalk.

Inside the house, a sparrow of a woman in a shapeless black dress greeted them. She smiled thinly at Karen, and looked at Charlie with piercing gray eyes. After speaking a few words in Hebrew, she disappeared down a narrow hallway.

Charlie followed Karen into a large living room with heavy overstuffed furniture, and an empty fireplace. A massive bookcase covered one wall. Each shelf contained rows of books, all neatly arranged. It was obvious that the house was well cared for, but seldom used.

Karen punched a number into her cell, and waited for a response. In seconds, she began speaking rapidly and for Charlie unintelligibly. Once she paused with a hand over the phone. "Control," she whispered to Charlie.

When she finished her call, she went to the window to peer through a set of heavy black drapes at the street outside. The room had a musty odor, and the drapes looked as if it had been months since they were last opened. She finally turned away, satisfied they had not been followed.

There was a large table with a small lamp in the center of the room, she sat down and motioned for Charlie to join her. "Let's see what you found."

He took off his jacket before sitting down, and emptied his pockets spreading the papers over the table top. Pulling a chair closer to Karen, he laid his jacket over its arm. A small thumb drive clattered to the floor." I forgot about that," he told her as he bent to retrieve it.

Karen glanced at Charlie. A blotch of purple had formed at the base of his neck where a blow from Markoff landed. She said nothing, he would find it soon enough himself. Karen still felt guilty that she had failed to warn him of the Colonel's return. It was completely unprofessional, and she prided herself on her competency above everything else.

As the two of them studied the documents, the sparrow entered the room carrying a tray of cold beef sandwiches, goat cheese, and a bottle of Israeli Red Zinfandel. She came and left in a whisper. Neither Karen nor Charlie paid her any attention. They were completely absorbed with the Colonel's papers.

The table lamp cast a pale yellow light. All of the documents were in Russian. Some typed, some scrawled, but all unintelligible to Charlie. Karen had spread them out over the table, and would occasionally pass one to Charlie to look at. None of them made any sense to him.

He ate a sandwich and washed it down with a glass of wine before picking up one of a set of black and white pictures among the documents. It was no clearer to him than the Russian documents had been.

He held the picture up to the light, then rotated it, then rotated it once more. The photo was in varying shades of gray, making it difficult to distinguish one form from the other. Eventually, he could make out a large block building sitting next to a street or a roadway. Rubble surrounded the entire area.

The next picture was similar, but taken from a greater distance and at another angle. Now Charlie could see that other buildings surrounded the structure in the previous picture. They were all in varying stages of collapse.

He held the photo to the light once more. In the background was a Ferris wheel. What in the hell was this all about he wondered. Certainly not Vienna, but where could it be, and why had the pictures been taken? He wanted to ask Karen, but she was concentrating her attention on a single sheet of paper she had separated from the others.

As Karen studied her document Charlie rose, stretched, and walked over to a large TV set on the other side of the room. He wanted to see if there was any news concerning a dead Russian. He adjusted the dials to bring in a better picture, but the color remained pallid, and the objects and people fuzzy and indistinct.

He searched for a remote, but finally resorted to manually turning the dial from station to station. The only thing he could find was a speech Vladimir Putin was giving to a grim-faced Moscow audience and on a local channel a group of Ukrainian folk dancers.

Suddenly, the dancers became awkwardly frozen in their presentation. The screen went blank, and a local announcer, feverishly describing a scene taking place in Independence Square, replaced the dancers.

Karen glanced up from her papers, then rose and joined Charlie. Occasionally, she would interpret, for him, what the newsman was saying.

The Ukrainian President, Viktor Yanukivych, had flown to a military base near Moscow for a secret meeting with the Russian President. While he was there, he stunned the EU negotiators and his own people, by rejecting a trade deal which he had agreed to sign just a few days before.

This was prompting angry protests in Kiev. Thousands of people were gathering in the square listening to speeches opposing the government's drift toward Russia, and away from the European Union. Many of them were waving flags, and singing the Ukrainian national anthem. Most were dressed in the blue and yellow colors of both Ukraine and the EU.

Some of the demonstrators were setting up barricades thrown together from metal fences and wooden benches, while others had occupied several of the surrounding government buildings. Soldiers in riot gear ringed the square, while others were strategically positioned on top of the taller buildings, armed with Kalashnikov rifles. It was obvious that Ukraine was on the verge of another political calamity.

Shaking her head, Karen retuned to the table. Taking a sandwich from the tray, she motioned to Charlie. "Let me tell you what I have found. We thought that perhaps Dimitri was involved in setting up a sex trafficking ring using Ukrainian brides as a focal point."

Charlie nodded, and poured another glass of Zinfandel.

"And we were right to a point," Karen continued. "The information I have—we have here, confirms that. It provides a list of names, dates, and overseas locations of young women sent, undercover, to perform intelligence gathering operations for Russia, similar to the type that the Illegals were doing in the United States."

"These girls were to replace them?" Charlie asked.

"Yes, but it was even more extensive than that. Several of the addresses are in the United States, but that is only part of the operation. Others were sent to Great Britain, one to Germany, two to Japan—they really like blonde women there. One even went to Israel. The Mossad will love to learn that."

"I don't understand," Charlie exclaimed. "Why, after just getting caught in the U.S. would they try to do it again?"

"You really don't understand. It worked for years there. It was only by accident that it was ever discovered. Many people still don't know exactly how they were eventually caught; or how much information they were able to supply to Moscow Center before they were deported.

"The KGB thinks long term. They are willing to wait years before their undercover agents become operational. By that time they have woven themselves into the fabric of society so that when they do become operational they have excellent cover."

"But why Ukraine?" Charlie asked. "Why not just use the Russian woman like they did before?"

"Do you recall, my telling you earlier that Dimitri was an expert on setting up false flag operations?"

Charlie nodded.

Karen continued, pacing back and forth. "They are operations that can't be traced back to their original source. This time it could be done from somewhere other than Russia. Where better to do that than Ukraine? You have a sympathetic government here. You have young women that are desperate to find a better life. And you can, if you wish, mix in your trained Russian woman with the innocent Ukrainians and no one knows the difference. That way, if agents are discovered, it is a Ukrainian problem and Russian-American relations are not jeopardized."

The ringing of the telephone startled both of them. Karen picked it up. "Shalom."

Charlie listened but didn't understand. He watched as Karen quickly paged through the documents.

She put down the receiver. "That was Control. They want me out. NOW. I told them before that I had shot the Colonel. They talked to Tel Aviv and the people there ordered an immediate exfiltration. They don't think his death will be investigated. There is too much crap going on in the country now for the authorities to concentrate on anything other than the demonstrations. Still, they don't want to take a chance. I have been in the country too long, and they need to see the information we found immediately."

"What about me?" Charlie asked.

"You are probably safe," she assured him. "You have just come to Kiev. It is quite likely that no one knows you are here.

"There is a copy machine in the other room, I'll make a copy of the list of names of the women, and you can give it to your people to translate. It should make up for not finding Emmett's killer.

"You don't have to mention me," she added. "I don't want them to know where I am."

"What about these photos, where do they fit in?" Charlie asked, holding up the black and whites.

Karen shook her head. "My guess is that the center building is some type of processing and storage facility. It may be for—I hate to tell you this Charlie, but it may be for chemical weapons.

"Some time ago, the Mossad learned that parties in Ukraine were communicating with Hezbollah for the transfer of chemical weapons. We didn't know who it was or where it was, but we did know there was a KGB connection. They have been using exotic poisons to get rid of their enemies for many years. Their activities are believed to be housed somewhere around Moscow in their top-secret laboratory Number 12. We started picking up chatter that the Russians were transferring some of their facilities to Ukraine."

"Why would they do that?"

"Another false flag operation. That was why we believed that Markoff was involved. They could sell to Hezbollah, or whoever else they wanted to, and it wouldn't be traced back to Mother Russia.

"You need to tell your people about it," she advised. "I don't have time now."

Karen left the room and returned shortly with a copy of the Russian documents. She handed them to Charlie, and headed up the stairs to collect her things.

In a matter of minutes she came down again, holding a bag, and went immediately to the window. She parted the drapes and peered out. "They're here," she told him, kissing him on the cheek and patting his blood encrusted ear.

"Sorry old friend. Wish it could have been longer. But nothing seems to last very long in my new world."

"Till next time," Charlie replied.

With that, Karen rushed out the door, leaving Charlie behind in a state of shock.

26

Charlie felt someone shaking him, and struggled to open his eyes. Once he was fully awake, he saw the little woman caretaker staring down at him. She was wearing the same stone-grey outfit she had on the night before.

"Time," she told him, nodding brusquely towards the table where he and Karen had been working. There was a carafe' of coffee and a dish of croissants where before their papers were strewn about.

When Karen left, it was late at night. Charlie was worn-out from his experience at the Catacombs, and his body ached from the blows of Colonel Markoff. He was too tired to go back to the hotel, and he curled up on the large leather sofa and fell asleep.

Now that it was morning, he didn't feel any better. It was still a monumental disappointment to find the Colonel was not the person who had murdered Emmett. It was some consolation to learn that Markoff was still involved in placing sleeper cells into the United States, and he would have to let Riordan know what he had found. Still it wasn't the same.

A slight sliver of daylight was visible through a break in the drapes. He looked out, and saw that the street remained empty before returning to the table. Two cups of black coffee and a stale croissant provided the necessary stimulant for him to think about what to do next. The photos he had looked at the night before were by the tray, and he noticed that the ZIP drive had fallen to the floor underneath the table.

There was a small bathroom off the study. Inside was a razor, shaving cream, toothbrush, and a half empty tube of toothpaste. Apparently, they were used to having unexpected guests. He looked in the mirror above the washbasin. The face looking back at him was more wrinkled and saggy than he remembered. He felt and looked like he had aged a decade since coming to Kiev. His mouth was dry, and his shoulder ached. He rubbed his eyes, and turned away from the reflection as quickly as he could.

Once Charlie cleaned up, he went in search of the sparrow. He found her sitting in the kitchen having breakfast with a heavyset man in shirtsleeves, wearing a Yamaka, and a shoulder holster. The blue-steel grip of a Walther PPK automatic protruded over its top. Compared with her companion, the woman looked even smaller than she had the night before. They both stared at him, without expression or movement.

"Taxi?" Charlie inquired.

The housekeeper nodded, and went for the phone, while Charlie returned to the study to collect his things. He had a number that Durand had given him, and punched it into his new phone. He was relieved to hear a recognizable voice on the other end of the connection and explained, as briefly as he could, that it was important that they meet. The station chief agreed, and by the time he finished his call his taxi was in front of the safe house.

It was a cold gray day. The streets were empty, which Charlie found surprising. He soon found out where the people were that morning.

The demonstrations from the night before had moved from Independence Square and were now on Taras Shevchenko Boulevard, massed around a large statue of Vladimir Lenin. The crowd was singing and waving Ukrainian flags as they toppled the huge monument to the Bolshevik leader.

189

The taxi swerved down a narrow side street to avoid the crowd, and soon pulled to a stop in front of the American Embassy. The number of Marine guards at the gate had increased considerably since Charlie's previous visit, (could it have been just the day before) and they were now more visibly armed. A sergeant glanced at Charlie's passport and waved him inside. The marine's interest focused more on what might be coming at him from the street, than the passage of an obvious American citizen.

Once inside, he repeated the process of the day before, and Charlie found himself once again following Nadia down the hallway to Durand's office. The clipping sound of her high heels, keeping time with the motion of her slender hips, momentarily diverted his mind from his problems.

Nadia had given him a knowing smile when she greeted him. He wondered what she might be thinking of him and his unnamed girlfriend of the night before. She had seen the two of them on their trip up the stairs at the Catacombs, but could have only guessed at their purpose.

Her smile was broader than before as she stood aside to let him pass by her through the now narrow entrance to Durand's office.

"You look like crap," the station chief roared in greeting.

"Thanks and a good morning to you too," Charlie replied, stiffly lowering himself into a chair by the desk.

"I hear you and some blond babe were at the Catacombs last night. Was she hot?"

"Just an old college friend that was passing through town," Charlie replied, hoping to shut off the direction the conversation was obviously taking.

Durand took the signal, and listened as Charlie weaved a story about the night before. "I found Colonel Markoff. It was like Nadia told us. He was using the Catacombs as his headquarters."

"Headquarters for what?" Durand asked reaching for a desk drawer.

Charlie shook his head. The last thing he needed that morning was a drink.

"For what the hell," Durand repeated his question, returning his attention to the tired looking man across the desk from him.

"Relax, let me tell you what happened, I'm too damned beat to play word games with you. I found Markoff," he began again. "But it was too late."

"Too late for what?" Durand could not contain himself.

"Too late," Charlie continued. This was going to be more difficult than he thought. He really couldn't blame Durand for asking, but it was difficult blending truth with deception. Now he more fully understood why the Agency people relied as much as they did on ambiguity.

"He was already dead."

"Dead?" Durand shouted, rising from his chair.

"He had shot himself."

"Suicide?" Durand asked incredulously." Why?"

"No idea. But he put a bullet in his forehead."

"Well that is usually how the Ruskies do it. Ever since the Bolsheviks. They go to the head if they go at all."

Charlie didn't know how Durand had become such an expert on Russian suicides, but he was willing to accept anything that served his own purposes.

"Well anyway, you got the guy that did Valentine. He deserves to be dead."

"There is a little problem here. He deserves to be dead all right. I'll grant you that," Charlie offered. "But as it turns out, Markoff wasn't the one that killed Emmett."

"How do...?"

"I found his passport, and the son of a bitch was basking under the sun in Cyprus at the time Emmett was murdered.

"But then who did kill the old man?" Durand asked, staring down at Charlie.

"I don't know. But while I was in Markoff''s room, I came up with a wealth of intelligence information," Charlie was quick to add before he got further side-tracked. He stood-up to face Durand, and began removing the papers he had stored in the deep pockets of his Barbour Jacket. When he was satisfied he had found them all he began spreading them across the surface of Durand's desk.

"What is all this?"

"These papers contain the names, and locations of deep cover agents that Markoff was running from Ukraine. He was mixing them in with the legitimate Ukrainian brides. Some of them have been sent to the United States to replace the Illegals that he was running there before they were found out."

"My God. We need to get these names to Langley ASAP."

Charlie nodded in agreement. "There is also this ZIP drive, but I don't know what's on it."

"That's a small little devil, isn't it?" Durand chuckled, walking over to his desk-top computer. He slid the drive into the side receptacle, and then punched a few keys in rapid succession. A list of names soon showed on the screen. "Looks like cryptonyms," he told Charlie. The addresses are not encoded. They wouldn't be much help if you didn't have the names."

"Oh, oh, look here. There is one of these bastards in D.C. We need to get this to Riordan right now," he added extracting the drive.

"So what the hell are these pictures?" he asked Charlie. "Man they do look grim." Durand observed, holding them up to the light. "They look like they were taken a day after the end of the world. Look here is one building standing amongst piles of rubble, with a dilapidated god-damned Ferris wheel in the background."

He turned once more to Charlie. "Where is this?"

Charlie shrugged, "I don't know where it is, but I have an idea what it is."

"And?"

"It has some connection to the production and storage of chemical weapons. I believe it is somewhere here in Ukraine. Do you recognize it?" he asked Durand.

"Hell no? But let me call in my Ukrainian expert," he smiled flipping a switch on his intercom.

"Nadia," he shouted. Then repeated his secretary's name more quietly.

It occurred to Charlie that a person might think that the head of intelligence operations in one of Europe's largest countries would have someone other than his secretary to rely on for local information. But what the hell, he decided, she did pretty well on identifying Colonel Markoff.

Nadia gave Charlie a knowing smile as she entered the office, and the very slightest of winks. He had obviously established his reputation with the young woman.

"Look at these glossies," Durand told her, shoving the pictures across the desk. "They are a little difficult to make out, but do you have any idea where these shots might have been taken?"

Nadia glanced at them briefly. "Of course I do. I don't know what that building is, but I know where it is."

"And?" her boss urged her.

"It's Prypyat."

"And you know that because?" Charlie asked, shocked that she came up with the answer so quickly.

"I know that because I was born there. It's a ghost town now, but it is--was the heart of the Chernobyl area."

"And you would know how to get there?" Charlie pressed.

"Well yes," she answered less confidently. "You see my parents fled from there after the nuclear reactor exploded. They never wanted to go back. It wasn't safe to go there for a long time anyway, so it made no difference. Once the government considered it was safe once again, a private company started to run tours several times a week. I was always curious, so I went on one of them. I wish I hadn't. It is dreadful there."

"Would you know how to get back if you had to?" Durand asked her.

"If I had to," Nadia replied softly, as she left the office to return to her desk.

"We need to talk with Riordan," Durand declared.

"The bubble?" Charlie asked.

"The bubble," Durand acknowledged, tapping on the wall behind his desk.

Two firm taps and the wall silently slid away. The light to the stairwell switched on, and the two men soon found their seats in front of the communication console. Durand threw a switch, and the dome descended with a puff of exhaled air.

He then took the binder from under the console, and looked apologetically at Charlie. "Never could remember numbers," he admitted, tracing Riordan's number with one finger and carefully dialing with his opposite hand. There was a slight hesitation as the code cleared the scrambler before it rang in the assistant director's office.

Riordan answered, and Durand signaled Charlie to begin his explanation. He dutifully went through his story of discovering Colonel Markoff's body. Riordan was more skeptical than Durand had been about the cause of the Russian's death, but Charlie had constructed the story and had nowhere to go with it than to, at least, be consistent.

The subject of the overseas conversation changed when Riordan learned that it could not have been the Colonel who had killed Emmett. It changed once more as Charlie described the wealth of information he had discovered in Markoff's room.

"He was running assets into the U.S. —*again*," Riordan roared.

"I have a list of the names and the locations where they have been sent," Charlie assured him. The sleepers have been mixed in with the legitimate Ukrainian brides.

Durand remained silent during the conversation, but he was becoming increasingly restless. He coughed nervously. Then he cracked his knuckles and scratched himself. He had to let someone else do the talking—filling in the details that he didn't have, and he was not used to playing such a secondary role.

Finally, they got to the subject of possible chemical weapons. "We think we know where it is that this crap is being stored for shipment," Durand inserted himself into the conversation.

Riordan exploded. "Stay the hell away from there. I have a different person from State calling me every day to make sure we are not taking any action in Ukraine that they don't know about. The pinstripers are getting flooded with reports regarding what is happening in Kiev, and they don't want to get between the Russian Government, the Ukrainian Government, and the EU. Our State has decided to let things take their course without us. Do you understand?"

Durand had never heard Riordan be that emphatic about inaction, and realized the pressure he must be under.

"But we can't just let the stuff sit there. If we are right about it, hundreds of people could die," Durand tried once more and was told by Riordan that was exactly what he was to do. "Let the stuff sit there."

Before the conversation ended, Charlie told Riordan that he was sending the file of operatives names to him, and that he had an additional ZIP file to send to Ken Madden to see if he could make sense of it.

Riordan agreed, and terminated the line.

The two men looked at each other. Durand shrugged, and began to insert the ZIP file into the appropriate slot on the console. A yellow LED flickered to acknowledge acceptance. He found the correct corresponding number for Madden, entered it into the keyboard, checked with Charlie, and depressed the send key. The compressed algorithms containing the cryptonyms of undercover Russian agents burst from the basement in Kiev, hurtled over Greenland, cleared the NSA at Fort Meade, Maryland, and landed in Madden's oversized lap top at Langley. A green LED on the console confirmed that the information had been successfully transmitted between the two systems.

Now it was up to the young IT whiz to check his registry of cryptonyms to see if he could make a match with any of those on Markoff's list.

The only thing remaining for Durand was to take the list of Russian agents and fax it to Riordan for translation and further investigation. The conversion from alpha to numeric was completed almost instantaneously between the systems in Kiev and Langley.

The work in Kiev was done. The digital trans-Atlantic handshake had been exchanged, and the computer console was shut down.

27

Chernobyl

Back in Durand's office, the two man stared at each other. "You know, for as long as I can remember," the COS began. "Well as least for the last twenty years," he corrected himself. "Ever since Ukraine became independent, the *wise men* at the CIA have been predicting it was likely there would be a civil war here. All this time Ukraine has been the powder keg that never blew. Now that there is a possibility it could happen, and possibly result in destabilizing all of Europe, my orders are to stand down. Don't, for God's sake, rock the damn boat."

The station chief was obviously distraught, but Charlie could think of nothing to say that would help.

"What are you going to do now Charlie — go back to Chicago?"

It was a good question, Charlie had been thinking about it himself. He had transmitted all of the information he had found in Markoff's office to Langley. That should be enough for them. Still, he had not found out who had killed Emmett, and that had been his objective. That was his job. That was why he was here.

When he was in corporate, that was what you did. You set objectives and, to continue Durand's boat analogy, you steered a course toward them. The problem was then you had an opportunity to analyze a set of facts. Here you just had to wing it.

"Well what *are* you going to do?" The question was repeated with a little more urgency.

There were too many questions, and too few answers. One thing he was sure of, it was entirely possible that in his search for Emmett's killer he had stumbled across the possibility there might be something that could kill many innocent people. If that was right, he had to stop it from happening.

"I am going to try and find out what is in that building at Prypyat," Charlie replied, surprising himself with the firmness of his answer.

"By yourself?"

Charlie had not quite thought that out. "If I have to…but actually I had hoped that Nadia could help me."

"Just the two of you amateurs mucking around Chernobyl for chemical weapons?"

"That's the plan. Do you have a problem with it," Charlie demanded.

"Do you have a better idea?" he added afterward.

"Yes I do," Durand replied rising from his chair. "I'll go with you…if Nadia agrees to drive."

"But Riordan was pretty firm about you standing down. He made it very clear that he did not want you to get involved. Not to rock the boat, as you said."

By now, Durand was pacing back and forth, nervously running his hand through his hair. "You're right, he made himself abundantly clear about that, but he is in Washington and I am in Kiev. It is a whole new world for us ever since Snowden released our confidential communications. We're traveling through unchartered waters without a compass. All of a sudden, the CIA has been replaced by the CYA, and I don't like it," he grimaced barely able to control his frustration. "When the agency needs risk takers we're getting bureaucrats, scared to death there will be blowback. I don't like that at all. That's not what I signed on for."

"So?" Charlie asked.

"So I am going there with you. At the very least, we have to find out what the hell is going on up there. Colonel Markoff didn't have those pictures for nothing. We can decide what we do once we figure out what we are dealing with."

Nadia returned to the office where Durand explained that they suspected there was something stored in Prypyat they needed to look into, and they needed her to help them.

At first, she was reluctant. She really didn't want to go back to Chernobyl. On the other hand, she liked her job.

"All right" Nadia agreed. Then she found out that they also needed her car.

Nadia's car was parked in the embassy lot. It was an old Moskva auto that her family owned. Charlie got in front beside her and Durand in back. Both men bent over as Nadia drove out the gate. They were using her car to draw less attention than a black SUV favored by most embassy officials. Anyone that might be watching was used to seeing only Nadia in the car, and that was how they wanted it to appear that morning.

After a couple of blocks, Nadia had not noticed anything unusual, and her passengers straightened up. They were still concerned that someone might follow them, and Durand began giving directions to prevent that.

Over his years with the Agency, he had become skilled in surveillance detection methods, as well as how best to frustrate them. "Turn here," he would order suddenly. Then later, "pull over," and the surprised Nadia would be required to park and wait so he could observe if anyone passed suspiciously, or parked behind or in front of them.

He would not have had to bother. As they proceeded through Kiev, it was apparent that the majority of the vehicles on the road were military, either on patrol for groups of insurgents or troop carriers moving additional support to demonstration sites. The vehicles crisscrossed the streets in front of them like brown bugs on a stagnant pond.

"You could rob the Central Bank of Ukraine," Durand observed at one point, "and no one would notice while these demonstrations continue."

When Charlie heard him say that, he felt more confident that no one would have time to become suspicious of the death of a Russian Colonel. In spite of the cold air seeping through the ill-fitting frame of the old Russian car he became more relaxed, and interested in his surroundings.

Outside of the city, the majority of the traffic was composed of convoys of riot police and accompanying military vehicles heading south to provide additional support to the Ukrainian troops already deployed. They gave the impression that the entire area ahead was being evacuated once again.

Further on, they began to pass through a series of small villages with neat wooden houses. Every modest home had its own window box and well-tended garden.

As a result of central planning, in each town they passed through, all of the houses were painted the same color; depending on which shade was being produced by the paint factory when that particular town's order was scheduled to be processed. As a result, the travelers would pass through a white town, which was a few miles from a brown town, before reaching a tiny hamlet composed entirely of green colored houses.

Charlie continually caught himself dozing, still tired from the night before. "What was it like living in Chernobyl?" he asked Nadia, trying to stay awake.

"I don't really remember living there," she replied sadly. "I was a small child when we left. My father was an engineer at one of the plants, but he was off the day the reactor exploded. He saw the smoke and knew what had happened. He immediately gathered the family together, along with a few belongings, and began to evacuate. I have heard him and my mother talk about it — not often, but sometimes. That was why I wanted to take that tour, to see for myself. Now I wish I had never gone."

Durand leaned forward from the back seat. "What does your father do now Nadia?"

"Nothing. He has leukemia and hasn't been able to work for some time."

"I am sorry," Durand apologized. "I wouldn't have asked you to come, but I think it's necessary to see what is inside that building, and you know the way."

"I understand," she replied, brushing a tear from her eye.

The kaleidoscopic imagery of their journey continued as they drew closer to their destination. They passed through an area that the returning peasants referred to as the *Red Forest*. Following the explosion at Chernobyl, a drifting radioactive cloud killed a large swath of tall pine trees, turning their formerly green needles into an eerie shade of crimson. New growth eventually surrounded the dead trees, but the lingering radioactivity had shaped them into grotesque patterns of permanently deformed life.

Further on, they sighted packs of wild wolves that had managed to reclaim their section of the deserted forest.

Later, a large flock of low flying black storks soared over the car. "A bad omen," Nadia told them. The men both hoped that it was not, but it was increasingly apparent to the travelers why the area was referred to as "the devil's playground."

As they drew closer to their destination, the travelers would occasionally see a few old peasants who had returned to reclaim their former homes in the decaying villages. Either because of their age, or declining health, they seemed to be unable to take adequate care of their cottages. The paint was faded and peeling, and the doors and shutters hung at odd angles on their loose hinges giving a macabre appearance to the crumbling communities.

On the outskirts of Prypyat, Nadia drove past a rusting graveyard of old trucks and helicopters that were used in fighting Chernobyl's fires, and then abandoned because of contamination.

Eventfully, they drove through the deserted streets of town that once was populated by families of workers at the Chernobyl nuclear facilities. Now, there were only ghostly rows of white and pastel apartment-blocks with their charred windows resting on rotted frames. Their few surviving occupants long ago moved to areas with a more benign environment.

Occasionally, they would see someone furtively scurrying around a corner or glancing out a window of an abandoned building eager to see, yet fearful of, an approaching car. A few people had returned to the town preferring to deal with what they were familiar with rather than stay in one of the many resettlement areas the government of Ukraine had established.

"If you wanted to hide something this ghost town would sure as hell be the place," Durand observed as they drove through town.

"I believe the building is over here," Nadia said turning a corner. They could see the structure in Markoff''s pictures, surrounded by piles of rubble from crumbling buildings.

Behind it, the abandoned and distorted Ferris wheel would occasionally attempt to revolve, as its worn gears yielded to gravitational pressure before catching hold once again. It was an eerie sight.

"There was a large amusement park built around that Ferris wheel," Nadia told them. "All kinds of different fun rides. Back in…happier days…." Her voice trailed off, and she turned away.

"The building looks empty," Charlie said. They had parked a block away, waiting to see if there were any signs of activity around it.

"Whoever was here may have left because of the demonstrations in Kiev. They have sucked all of the government people back to protect the Administration," Durand added.

They waited a little longer then parked in front. Charlie glanced back at Durand before opening the car door and approaching the building. Durand followed. Nadia hesitated, but didn't want to stay in the car alone. Just being in the god-forsaken place made her uneasy.

"The damn door's locked," Charlie said, turning the handle back and forth.

"What did you expect?" Durand growled, trying it for himself.

It was a large building, exhibiting varying stages of decay and neglect. Whatever was inside didn't appear to require that the structure be maintained with any degree of regularity. "They are probably going to use it for only a short period of time, before leaving it vacant again," Durand observed, as the three of them walked around the old structure.

The back of the building was shielded from view by what once was a wall, but was now only a mass of crumbling cement blocks. There were several windows in the rear, all bearing large cracks. Charlie took out his handkerchief and wrapped it around his fist before punching out the window closest to him. After he had finished, Durand removed his shoe and smashed any remaining shards of glass with its rubber heel.

The window was shoulder high, and when the men finished they turned and stared at Nadia.

No, no, absolutely not," she declared, realizing what they intended, and backing away. The two men kept staring at her and smiling.

Finally, shaking her head in defeat, Nadia came forward and gingerly placed her foot in a cradle of hands. Once she had steadied herself, the men boosted her through the empty window frame. Durand grinned at Charlie as they watched Nadia's well-formed derrière disappearing through the opening.

By the time the men returned to the front of the building, Nadia was standing in the unlocked doorway dusting herself off. Inside there were signs of a rapid departure. All the lights had been left on, and papers strewn about the floor. Dark shadows had captured the corners, and white hazmat suits and masks hung empty on their hooks like deflated phantoms.

The conflicting odors of stale cigarette smoke and acerbic chemicals filled the air. Empty beakers and bottles stood on a long work table in the center of the room, stacked alongside racks of varying sized test tubes. Cluttering the floor below the table were storage containers marked sodium fluoride and potassium fluoride. Slender lead-lined canisters stood side by side on a far wall resembling columns of lethal soldiers.

Durand pursed his lips exhaling, "son-of-a bitch they're making saran gas."

The three of them stood staring around the room, mesmerized by what they saw and what they feared.

Finally, Charlie walked over to the desk and began thumbing through the stacks of papers. Most were in Russian, but he could make out the signature of Colonel Dimitri Markoff on some of them. Probably some sort of work orders he decided. Other documents bore the address of the Moscow-based K12 laboratory, presumably the originator of many of the chemicals in the building.

There was a sense of urgency felt by all of them. The streets of the town had been empty when they arrived, and the warehouse abandoned, but still none of them felt confident that someone would not burst through the door at any moment.

Nadia was, leafing through a stack of papers. "Look here," she exclaimed, "this is a bill of lading. They plan to be shipping those canisters out of here very soon."

"Where to?" Durand asked, as he studied the materials on the laboratory table.

"I can't tell the final destination, but they go from here by train to the port of Oktyabrsk," she replied, continuing to leaf through the papers.

"That's a Russian controlled seaport on the Black Sea, just up the coast from Odessa," Durand confirmed. "For most of its existence, Oktyabrsk was a top-secret naval installation and it was a critical part of the Soviet Union's military supply chain. Now, even after independence, it is like the damn place is frozen in a kind of Cold War time warp. That's why, at least one of the reasons why, control of this former satellite state is critical to Putin.

"The port theoretically belongs to Ukraine," Durand continued. "It is on Ukrainian soil, but it is functionally controlled by Russian oligarchs close to Putin. The place is headed by a former Russian Navy captain, and owned by a business magnate with ties to the Kremlin. Major Russian weapons exporters have offices there, alongside a number of Ukrainian and Russian shipping and logistics companies. They refer to it as the *Odessa network* of arms shipments."

"That's pretty dramatic," Charlie grinned. "It sounds like the title to an old movie. How do you know so much about it?"

"It's easy," Durand replied. "The information was in a report prepared by a Washington-based nonprofit group by the name of C4ADS. The Agency sent me a copy because it had to do with Ukraine. It was also important to them because Oktyabrsk is the point of origin of arms shipments to many countries like Sudan, Congo, Burma, China, Angola and Iran," he added as an afterthought.

"All of them are countries with a history of brutal repression of ethnic and religious minorities," Charlie observed. "It fits the Russian paradigm perfectly."

"Well this particular shipment is headed for Syria," Nadia told them, setting down the document and picking up a map that was laying on the desk.

"How do you know?" both men asked in unison.

"Look here at the maifest. The containers are to be loaded on a ship with the name *Kapitan Kukushkin.* It sails from the port of Oktyabrsk, through the Black Sea to Istanbul. From Turkey, the ship enters the Mediterranean heading towards Egypt, then up the coast past Israel and Lebanon, before unloading at Tartus or Latakia in Syria."

Charlie had been taking notes. "Two ports? They unload at both ports?"

"No, I don't think so," Nadia told him, studying the route. "It's penciled in here that they will be notified later which port to choose."

"How? How will they be notified?" Durand asked Nadia.

"I can't tell exactly" "There are some strange names written here, along with accompanying numbers."

Charlie copied them down.

"Let's get out of here before we have company," Durand told them. "There is nothing more we can do."

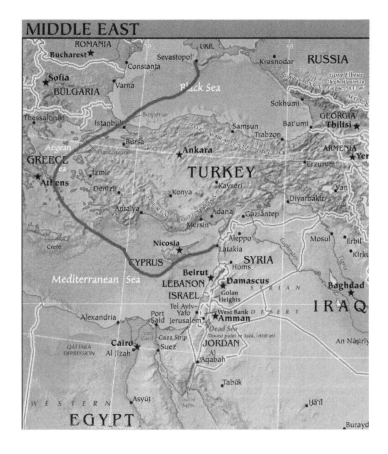

28

Kiev

On the return trip to Kiev, the conversation between Charlie and Durand focused on what they should do next. Now they clearly understood the significance of Markoff's pictures, they were both convinced that some steps must be taken to prevent the saran canisters from reaching Syria. Their discussion revolved around what could be done, and who was to do it.

Because of the nature of their discovery, they realized a person could not just rush in and blow the place up—yet that was what they both would like to do. They fully realized if that was to be done, or some similarly aggressive venture, it would spread poison chemicals all over northern Ukraine. Obviously, that could not be the solution; the area had already suffered too much for mounting such an aggressive alternative.

Nadia paid little attention to their discussion, it was growing dark and she had to concentrate on her driving. The young woman was not accustomed to operating her car at night, and to make her task worse, it was beginning to rain.

She was also furious at her boss for making her crawl through a dirty window frame. It was embarrassing and undignified for an administrative assistant. She shook her head to clear the anger, and concentrated all of her attention on the road ahead.

By the time they reached the outskirts of the city, the rain had intensified to a downpour. It was coming down in wind-driven horizontal sheets that typically precede the arrival of winter in Ukraine.

Inside Kiev, in spite of the heavy rain, the demonstrations had intensified. More people had joined the opposition, requiring more troops to contain them. The soldiers were dressed in blue camouflage outfits and large protective plastic helmets.

The protestors, on the other hand, had donned black plastic garbage bags over their clothes to provide at least partial protection from the frigid rain. With their heads protruding from slits slashed in the top, they resembled a vast field of black mushrooms, watched over by armed men from a distant planet.

The three travelers stared in astonishment as they viewed the angry crowd from a protective distance. The city's lights had recently come on and their translucent glow, shining through the downpour, added still another dimension to the already bizarre scene unfolding in front of them.

Later they were to learn that, during their journey to Prypyat, a local activist reporter had been badly beaten and hospitalized because of her reporting on the financial excesses of the country's Interior Minister. When the story became public, it resulted in an immediate increase in the size of the crowd, and added to the intensity of their protests.

Nadia let the men off at the Dnieper Hotel with a cautionary warning from her boss to forget everything she had seen that day. She certainly would have liked to, she thought pulling out of the hotel driveway, but she doubted she would ever be able to do that.

Durand had decided to join Charlie at the hotel in order to continue their conversation. In a secluded corner of the lobby, the station chief described the plan of action he had been turning over in his mind since leaving Prypyat.

"There are still some of my assets that I can convince to help me deactivate those canisters," he explained to Charlie.

"How would you contact them now with the city shutdown," Charlie asked.

Durand shook his head. "I have a series of dead drops for each of them that they are required to check. I might be able to get to some of them that way," he replied unconvincingly.

"Then what would you do?"

"I am not sure....but we could decide that once we got there."

"That's the best you have? You can decide when you get there?" Charlie asked angrily. "That's no plan at all. There is no way you can tamper with those chemicals without spreading them all over the Chernobyl area."

Durand stared at him. "Well it's the best I have for now. Maybe I will think of a better one on the way."

"And if you are caught? These demonstrations can't last forever. Eventually they'll run out of steam. Once that happens—and you don't know when it will happen—that place will be protected. You get caught, and it will be your ass. You know what Riordan told you. It will be the end of your career."

"Look Charlie," Durand began, and then hesitated as two men walked past them on their way to the bar. "My career is essentially over now. Kiev station is the highest I am going to go. It's my last rung on the ladder. And my wife doesn't like it here anyway," he said with a snort.

Durand's candid admission surprised Charlie. It was uncharacteristically frank, particularly coming from someone working for the Agency. Their style was to rely on ambiguity, even in their personal feelings. Charlie felt sorry for him.

"Look, before you do anything rash let me work on it."

"You Charlie? Hell, you're a nice guy, but you're just a NOC. You're good at what you do, but you're not even with the Agency, just working under non-official cover. What can you do?" Durand blurted.

"Yeah," Charlie replied, assuming a distinct accent, "Like we say in Chicago, 'I know a guy-- *I got connections.'* Let me work on it, and let's see what I can come up with.

"We can talk tomorrow. Them canisters' ain't going away right away anyway," he added with a grin.

Durand poked him in the arm good naturedly, and left the hotel. Nothing had been settled, but nothing was going to be done immediately either.

Back in his room, Charlie sat on his bed recharging the encrypted phone he had brought with him. The real phone, as he thought of it, not the throw-away burner with the prepaid card he had purchased locally. There were a number of calls he planned to make, and he didn't want the phone to die on him in the middle of a conversation.

Before, he had been reluctant to place any confidential calls from his room, but as they were leaving the embassy for Chernobyl, Durand had made arrangements with the *sweepers* to go over his hotel room and scour it for hidden listening devices.

Charlie was familiar with how they worked. They were meticulous in checking for any possible location that might contain a bug, and he was confident his room was swept clean.

The most important phone call he had to make was to Karen. He had failed to mention to Durand that his *guy* was, in fact, a girl and his *connections* were not with the mob, but with the Mossad.

He punched in the number that Vincent St. Claire had given him in Vienna. The one on the grid. He smiled, recalling Vincent's explanation of the secure system that he and other select intelligence agents used.

When he finished, he let the phone ring twice and hung-up. He waited a few minutes before re-dialing, and this time letting it ring three times before hanging up. It was a protocol he and Karen had used before.

Now he laid back on the bed, waiting to hear from her. It was at times like this, when he was alone in a darkened hotel room, that he wondered if he was really doing the right thing. Perhaps he should just pack his bag and get the hell out of Ukraine. So far, he wasn't any closer to finding who had murdered Emmett, and instead had become involved in the killing of a Russian Colonel.

Certainly, if you believed what Karen had said—and he did--Dimitri deserved to die. But where was the morality of it all. What happens when his personal responsibility confronts morality? It was the same dilemma he always faced when he entered their world. Dark thoughts on a dark night are the worst.

The ringing of the phone beside his bed brought him back to the reality of the moment.

"Charlie, I was wondering when I would hear from you," Karen announced from the other end of the line.

Charlie smiled at the sound of her voice. She was self-assured as always, and hearing her brought back many memories. He felt confident that she would be able to find a solution—at least to his most immediate problem.

He began by referring her to the photos they had discovered in Dimitri's room. She remembered them well. After that, Charlie described the trip to Prypyat and discovering what the Russians had hidden in the building there.

"Canisters of saran gas? Are you sure Charlie?"

"That's what they are referred to in the shipping documents," Charlie assured her.

"The problem is Karen, we don't know what to do with them. We can't burn the place down, or blow it, up for obvious reasons. On top of that," Charlie continued, "The station chief here has been ordered by Langley to stay low while Ukraine is trying to decide if it should align itself with the EU or Putin's Russia."

"I can sympathize with Durand, I have seen that attitude at the Agency myself," Karen confirmed.

"Is there anything that some of your people here can do?" he asked.

Karen paused momentarily, "I doubt it, they would be faced with the same dilemma that you are," she replied. They are just as interested in maintaining their position in Ukraine as the Americans, and they would have a great deal more to lose than your people."

Charlie's stomach churned. That had been his plan — his only alternative.

"We can't stop them, but we can track their progress," Karen added. "We can send one of the men from the Synagogue in Kiev to keep us informed when the canisters begin to move. Do you know the name of the vessel that will be transporting them Charlie?"

"Kapitan Kukushkin is on the manifesto," he replied. It departs Oktyabrsk...."

214

"The naval port north of Odessa?"

"That's Right. On the Black Sea Durand told me. From there it stops in Istanbul, and then proceeds on into the Mediterranean."

"Do you know the ship's final destination? Where does it unload their chemical weapons?"

Charlie paused before answering. He heard footsteps outside his door, then trailing off down the hallway.

Getting paranoid, he decided. Not a good sign. It was at times like this when he knew he was never made for the spy business.

"Not exactly," he replied to her question. "There are alternative destinations listed. Both of them are in Syria."

"Syria? That's no surprise," Karen observed dryly.

"One is the port of Tartus and the other is Latakia. Are you familiar with them?"

"Only slightly," Karen replied. "They are both Russian controlled Syrian ports that are used as a supply line to feed arms to the Assad regime. Can you tell, from your papers if the ship goes to both ports, which one is first?" she asked.

"I presume it would be Tartus, but I'm not sure. Nadia-- she is Ukrainian and works for Durand—said there were some notes about receiving instructions where to go while they were in route. She thought that it could be one or the other."

"Do you have the notes?" Karen asked.

"Yes," he assured her. "I copied them, but I don't understand them. I think that they are cryptonyms and non-sequenced numbers," Charlie replied, changing his position on the bed. Karen's questions were making him nervous. So far, he had been unable to give a definite answer to most of them.

After a moment's pause Karen asked, "Do you have a one-time pad? The Agency is crazy about the damn things."

Charlie assured her that he did. She provided him with some assistance and suggestions on how best to use it. "I'll call back as soon as I have something," she told him before hanging up.

He thought about their conversation, He had hoped that Karen's' people in Kiev would be able to do something to nullify the chemical threat that he and Durand had found. That was obviously not to be the case. He still had hopes that she could come up with something. He was confident that she would.

He concentrated on transcribing the information regarding the route the Kapitan Kukushkin was to take, and the form of the ship to shore communications that would eventually specify its final destination. Once he had finished, he inserted the jack into his phone and the encrypted algorithms began to flow by bits and bytes between his hotel room in Kiev and Karen's location in Tel Aviv.

His next call was to Vincent St. Claire. He had to advise the old man of his failure to locate his friend's killer.

"Hello Charlie, I have been waiting to hear from you," Vincent announced from his home in Vienna.

"Is that Puccini I hear in the background? Charlie asked about the muted melody coming through his receiver.

"You are very astute, my boy."

Charlie smiled, it had been a long time since anyone had referred to him as a boy.

"That is another element that Emmett and I shared, our love of Puccini. In this case, it is *Turandot*. I have always found the story significant. The opera is set in Asia, as I am sure you are aware, and involves Prince Calaf who falls in love with Princess Turandot. In order to win her hand, the Prince must solve three riddles. If the poor man comes up with the wrong answer to any of the riddles it results in his death.

"That is what you and I do Charlie. We try our best to solve riddles."

"Well I hope the failure to do so doesn't necessarily result in my death," Charlie replied. "So far, I haven't been particularly good at finding answers. That's the reason I called. While I did locate Colonel Markoff, I am afraid he was not the person who killed our friend."

With that as an introduction, Charlie went on to describe exactly what had occurred. He included meeting and working with Karen, Dimitri's death, the violent demonstrations in Kiev, and finally locating the chemical weapons in Prypyat.

By the time he finished his story, the music had ended in Vienna. "You are doing the right thing Charlie," Vincent declared. "Those canisters must be safely disposed of. We will just have to wait and see what Karen can come up with. She is a very resourceful woman, and so is the organization with which she is associated. It is vitally important to the Israelis that the supply of saran gas does not get to the Syrians."

Before their conversation ended, Vincent asked Charlie to provide him with all the information he had. "It seems very strange," Vincent added. "I was sure that it was Markoff who was responsible for Emmett's death. We know that he was the control for your American Illegals. It is curious how he was able to leave the country just before all the others were arrested. All of them but him presumably.

"I will check with some of the fellows I still know at MI6. They are a good lot and of course, I will see what assistance I may be able to garner from the old boys at GCHQ. They are not quite as effective at what they do as your NSA, but they can still be helpful when they want to," he chuckled.

After finishing the call to Vincent, Charlie checked his watch. It was far too late to call Beth. He would do it tomorrow he decided before dropping off to sleep.

29

The phone was ringing--ringing loudly. It had been for some time, but Charlie thought it was his travel-alarm, and tried to ignore it.

"Did I wake you?" Karen Kincaid's voice came from the other end of the line.

"No, of course not," Charlie lied, sitting up in bed. "It took me a minute to get to the phone." No man likes to be caught sleeping, particularly by a woman. Charlie Connelly was no exception.

"That's good," she chuckled. "I wouldn't want to wake you. "

"I have some important information," She told him, changing the subject. "When I talked to the people here, they were shocked by what you found in Prypyat. I should have paid more attention to Dimitri's pictures. I was so wrapped-up in the other information about his encrypted contacts, and running undercover agents among the Ukrainian brides, I failed to give them adequate attention. I am embarrassed, but I am glad you followed up on them Charlie. That was good work."

He was pleased to receive praise from a professional. Particularly Karen.

"The people here…" she began.

"The Mossad?" Charlie interrupted. He felt he needed to be sure.

"Yes Charlie the Mossad. They are very concerned with your shipment. Our leaders made crystal clear to Damascus, early on in their conflict, that any transfer of their chemical arms to our enemies would be crossing a *red-line*.

"We know, from our sources, that their chemical programs are overseen by an elite Syrian military unit with close ties to the Hezbollah. Last year we struck inside Syria at least five times to take out chemical weapons bound for them. One of those strikes was at Latakia. We thought that we had succeeded in shutting them down. Now it looks like the Russians are trying to resupply them with the shipment on the Kapitan Kukushkin."

Karen's voice rose as she described the Russian involvement. It was obvious she was very concerned.

"We were confident that our eavesdropping network was capable of picking up information on their arms shipments, but after the Snowden affair they have all modified their methods of communications to evade NSA snooping. It has limited our ability to track them as well. This whole area is a spider web of conflicting interests. The only thing they all have in common is their abiding hatred of Israel."

Charlie reminded her that the notes they had found contained information that, once at sea, the ship was to receive land-based communications directing them to their Syrian destination.

"I know. I know," she told him emphatically. "We were very interested in that, and we are pursuing it further. We are picking up some chatter out of Cairo, but so far we have been unable to locate its origin or its exact location."

"What do you plan to do about it?" Charlie asked. By now, he was fully awake.

"The first thing we plan to do is to put a transponder on the Kapitan Kukushkin. We have people working the docks in Istanbul that keep us informed of ships and shipments they believe would be of interest to us. They are well paid, and will do what we tell them to do. Once the ship docks, one of them will slip on board and hide the device where no one will find it. That way we can track the ship's progress through the Mediterranean."

"And then what?" Charlie asked. It was important for him to know what action they planned to take. He was afraid they would only track the shipment to its destination, and then do nothing further.

"Then we will either sink it or board it. Whichever way we decide the chemical weapons will not reach Syria. Or anywhere else," she assured him.

Her blunt response surprised him, but that was what he wanted to hear. Karen's voice had such a strong ring of confidence he knew he could put those deadly saran canisters behind him. It was a tremendous relief.

"And Charlie," she added. "It's vital for us to learn exactly who is telling the ship in which port they are to unload. Our back room analysts are working hard to find the answer. I'll be in touch with you when we learn more."

Karen ended the conversation, and Charlie hung up the phone. Afterwards, he thought about what she had told him. He was pleased to hear that the Mossad was going to intervene with the Kapitan Kukushkin. It was a tremendous relief, but it brought him no closer to finding the person that killed Emmett. He feared now he never would.

Charlie showered and shaved and then went downstairs to the breakfast room. It was beginning to fill with visiting business men, international agency people, and quite a few who appeared to be the previous night's participants in the Romance Tours.

Some of them sat at a table alone. Female companions, apparently from the previous night's outing, accompanied others. Some of these young women seemed happy, while others stared across the table at their companion with a decidedly dour expression. Apparently, not everyone's dreams had been fulfilled.

Outside the hotel, Kiev was beginning wake to its daily routine. The storm from the night before had passed through the city, and moved on to batter the Ukrainian steppes. The demonstrations had assumed a rhythm of their own, ebbing and flowing depending on each new political revelation.

A scattering of school children, weighted down by their bulging book bags, trailed past the hotel on their way to class. Following behind them limped a tired old babushka. Her scarfed gray head and tattered sweater provided a distinct contrast to the attire of the more youthful students. Shops along the soaked sidewalk, in order to prepare for the day's anticipated business, were beginning to open their tightly shuttered entranceways.

An ancient Soviet-built streetcar clattered past, and after a moment's hesitation Charlie climbed aboard. He was becoming more familiar with the city, and knew this one would pass by the American Embassy. He was anxious to meet with Durand to assure him the shipment of saran would be taken care of without requiring any American involvement.

The trolley passed the golden domed St. Sophia Cathedral, with its wedding-cake baroque style bell tower. Shortly afterwards it deposited him a block away from his destination. He wanted to assure himself there was no one traveling with him who would associate him with the Embassy.

The marine guards appeared more relaxed, and less heavily armed than the day before. Apparently, they were also in tune with the varying tempo the demonstrators set.

A young corporal inspected his credentials before waving him through the gate.

Once inside, an unfamiliar young woman led him to Durand's office. "Where is Nadia this morning?" Charlie asked, as the station chief glanced up from his desk.

"Gave her the day off. Thought she deserved it," Durand added. "She was damned helpful yesterday."

"She was surprisingly so. I think she was upset when you asked her to go through the window. Are you sure she will keep her mouth shut about what we found there."

"Pretty sure. As sure as you can be in this circus we live in. She has no time for the Russians. Thinks they were responsible for Chernobyl. Which of course they were."

"Look at this," he added, holding up a copy of the Kiev Post. "They found your Colonel."

"And?" Charlie asked, taking the paper and sitting down by the desk.

"And nothing," Durand grinned. "Just like I told you. It just says that a Russian Colonel was found dead of unknown causes in his apartment at the Catacombs. Period. The SZRU is too busy keeping track of the anti-government demonstrators to worry about one Russian more or less in Ukraine."

Charlie located the article. It wasn't easy. It was just a small item among a long list of daily death notices.

"Sad," Charlie said, tossing the paper back on the desk, relieved to learn he was apparently safe.

"Isn't it though," Durand replied with a grin.

"The reason I wanted to talk to you," Charlie began, "is I have been assured that the shipment will never reach its destination. You and I don't have to worry about it anymore."

"And does this assurance come from people you have confidence in?" Durand asked.

"The utmost," Charlie assured him.

Durand leaned back in his chair and stared at his visitor.

Charlie stared back in return.

"Can I give the people at Langley this assurance?" Durand asked. Before Charlie could reply, Durand added, "and if they knew where this information came from, would they feel confident as well?"

"Absolutely," Charlie assured him.

"Very good," Durand summed-up, moving on to a new subject. "Now, I have some more information for you. This came back in our overnight packet," he told Charlie handing him a decoded message from Ken Madden.

The IT whiz had worked on the cryptonyms that Charlie had sent him from the thumb drive he had found. He had also looked at the information given to Riordan regarding Markoff's insertion of a new group of Illegals.

The thrust of Madden's reply was that Riordan had turned over the information about the undercover agents to the FBI. It was their job to investigate things on American soil, and he didn't want to intervene or antagonize them at this point.

Regarding the list of code names, Madden had compared them to the registry of active cryptonyms that the Agency maintained. One of them, HERCULIES, was familiar to him. It was the name Ralph Gross often used. The message said that it was puzzling to them how Markoff became aware of the name, but since they knew Gross was not a threat, they concluded the rest of the names were fictitious as well. A dangle they called it, a wild hare of some sort. Not a counterintelligence problem.

Unwritten, but understood by both Durand and Charlie, was the implication that Langley had more important things to do than chase a will of the wisp they knew to be a false lead.

Charlie read it and shrugged. "So be it," he said angrily, rising from his chair and handing the message back to Durand. "That's the best I can do. If they don't want to follow-up, to hell with it."

"So you're giving up?" the station chief asked incredulously. When there was no answer, he tried again. "What now? What are you going to do now Charlie?"

"I don't know, unless you have some suggestions I seem to have hit a brick wall. Time to fold my tent and go into the night—or however the saying goes."

Durand shrugged. He had no other suggestions.

Outside of the embassy, Charlie decided to walk back to the hotel. He was angry Riordan had dismissed the list of cryptonyms so readily but, as he told Durand, what more could he do.

On his way, he passed the Chernobyl museum and decided to go in and look around. Inside there were photographs of the devastated area. They were shockingly graphic and difficult to view. Alongside the pictures were numerical tables and graphs detailing the resulting radiation and contamination that occurred when the main reactor exploded.

There was also a separate room of the museum that contained pictures and identity cards of people who had died as a result of the explosion. On the opposite wall, there were frightening photos of deformed animals and humans that stemmed from the contamination. It was all very sobering when you realize that much of the lingering after-effect was a result of Russian management attempting to downplay the gravity of their problem.

Charlie wondered, during the remainder of his walk, if he had done all he could with the information he had obtained.

30

Langley

Riordan stared out of his seventh floor office window. Ralph Gross' file lay open on the desk in front of him. He had meant to retrieve it earlier, but he first needed to obtain the combination to the man's safe. He had his own list of combinations for people on his staff, but somehow Ralph's was not among them.

He had started to page through it, but his mind drifted toward more immediate problems. The CIA was in the middle of another reorganization. He had been through a lot of them during his career, but now he felt less sure of his position than before.

Every time the Agency is confronted with a new problem, or has screwed-up on an old one, the immediate reaction is to reorganize. This time it was another attempt to become more responsive to the ever-changing pressures in the Mideast. The war in Iraq was considered finished, at least as far as the U.S. was concerned. Afghanistan was winding down. Iran was still a problem, and Russia was beginning to be more assertive in Ukraine.

The Agency mandarins were naval-gazing on how best to react, in such a fluid global environment, to the Administration's wishes. Riordan didn't have any idea where this was going to go, or how he would eventually fit in. If at all. Part of his responsibilities were left over from the Cold War. That was why he had Emmett on board.

He was still worried that Emmett's death would come to light, and his cover-up along with it. He had hoped Connelly would be able to track down the person that killed the old man, but he was beginning to lose confidence. Charlie had produced for them in the past, in an unofficial role, but perhaps this was asking too much.

Connelly had been able to provide the Agency with information on the new undercover agents Colonel Markoff was sending to the U.S. as brides. That was a hell of an accomplishment he realized, but he had decided to turn this information over to the Feds. That was what he was supposed to do. He would like to have followed up on it himself, but this was not the time to be playing games. Play it safe. That was the motto in times like this.

"Don't rock the boat," the Admiral was constantly telling him; Actually, it was "don't rock the *god-damned* boat." The Admiral was also feeling less secure the longer he held down the Director's position.

Riordan had put his assistant Bill Brady on the management review task force. That was what assistants were for--to take the crap so the boss didn't have to. Brady was good at it, but even he couldn't figure out where this train was headed.

Riordan picked up the file once again. He hated to do this part of his job. Combing files was not his pattern. He liked action. Gross and he were the same in that regard. That was why they got along so well.

Although he did think it odd that Markoff had Gross' cryptonym on a list in his Kiev room. It was hard to figure out how he got it, and even more difficult to understand why he had kept it.

As Riordan paged his way through the file, he wondered if Gross could have become compromised. Try as he might, he could not come up with a reasonable answer. Sure, Gross was assigned to work with the FBI in their attempt to uncover the Illegals. He had asked to do that.

And, it was he who had turned over the name of one of the principals involved.

Riordan tried to refresh his memory. Actually, he recalled, he had not been all that involved, but Gross had kept him informed. It was a complex "deep cover" operation based on the use of long-established false identities, secret rendezvous, and old school intelligence techniques like invisible writing; as well as more innovative approaches that involved a private wireless network through linked laptop computers.

A picture in the file of Anna Chapman, the buxom Russian spy, caught his eye. She would sit near a window of a coffee shop where she, like many others there, would have a latte' and work on her laptop. At the same time, arrangements were made for a minivan, driven by a Russian Mission contact, to drive past her location. The vehicle was equipped with secret computer capacity that enabled Chapman to send material from her laptop directly to his, without going through standard commercial networks and leaving a trail.

It appeared from reading the file that someone had tipped off Gross who, in turn tipped off the FBI. The *cousins* then had sent one of their agents, who posed as a Russian consulate employee, to meet with her at the coffee shop and tell her that the protocol was changing. In the future, she was advised, there would no longer be "laptop to laptop" communications, but instead, that was being replaced by "person to person" communications. She agreed.

The FBI soon arrested her, and the other Illegals that were involved. They were all immediately tried, and the arrangements were rapidly set in motion for their immediate return to Moscow.

Riordan quickly paged through the rest of the file. He was getting bored with this. He had found nothing that would have implicated Gross, other than the question of how he got hold of the information he had passed on to the FBI. But what the hell, Riordan decided, that's what good agents do. They keep their sources secret.

Normally, he would have called Gross into his office and asked him about it. The problem with that was the Admiral had sent him to Cairo on a clandestine mission. That seemed a little odd as well. Riordan had thought about asking the Admiral about it but with a reorganization being in play, he didn't want to go to him and admit that he was not fully informed on everything going on in his own organization. Not a good time for that he decided. Not a good time at all.

Still, he did feel that he should do something.

"Get me Barbara Richards," he told his secretary Linda. She was the staff analyst he decided, so let her analyze this. The more he thought about it, the more convinced he became that this was the correct course of action. She was not as close to Gross as he was, and there might be a slight level of competitive animosity. That made her all the more independent. Clear eyes—clear mind, that was the thing.

That was how Barbara found herself leafing through the file she had been handed by her boss. It was the last thing she wanted to do. She knew Riordan and Gross were very close—in a masculine sort of way— a way that she could never be with her boss. It wasn't fair, but she was realistic enough to recognize that while things were improving for women at the CIA, they would never be equal in her lifetime.

Before becoming a staff analyst Barbara had spent many years as a field agent. She liked that better, but when she was offered a job as an analyst on Riordan's staff, she jumped at it. It was a good career move, and a single woman has to consider her career.

After thinking about it more, she decided that she wanted to be thorough with her analysis, but she also wanted to get rid of the job as quickly as she could. Quick and thorough, that was how she would approach her assignment.

It was strange how Gross had found out about the Illegals, even stranger how quickly they were tried and exchanged. Usually such cases take months to unfold.

On the other hand, the Agency was built on strangeness. If everything was clear, there would be no need of them.

Why would Gross want to do anything that might jeopardize his position with the Agency? Why would *anyone* do that, she wondered?

The MICE test she decided. That was it. That was what Riordan always told her—and anyone else that would listen. There were basically four reasons people betrayed their country he said. Money, Ideology, Coercion, or Ego.

Might as well start at the top, she decided picking up the phone. She would begin with money. That was what brought down the Agency mole Aldrich Ames—money.

"Hello Agnes," Barbara began in her warmest most cajoling voice. "How are things going at the company bank?"

It wasn't easy. "She really shouldn't have access to someone else's account," Agnes informed her several times--before finally giving her the information she wanted.

That is what friends are for, Barbara knew. It was *the old girls network* at work she thought, smiling to herself.

Looking at the data Agnes had transmitted to her computer she discovered there were several, large and continuing deposits in Ralph Gross's account. There were also substantial withdrawals, indicating a big spender. If he was getting his money from an illegal source, would he be dumb enough to deposit it in the Agency's bank?

Perhaps--others had done it. She thought again of Aldrich Ames, Nobody thought anything about it until he was arrested. Why wouldn't Gross do the same thing?

Barbara leaned back in her chair. If she were a man she would put her feet up on her desk, but that wouldn't do. Anyway, her legs were not long enough to do it comfortably. She knew. She had tried it once.

Barbara searched through her desk for her notebook of names and numbers she kept to herself. She soon found what she was looking for, Sergey Ivanovich. Funny little man. Sad little man. He had been a defector. *A walk-in.* Turned himself voluntarily over to our Moscow Station.

Sergey was a file clerk with the Russian First Directorate. He held a low level position, but had access to a considerable amount of information--which he had memorized. Our Agency people had scrubbed him in Moscow before they sent him out, undercover, to Helsinki. Once they got him there, they put their new asset on an army cargo plane and flew him to Washington.

Barbara remembered the debriefing he received after he got to Langley. At first, it was thought that he would be able to provide valuable information on the organization and workings of the First Directorate. They put him up in a safe house well outside of the Distract. During the interrogation, they promised him a new name, a new home, and a steady income. That was what he wanted — a better standard of living.

Later the process became acrimonious. That was when James Jesus Angleton, the CIA's master mole catcher, got hold of Sergey. JJ decided that his information was crap—worthless—not to be believed, since it didn't support what Angleton thought that he already knew.

Poor old Sergey, Barbara thought, he was discarded with half of what he had been promised. The Agency didn't want him to go back to Russia with what he had learned while he was here—names—techniques—secret locations and the like; so they gave him enough to make his life better than what it was in Moscow, and forgot about him.

But she had not. Barbara remembered him well. She really believed him, and thought he got screwed by Angleton. She had been part of the interrogation team. The two of them, she and Sergey, got along well together, she recalled, dialing his number.

They agreed to meet for lunch near the hotel where he stayed. It was a seedy place but clean, and he seemed genuinely happy to see her. To see anyone she decided. He had said all along that there was a mole operating at Langley. He repeated his story. He didn't know who it was, but the mole had the code name of HERCULES. Sergey had seen it in the files.

Barbara picked up the check. She was glad to do it, and Sergey was glad to let her.

When Barbara got back to her office, she wondered what to do with the information she had found. Her analysis had been thorough, and it had been quick. Those were her objectives, but now what the hell should she do with it.

The problem was that she had an answer her boss wouldn't like. Gross was his guy. She had heard him say that many times. He must have had some inkling or he would not have given her the file. She tried to evaluate the pros and cons of what she should do next. Her difficulty was that it was mostly cons, and very few pros.

What the hell, she decided. She would do what she should do. She picked up the file and headed down the hallway to Riordan's office.

Riordan was still at his desk, and looked surprised to see her.

She told him what she had found: the inordinately large bank deposits, and the hit she got on the cryptonym HERCULES. She also told him her source.

Riordan didn't like what he was hearing. On the other hand, he had also believed Sergey when the Russian was first vetted by the Agency. He never liked Angleton — thought he was an ass, but he was the official spy catcher. The Agency's anointed mole whacker, so what could Riordan do.

The deposits were a little odd as well. Riordan knew precisely what Gross drew down in salary, and it was not anything close to the deposits he made in the Agency's bank.

He and Barbara discussed their options. When they put the threads together they didn't make a whole cloth, but then they rarely did. The facts didn't prove anything, but they didn't have to in order to raise the level of suspicion.

That was how Barbara ended up on the night flight to Cairo. Just to look around mind you. Stay low. See what Gross is doing there. Don't confront him, and report back to the boss.

31

Kiev

By the time Charlie reached his room at the Dnipro, he had decided to call Beth, and tell her he was coming home. After leaving the Chernobyl Museum, he considered staying a few more days in Kiev to see if anything further developed. The more he thought about it, the more that approach seemed to be a waste of time.

The city itself was on the verge of erupting into a full scale conflict. Colonel Markoff was dead, and the longer Charlie stayed in Kiev the greater the probability he would become linked to the Russian's death.

Charlie tried to evaluate his chances of uncovering additional information, and the more he thought about it the more he decided that it was all trending to the downside, with no upside in sight.

There were also no additional leads to follow to Emmett's killer. At least not where he was now.

If Charlie had learned anything in his long corporate career, it was that you should not give up pursuing your objectives until you had exhausted all of your alternatives. On the other hand, when you decide there are no more alternatives to pursue, it is time to throw in the towel. After a few more minutes of reflection he was firmly convinced he was definitely at that point.

He took out his phone to punch in Beth's number. Before he could do that, the phone began to ring. Startled, Charlie dropped it on the bed. Quickly recovering he retrieved the device, and recognized Karen's voice on the line.

"Charlie?"

"Yes Karen its Charlie," he replied, surprised yet pleased to hear from her.

"You're still in Kiev?"

"Still in Kiev," he replied, fumbling for the light switch by the bed. There is nothing darker than a dark hotel room, and this one was no exception. "But, I had just decided that it was time to leave. There is really nothing more I can do here."

"Well, I'm glad that I caught you. We have just learned the movement of chemical weapons has already begun, much earlier than we expected. Earlier than they expected as well," she chuckled."

"How did you find this out?" Charlie asked, surprised that she was that well informed.

"Ever since I alerted our people in Kiev to what we found in Prypyat, they have had their watchers covering the place. They called to alert us. It seems that the demonstrations are beginning to spread throughout Ukraine, and the Russians want to get the canisters out of the country before all the rail lines and ports are closed down."

"So they are moving faster than we thought, but what does that have to do with me?" Charlie asked. His palm was beginning to sweat, and he nervously switched the phone to his other hand. He feared where this conversation might be going.

"Because the shipment has started to move, the chatter between Cairo and Kiev has increased exponentially, and we are beginning to get a better fix on the origin."

Charlie hesitated. "That's... good," he finally replied, still unsure what it might have to do with him.

"Most of the communications are like I told you" Karen explained patiently, "between Cairo and Ukraine, but some of it is also floating between Cairo and Langley."

"Langley — that's not possible," Charlie exclaimed incredulously.

"That's exactly what *we* thought," she continued. "It was pretty well scrambled, but we checked it, and checked it again, before finally cracking the encryption algorithms and concluding that it had been with someone at the Agency. Now we think it is important that you drop off here on your way back to the States."

"That's not exactly on my way," Charlie protested lamely. "What can I do in Tel Aviv?

"We have some pictures we want you to look at. Not many — just a few. We are hoping you might recognize one of them."

Charlie frowned. It seemed utterly implausible that he might be able to pick out the photo of someone connected to the Agency. Karen had added that it was someone they believed to be working for Riordan. He had only met with the people there very briefly. He didn't know if he would recognize them again if he saw them. It seemed further unlikely that someone working for Riordan would be involved in the movement of chemical weapons from Ukraine to Syria. But then, what did he have to lose. Just another day or two, and he had already invested so much of his time, what would that matter?

He eventually agreed. It seemed like he always did.

The rest of the conversation between them involved the flights he might be able to catch out of Kiev, and the connections he could make to Tel Aviv. Karen assured him that the Mossad would green-light him with EL AL.

Then it was the call to Beth, telling her that he might be a little longer than he expected.

She was not at all surprised.

He thought of his wife as he did often when he was alone, usually at night—particularly at night. But now his reflections centered on Beth the college girl, as she was when they first met. A long time ago, and a long way away, but the memory still clear and appealing. He passed his hand across his face and willed the memory away.

He looked at himself in the mirror and saw a stranger — an older man he barely recognized. Not at all the man that he remembered. Each morning he looked at the same face but never saw. Today it was different—far different. There was no sign of that college boy that fell in love with that Midwestern college girl.

He waved that memory away as well. He would have liked to go home, but he had a responsibility to find who had killed his friend. As best he could. Wherever it took him. Until he was satisfied that he could search no longer — or he found the killer.

He looked for a cab outside the hotel. The streets were empty. This morning there were no passing school boys, and the small shops around the hotel remained closed. The fighting between the two factions had intensified, and those who were not directly involved were trying to stay out of the way.

Earlier, the atmosphere where the demonstrations were taking place had the feel of a rock concert, but now they had become increasingly militant and had left hundreds injured.

238

It was being referred to over Moscow's independent radio station *Ekho Moskvy* as the "Maidan" movement, after the square occupied by the anti-government protestors.

Men in helmets, brandishing clubs, had launched forays from the square hunting for troublemakers. Banks, cafes, and shops in the area had all closed and the government had given the police more power to close access to the areas around Kiev, as the demonstrations spread throughout Ukraine.

Finally, a cab pulled to the curb, and Charlie directed the driver to take him to the airport. As they drove, they could see down Grushevsky Street where thousands of protestors were clashing with riot police. The demonstrators had been throwing rocks and Molotov cocktails as well as burning tires. Police were responding with truncheons, tear gas, concussion grenades, and guns.

It was a chilling scene, and in considerable contrast to his arrival only a short time ago. Charlie was glad to be putting Kiev in the rear view mirror. He considered himself fortunate to be getting out, as the driver attempted to select a route that would keep them away from the ongoing violence.

The airport terminal was nearly empty. All incoming flights had been cancelled, and removed from the arrivals board. The Ukrainian Government was having enough problems without allowing additional potential trouble makers to enter their country.

Charlie found a place where he was sure he would not be overheard, and took out his recently purchased cell phone. He looked around once more before placing a call to Durand. He wanted to let him know that he was leaving Ukraine.

The number rang several times, and Charlie was about to give up and try again when he heard a gruff "Yes?" Not too appropriate a response for an ostensible Commercial Attaché Charlie thought. But then, these were trying times in this almost paralyzed and certainly polarized country.

After Charlie was able to identify himself Durand's tone changed considerably. He was sympathetic to the reasons for Charlie's departure. He had expected as much, but was surprised to learn that he was on his way to Israel instead of the United States.

Charlie explained that the chemical weapons had begun to move, and he was going to see if he could help some people in Tel Aviv intercept them before the canisters reached their final destination in Syria.

Durand had never completely understood his friend's connection to the Israelis, but he had been around the intelligence community long enough to avoid asking a question he was sure would fail to generate a valid answer. It was none of his business anyway; he had done what Langley wanted him to do and that was enough for him.

After his conversation with Durand, Charlie no longer had any use for his burner and, after removing the SIM card, tossed the cheap receiver into a trash can on his way to the men's room. Once inside, he went into one of the empty stalls and crushed the SIM card under his foot and spread the remains around the tiled floor. Satisfied that there could be no trace of his conversations in Ukraine, Charlie re-entered the lobby to check-in.

Looking around the terminal, there appeared to be more security than travelers. Each of the camo-clad military men had their Ak-47s at the ready, as they carefully scanned the travelers. There was also a number of broad-shouldered men in civilian clothes, with perceptible Berretta-bulges underneath their tight fitting jackets.

There were only two counters that remained open, one for Austrian Air, and the other for ELAL. Charlie approached the desk, and handed his passport to the young woman agent.

"Mr. Connelly, we were told to expect you. Just a minute," she smiled, and pushed a button underneath the counter.

Almost immediately, a tall man in a gray suit and tie appeared through a concealed doorway behind the check-in counter. "I'm to help you board," he told Charlie reaching for his bag.

At the customs area, the man nodded to the agents who were inspecting passports and interrogating the waiting travelers. One of them waved them through to the baggage inspection area.

Charlie watched the other passengers waiting in line as their luggage went through an extensive search. All electrical appliances, such as a razors or hairdryers, were plugged into a row of available outlets that strategically lined the terminal's wall. Any tubes of toothpaste or bottles containing liquid discovered in the luggage were immediately discarded in large garbage cans before the offending passengers could pass through to their waiting flight.

Outside of the terminal, as the other travelers filed aboard an idling bus, the ELAL agent directed Charlie to a waiting automobile that transported him directly to his plane. Once all the other passengers were finally on board, the Boeing 738 taxied down the runway.

The plane was trailed on each side by a speeding jeep containing heavily armed guards. When the plane was safely airborne, it dipped its wings and the vehicles turned and sped back to the terminal.

Charlie adjusted his seat, and settled in for the flight. Shortly afterwards, he was approached by a slender blond attendant carefully carrying a tall chilled glass. "I have been told that a Bombay martini is a prerequisite for your comfortable flight," she grinned before returning to the galley and her whispering associates.

You have to hand it to the Mossad—and Karen he decided. When they green-light your departure they cover all of the bases.

32

Tel Aviv

The twin engine 738 completed its three hour flight from Kiev to Tel Aviv, and rolled to a stop close to the newly refurbished terminal at Ben Gurion Airport. The attendant opened the cabin doorway as soon as the plane's twin engines were shut down. By the time Charlie deplaned there was a black limo idling by the bottom of the stairway. Karen was casually leaning against it, waving at him to join her.

Seated beside the driver was a small man with a gray sliver of a mustache that seemed to accentuate his slender features.

"This is my boss Ben Widra," Karen offered, after their car was underway.

"Awfully nice of you to make a detour on your way home," Ben said, extending his hand to Charlie in the backseat.

It was a very cold hand, but offered with a warm smile.

"We greatly appreciate your help in locating those chemical weapons," the man from the Mossad continued. "Quite ingenious, and appropriate really, to secret them away in a place no one would ever think of looking for them. The dead zone--really," he intoned, shaking his head. "Damned clever," he added, with ill-concealed admiration.

By now, the black limo had picked up speed. Apparently, it was a common sight on the roads around Tel Aviv. Charlie noticed that none of the drivers gave the speeding car a second glance.

The streets of Tel Aviv were as he remembered them—neat, clean, and busy. The city had always reminded him of a town in California—San Diego perhaps. Jerusalem had the ancient culture. Tel Aviv had the commerce.

It had been some time since he had been in Israel. He used to come often when he was on the international circuit for Apex Electronics. But that ended with the suicide of the principal of the company that manufactured products under license for the Israeli market.

The old man who owned the company was a colorful hard driving entrepreneur that got his start running guns for the Haganah, when Israel was under the British mandate. After the country gained its independence, his former associates in the underground became influential in the newly formed government. In return for his past services, they provided him with a monopoly for the distribution of beer in the thirsty country. He invested his profits in new enterprises, including the production of Apex products.

Unfortunately, the old man also invested heavily in his only son by buying him a bank in Switzerland. When the bank eventually failed, the son became wanted by Interpol, and the old man leaped to his death from the top of one of the many buildings he owned in Tel Aviv.

That was the sad end of Charlie's trips to Tel Aviv, but from what he could see the city had not changed that much during the intervening years.

The flood of memories ended as the car pulled to a stop inside the Mossad compound. The headquarters area had a campus like feel about it. The grounds were well landscaped, and the buildings' designs were modern but functional.

Ben led the way to his large office on the top floor of the main building. As the three of them sat around his mahogany desk, the bright fluorescent lighting caused the man to appear even paler than before. While Ben searched for something in his desk, Charlie studied him and decided that the man's life was reflected in the features of his face. It was a hard life that he saw, one filled with responsibility and sadness. For the first time, Charlie noticed a jagged scar running from the lobe of Ben's ear into his tight fitting shirt collar.

"Ben is in charge of the Collections Department," Karen explained, bringing Charlie back to the task at hand.

"The Collections Department," Charlie grinned at the reference. That sounds like you are working for a finance company rather than an intelligence agency."

Finding what he was looking for, Ben laid a folder on his desk and turned his attention to Charlie. "Perhaps the term losses something in translation from Hebrew," he smiled. "What we are mainly responsible for is collecting information overseas and then acting on it when it becomes necessary to do so.

"The other principal organization of the Mossad," Ben added, "is the Political Action and Liaison Department. It has the responsibility for working with the allied foreign intelligence service.

"They were the people," Karen intervened "who worked with your people on the Stuxnet malware that disabled Iran's nuclear centrifuges."

"Allegedly," Ben grinned.

"But sometimes," Ben smiled, "there is an occasional gap in the cooperation between our two organizations.

"Right now, my chief concern is stopping the flow of the chemical weapons the two of you discovered in Ukraine. We are afraid if they get to Syria they can ultimately be used to intimidate or, in a worst case scenario, annihilate us.

"We are a very small country. Our population is not much larger than your metro Chicago area so we are very vulnerable. But then Charlie you know all that. I understand you have been here many times, and know us very well."

Charlie wondered how the man knew that, but before he could ask Ben continued.

"That is why we need to know who is coordinating the shipment out of Cairo."

Ben opened the folder and passed it to Charlie. "We operate a reasonably large stable of operatives in Egypt. Have done so for many years. They have come up with some photographs of people they think may be involved with the transfer. We are reasonably confident that we can stop this shipment from reaching its destination, but we need to be sure that there is not another one we don't know about."

"It was just by accident that we came across this one," Karen added. "If you hadn't been searching for Markoff we would have never known what the Russians were doing in Prypyat."

"Have you looked at these?" Charlie asked Karen.

"Yes I have, but there is no one there I can identify. I have been gone from the Agency too long."

Charlie studied each picture closely. Some were clear. Some were not. In some cases there appeared to be several shots of the same person, while for others there was only a single photo. They all appeared to be either American or English.

As it seems frequently to be the case, it was not until Charlie reached the last picture in the folder that he saw someone he recognized.

"That's Barbara Richards," he exclaimed. "But what the hell is she doing in Egypt. She does work for Riordan, but I am sure that she has nothing to do with the transfer of chemical weapons to the Syrians."

Ben and Karen looked at each other, and then they both looked at Charlie.

"Are you sure that is who it is?" Ben asked.

"Pretty sure, I only met her once, but she took me to the file room...and she is a damned good looking woman," Charlie added defensively.

"Would she know you if she saw you on the street...in Cairo?" Karen asked.

"Probably not, if she had no reason to know that I was there."

"I fully understand," Ben told him with a thin smile crossing his face. "That is why we believe you are the person we need to go to Cairo."

Charlie was ready to decline, but Ben continued. "I understand this all started because you were asked to find the killer of Emmett Valentine."

Charlie shrugged his agreement.

"I knew Emmett very well," Ben added. "He was a very courageous man. A fierce warrior who knew his enemy. There aren't many of his type left, at a time when they might be needed the most.

"As I believe you are well aware, the Russian Bear is very active in our area of the world. Secretly re-supplying Syria with chemical weapons is not the only thing they are doing. Each time they succeed, they get stronger.

"I have a bargain for you," Ben offered staring straight at Charlie. "You are a businessman I know, and businessmen value a bargain. I also understand that you

247

know Vincent St. Claire. We speak often—kind of an old boy's network if you will.

"We are pursuing some possibilities that might be helpful to you. In short Mr. Connelly, you help us, and we help you.

"What have you got to lose?" Ben concluded.

Charlie looked at Karen. She nodded in agreement.

After further discussion it was decided among them that if Barbara was not directly involved with the shipment there was a reasonable chance that she could lead to whoever was involved. Perhaps it was not a good chance, but in reality, it was the only chance they had.

The Mossad had been monitoring the flow of communications out of Egypt and while they could make some sense out of it, they had not been able to trace it back to its source.

In past cases, they could enlist the assistance of the NSA to tap into, and interpret the flow of communications. But in this case, since they suspected that someone with the CIA was involved, that didn't seem to provide a viable alternative.

It was agreed then that Charlie would go to Cairo—for just a short time. He would see if he could make contact with Barbara Richards and try and find out if she was a friend or foe. Then he would report back to Ben or Karen whatever he found.

Ben would make sure that someone would meet Charlie, and provide any assistance he could.

The meeting over, Charlie found himself on the way back to the airport, and wondering when this would all end and, most of all, if he was doing the right thing in pursuing it as much as he was.

Perhaps he should just chuck it all and catch a plane home, he wondered as the cab pulled up to Ben Gurion airport.

What was it he tried to remember — *in for a penny, in for a pound* — that was it he decided, as he approached the Olympia Airlines desk clutching his ticket to Athens.

33

Cairo

The Olympic flight from Athens groaned to a stop in front of Cairo's ancient terminal. One of the early deplaning passengers was Charlie Connelly. He was tired, and glad to get on the ground. He had taken the long way around from Tel Aviv, but thought that it was better for his purposes than going direct.

In the old days, this was the way you had to do it. When Charlie first traveled in the Mideast, there were no direct flights between Israel and Egypt. Political nonsense prohibited travel between the two countries. Even then, if you had an Israeli customs stamp anywhere on your passport you couldn't enter Egypt, regardless of where you came from.

He had always asked the Israelis' to "stamp it on the side," when entering their country. They understood. They did it all of the time. They would put their stamp on a separate piece of paper and stick in your passport. When you left the country they would remove it, and there was no visible evidence you had ever been there.

Things had changed, and there was now sporadic air service between Tel Aviv and Cairo, depending on the prevailing political climate at the time of departure. Charlie had decided that the old ways are sometimes the best ways, and had restructured his route through Athens.

His current passport carried no evidence he had recently been in Israel. The Mossad had seen to that, but it seemed safer to take the long way around. He was reasonably certain that Egypt's General Intelligence Service

(GIS) kept close track on who might be entering their troubled country now that the "Arab Spring" had become their "winter of discontent." Because of the nature of his visit, he was not particularly interested in attracting any more attention to his arrival than was necessary.

Cairo's streets were crowded, and the air polluted. The same as it was when he had traveled there before. One thing had changed considerably. The taxi driver now seemed more apprehensive, and his attention darted from side to side with increasing frequency the closer they got to the center of the city.

As the taxi circled Tahrir Square, there was considerable evidence of the recent demonstrations. Fallen masonry, sheared off from the surrounding buildings by powerful explosions, was stacked in giant piles scattered indiscriminately around the square. Crews of workers were busy sweeping up shards of glass that had fallen from windows and storefronts.

Protective barricades were stacked in front of the city's famous museum, and armed guards patrolled the perimeters to safeguard the antiquities from future protestors.

The driver commented that the day was relatively peaceful. The preceding weeks had been marked by a grim pattern of spontaneous, but still violent, demonstrations. The protests had plagued the country for many weeks.

It seemed to Charlie the entire world was in turmoil. Kiev had been burning, Tel Aviv was being mortally threatened by its neighbors, and Cairo, which had provided some semblance of sanity to the Mideast, was now in a continuing state of revolt against one political faction or another. Underlying all of this unrest, Russia's global intelligence operations were playing a not so subtle hand, while America was seemingly preoccupied somewhere else.

The Hilton's lobby was virtually empty. The tourists and foreign commercial visitors, who usually composed the majority of the hotel's guests, were cautiously staying home frightened by the continuing violence in the streets. There were only a few men dressed in their white robes, aimlessly roaming the deserted lobby.

It didn't take Charlie long to unpack, and after a shower and a change of clothes he stretched out on the bed staring at the ceiling. He thought that one of Ben Widra's people would meet him at the airport, but that was probably not appropriate. Now he wondered what to do next. He wanted to find Barbara Richards, and through her uncover who was giving directions to the ship carrying chemical weapons to Syria. He also worried that he had reached a dead-end in his search for the killer Emmett Valentine.

So many questions so few answers he thought, staring at the ceiling fan as it made its continuing rotations above his head.

Charlie was about to doze off when he was aroused by a sharp knock at his door.

"Room Service," announced a dark complexioned hotel employee striding into the room, and quickly closing the door behind him.

"I am your contact here in Cairo," the man announced, setting down the large tray he was carrying.

Charlie had been expecting to be contacted, but was surprised that it was by room service.

"Call me Jonathan," the waiter instructed, removing the lid from a plate on the tray.

"You're too pink—too American," he chuckled as he arranged an array of small bottles on the plate.

"Sit down," he pointed to a nearby chair. "I have been told to try and make you look Egyptian." Staring intently at Charlie's face the waiter shook his head, "That will be impossible, but I will do what I can."

As Jonathan proceeded to apply cosmetics to darken Charlie's complexion he explained he was an agent with the Mossad who had been told to assist Charlie in any way he could, and had been given suggestions from Tel Aviv on how that might be accomplished.

"You're Egyptian?" Charlie asked, leaning his head back.

"Yes."

"An Egyptian working for the Mossad?" Charlie tried once more.

"Yes that's right. I am an Egyptian working for the Mossad. You're wondering why, I imagine."

"As a matter of fact," Charlie laughed, closing his eyes so Jonathan could work on that area of his face, "I was."

Jonathan paused momentarily and stared at Charlie. "The answer is—the answer always is I would guess—money.

"I have a very attractive wife," he went on to explain. "That has resulted in many children. Now that I have them, my wife tells me, I have to educate them, and that is hard to do on a waiters pay," Jonathan complained, dabbing something dark on Charlie's eyelids.

A little more forcefully than Charlie thought necessary, but he grimaced and kept silent.

"Even with the tips," Jonathan added, moving on to Charlie's chin.

"On the other hand," he continued, "the Mossad pays well as long as I can be helpful to them, and I have worked for them a long time."

"You are Muslim...?"

"And they are Jewish," Jonathan finished the sentence for him. "Actually I am not a Moslem, I am Coptic--a Coptic Christian. I guess that makes me a *mister in-between* as they say. We are hated by the Islamists, and tolerated by the Jews."

When the make-up was applied to Jonathon's satisfaction, he handed Charlie a small Ruger 9mm pistol from under his hotel vest. "It's double action with a 7 plus 1 capacity. They said you might need this, but to ditch it before you leave."

Charlie took the gun--it was small but looked mean and powerful-- and gingerly put it away in a drawer.

Afterward, he went into the bathroom to look at himself in the mirror. The face that stared back at him looked pretty much as it had before, only a little darker with a slight stubble. He was disappointed. He had hoped for Omar Sharif, but instead got only an aging Charlie Connelly.

He returned to Jonathan, and spread the pictures he had received from the Mossad on the table between them. The agent studied them closely. "I took a couple of these," he admitted, but I don't know who they are. They just looked a little different. A little suspicious. The others are too fuzzy. They could be my brother for all I know," he conceded.

"The only one I have seen around the hotel recently is this one," he grinned holding up the photo of Barbara Richards. "Last night the same woman came into the bar, spent an hour or so over one drink and left. She seemed to be looking for someone herself, but as far as I know, whoever it was never showed up."

Jonathan finished putting away his applicators and jars of cosmetics. He examined his handiwork and shook his head. "That's the best I can do," he shrugged, and headed toward the bathroom to wash his hands.

On his way, Charlie heard him grumble, "Even the Mossad can't expect me to turn an Irishman into an Arab overnight."

"Are there any men who are staying at the hotel who seem suspicious to you?" Charlie asked when Jonathan returned.

"Half the people in the hotel, and all of the non-Arabs could be suspect. Who would come to Cairo with all of the problems we are having?

"No one," Jonathan frowned, answering his own question. "Unless they are suspicious--or crazy," he added as an afterthought.

On his way out, Jonathan stopped. "By the way, I forgot to give you this," he told Charlie handing him a small cell phone he unclipped from his trouser top, while balancing the empty tray with his other hand.

"Getting old I guess. My number is the only one in it. Just hit *send* if you have any question...or anything else.

"Or you want room service," he added, heading once again for the door.

Standing in the open doorway, he turned back to Charlie. "Those pictures..." he began. "There is one Anglo I have been particularly curious about. Each day he goes to the center of the bridge over the Nile, heading toward Tahrir Square. Just the center of the bridge. Never all of the way. He just stands there looking at the water. Finally, he turns away and comes back to the hotel."

"He could be meeting someone?".

"Perhaps. Then it could also be some type of a dead drop that I can't see from where I am," Jonathan replied. "Or it could be nothing at all.

"Maybe I will ask the Sphinx," he added, closing the door quietly behind him.

34

The sun setting behind the pyramids on the outskirts of Cairo had a magical effect on the Lobby of the Hilton hotel. Earlier, the area had been relatively empty, with only a few people milling about. Now, it was far more active.

Men from nearby Arab countries, dressed in long sleeved white Dishdashahs and checked headscarves found their place in the hotel's long bar area, where they were favoring Johnny Walker Black Label, Makers Mark bourbon, and other liquid pleasures unavailable to them in their own country.

Attractive young women, in revealing western style clothing, sipping French wine, and giggling at whatever their companion said, accompanied several of the visiting Bedouins. Other men sat singularly, hiding their interests and observations behind large aviator-style Ray-Bans.

A local string ensemble now replaced the harpist, who had entertained during the afternoon. The hotel management hoped that the strains of the *Intermezzo* from *Cavalleria Rusticana* would contribute to their desired atmosphere of peace and tranquility.

The relative calm inside the hotel was in marked contrast to the increasing turmoil on the surrounding streets. Earlier in the day, Egypt's interim prime minister had announced the resignation of his cabinet. The resignation came amid a host of strikes, including one by public transport workers and another by the garbage collectors.

This labor unrest, along with a prolonged shortage of home cooking gas, was having a dramatic impact on the city's working population. They were, once again, taking to the streets to express their growing frustration with the country's leadership.

So far, none of the external turmoil served to dampen the evening's cocktail hour inside the hotel. Charlie found an unoccupied overstuffed chair beside a small table in a remote corner of the lounge. He sat, observing the people around him and enjoying a double Bombay martini.

His favorite drink provided only slight consolation. He was tired, and he was rapidly becoming fed-up with his assignment. It would have been better if he felt he was making progress, but that was not the case. He was no closer to finding Emmett's killer than he had been before. And poor Marissa Dolan, he thought, she apparently had been poisoned only because of the slight chance she might know who had done away with her boss.

Now, here he was in a bar he had been in many times before in his work-a-day world, hoping to find someone who was sending signals to a rogue Russian cargo ship carrying chemical weapons to Syria.

He had been sitting there for some time, reflecting on the odd set of circumstances that brought him to Cairo, when Barbara Richards entered the lounge.

At first, Charlie didn't recognize her, or at least didn't admit to the possibility that it could be the same woman who guided him to the file room, and helped him with that twit of a file room custodian. But he knew it was her. It had to be her. If nothing else, he recognized those long well shaped legs that he followed down the hallway at Langley. She was also the same woman in the picture that Ben Widra had showed him in Tel Aviv.

But what was she doing in Cairo? Looking for him? Perhaps, but why send her to look for him, when Riordan didn't know he was coming to Egypt? It wasn't that he was trying to deceive Ray. He just hadn't had time to tell him.

Barbara created considerable attention among the unattached, and some of the accompanied men as well. She was a strikingly attractive woman, with the ability to enter a room and cause all eyes to focus exclusively on her.

This was not necessarily an advantage for a person employed in her line of work. It was better to go unnoticed and immediately forgotten. Just a passing face in the crowd was preferred--but tonight she intended for her appearance to provide an extra advantage.

Since her arrival, Barbara had been unsuccessful in attempting to locate Ralph Gross. Her boss, Ray Riordan, had told her that Gross was staying at the Hilton. He always did he said. He liked the long bar. But, so far, she had been unable to locate him.

If the people behind the hotel desk were telling her the truth, and she was not sure that they were, there was no one by that name registered. Even after she slipped the man a folded fifty. She was familiar with the Mideast, and had worked there before. She completely understood that her $50 could be insignificant compared with an offered someone's $100 to keep quiet, but the baksheesh market was hard to assess.

On the other hand, she could understand that it would be unusual for a working agent, even one not undercover, to use his real name. It was second nature for someone in the Agency to remain anonymous outside of home base, but what name would he use?

This presented a problem for Barbara. Since she had been unable to locate Gross, her present strategy was to have him find her. She decided it was an effective plan as she observed the many male eyes following her entrance to the bar.

A pair of those eyes belonged to Charlie Connelly. He watched her languidly take her place on a vacant barstool.

259

The bartender recognized her from the night before, and hurried to mix the gin and grapefruit juice required for the Moneypenny cocktail that she ordered.

It was only a matter of minutes until one of the unattached men approached her, offering to pay for her drink. His whispered offer was rejected immediately. Whatever was said must have been stinging, the man quickly turned away as if he were slapped. Afterwards, Barbara was left entirely alone.

Until Charlie slid into the empty chair beside her.

She glanced at him, and then turned away, studying their reflection in the mirror behind the bar.

"Charlie Connelly?" Barbara whispered, glancing sideways. "Why are…?

"Barbara Richards? What the…?" His question, and hers, went unanswered. It was unnecessary. By then they both had, with certainty, recognized each other.

With a nod of his head, Charlie led Barbara to his table. All the men in the room wondered what that scruffy, sickly looking western male had to attract such a beautiful woman, after the handsome Arab had failed.

A waiter approached, but was summarily waved away. They had a great deal to discuss, and wanted no interruption. After the man left, Barbara looked closely at Charlie.

"Are you well? You look different. Your skin is dark."

"I'm well," he assured her.

"Then you need a shave—badly," her hand brushing his cheek. "And that scab on your ear?"

Charlie didn't want to tell her that he was supposed to be in disguise. So he would fit in—not stand out, as Jonathan had assured him.

They had a great deal to discuss.

"We got the cryptonyms that you found in Markoff's apartment," she began. From there she went into detail relating how Ken Madden had scrubbed the IT data files of names, and *HERCULES* had struck a respondent chord. It was one Ralph Gross had sometimes used in his classified messages, she informed Charlie in a whisper.

As she talked, Charlie had been sucking on the lemon twist he had extracted from his martini. When he heard her mention Ralph Gross, it focused his attention.

"I have heard of him. The big guy who works for Riordan? Arms like ten pins? Shoulders of a linebacker?"

"That's the one." Barbara confirmed with a faint smile. "Ray didn't believe it, but there were some items in a file that were curious. Also, some bank deposits that were highly questionable. He still didn't want to believe anything bad about his friend, but then he hadn't been hearing much from him lately so he sent me to check-up on him.

"But damn it, now that I am here I can't find him." she continued shaking her head. "There is no one registered by that name. I have been wandering around and haven't seen him. I am one lousy spy if I can't find someone I work with in a hotel where he is supposed to be staying. "

"And you Charlie—what in the name of God are you doing in Cairo? The last I heard of you, you were in Kiev."

Charlie had been wondering that as well, but wasn't ready to admit it. "Well," he began, and told her as quickly as possible the circumstances that brought him to the land of the Pharos.

"So someone here is sending signals to a ship headed for Syria, and you are supposed to find who it is and stop him?" Barbara asked, signaling the waiter to return.

"Another," she ordered. Charlie waved his hand at his half-filled glass. One double was enough for one night.

"What about the NSA?" Barbara asked. "They should be able to pin the signals down."

"The problem is that the signals go out in very short bursts, in an irregular sequence at odd intervals, and they get lost in all the crap that they are collecting. If they *can* isolate them, the chances are they will get lost in some bureaucratic black hole before they get to someone at Langley.

"There is another small problem," Charlie continued. "The weapons are on a Russian ship, and we are supposed to be working with them to destroy the weapons Bashar al Assad already has.

"Some of my contacts," he added in a whisper, "believe it is better they handle it themselves without involving the U.S."

"The Israelis?" Barbara asked, slowly sipping her drink.

Charlie nodded, glancing around.

The lounge crowd dwindled as the evening progressed, and the noise level had subsided. The two of them were beginning to stand out more among the remaining customers, and they found themselves having to whisper not to be overheard.

It was also becoming apparent to both of them that they were interested in finding the same man. "Our interests have converged," Barbara declared.

As they rose to leave, the music swelled behind them. It's a case of harmonic convergence Charlie decided, leading the way to the lobby.

Before going to their rooms, Charlie paused to tell Barbara that he had a connection with the Mossad who had

262

seen someone from the hotel walk to the bridge over the Nile each day at noon, and he appeared to be waiting for some form of contact, either a pass-off or a dead drop.

Thin as it was, it was the only lead they had, so they decided to join the man on his next visit to the bridge.

35

Charlie stepped out of his hotel room door, hesitated, and turned back. Inside the room, he removed the Ruger pistol from the dresser drawer and stared at it. It was an ugly but effective looking weapon, and it felt cold and deadly in his hand. He checked to make sure there was a bullet in the chamber before slipping the gun into his jacket pocket and quickly walking out the door.

In the elevator, he wondered why he had not heard from Vincent St. Claire. The old man had said he would check with his British contacts regarding the code name *HERCULES*, and let him know what he found. It was unlike Vincent to not follow-up.

Barbara was already in the lobby, nervously pacing back and forth. She was wearing a blue hijab wrap that only partially concealed her blond hair.

The night before, the two of them agreed to try and find the man on the bridge Jonathan had mentioned. It was nearing the time he was supposed to be there.

Charlie scanned the lobby and found the Mossad agent stationed by the revolving door. He had agreed on the phone to stay behind and watch what might happen.

They argued briefly over who should go first--who should lead and who should cover. Barbara won. She was familiar with Gross, if indeed it was Gross, and would be better able to identify him.

"All right?" she asked, entering the revolving door.

"Good luck," he replied, waiting to follow a few steps behind.

A crowd had gathered on the street outside, and was moving toward Tahrir Square. The demonstrations had already begun there, more violent than the day before. Frustration had reached a boiling point. Life among the citizens of Cairo was becoming increasingly difficult, and no one was listening to their demands. Overnight the military backed government had made additional changes, but the people believed they were merely different faces with the same inaction.

Today, military personnel had been added to the constabulary that was attempting to channel the crowd. The combination was more threatening than before. Guns were held at the ready, and the pushing and shoving between the demonstrators and the military was more evident and more forceful.

In the center of the milling crowd, black-clad Egyptian women shrilly ululated their loud displeasure, adding their sharp tongues to the unpleasant clamor of the moving throng.

Barbara tried to slip deeper into the crowd as she edged closer to the center of the bridge. She paused to catch her breath, and looked down at the muddy waters of the Nile flowing beneath her. She was jostled forward, and had to struggle to maintain her balance.

Charlie followed a few paces behind. Not too close, but close enough to keep her in sight. He felt the pistol in his jacket pocket. Would he use it? Could he use it in the crowd if it was necessary? His finger found the safety, and thumbed it off just in case. His palm was damp as his hand tightened on the pistol grip.

Stray dogs had joined the throng, looking for food or affection—or whatever Egyptian dogs search for. They weaved in and out of the crowd, and one nipped at Charlie's ankle as he passed underfoot.

Barbara searched for a familiar face. She was nearing the center of the span, and hesitated. There was a man standing apart from the passing crowd, staring in to the dark wasters below. She couldn't see his face, but his figure was familiar. The broad shoulders and thick neck, bulging above the collar of his caftan, was one she was certain belonged to Ralph Gross. But what was he staring at, with his back to the crowd.

Suddenly she realized, it wasn't the water he had fixated on, it was his watch. He turned away just as a tall woman, in a black burka and veil, passed behind him. They reached out to each other, in a tightly choreographed and almost unseen motion.

Barbara leaped between them, clutching at their outstretched hands. Gross instantly recognized her, and gave her a massive shove. Barbara tried to catch herself from falling, but it was no use. She fell to the ground, covered instantly by trampling feet.

The veiled woman reached down to grasp at Barbara's hand, but she was carried backward by the motion of the crowd; finally turning with the flow and going unwillingly with them toward the opposite side of the bridge.

Charlie saw what had happened and leaped forward attempting to reach the muscular Ralph Gross. The man was too powerful, and pushed him aside. As Charlie fell forward, the gun he was clutching in his pocket discharged. The sound went unheard, just another sound among many in the noisy milling throng.

Gross grimaced clutching his chest, then moved away, becoming lost in the crowd. A streetcar pushed its way slowly across the bridge, and he grasped desperately at the doorway, hoping it would carry him to the other side.

Charlie knew he should chase after Gross, but instead turned towards Barbara who was attempting to pull herself upright on the bridge railing. "I got it," she screamed in his ear, clutching a tightly rolled piece of parchment.

He shielded her body with his, holding her tightly against the concrete structure until the crowd passed, moving on like a wave to Tahrir Square.

The two of them tried to catch their breath. "Where did he go?" Barbara asked finally, when she could speak again. "It was him," she added. "It was Ralph Gross."

"I don't know where," Charlie, told her. "I didn't see. Maybe back to the hotel. He was headed that way."

He remembered the phone Jonathan had given him, and dug it from his pocket. He quickly punched *send.*

"Yes?"

"He's headed your way."

The phone went dead.

He took the rolled up piece of paper from her hand. "What is this?" he asked looking at the note.

"What in the *hell* is this?" he asked again, as they both studied a set of drawings running horizontally across the parchment.

"They make no sense. No sense at all," Barbara replied shaking her head, her hijab falling to her shoulders. "But they must have been important for him to have gone to all of this trouble to get them."

"And who would give them to him, and why? Charlie asked.

Before returning to the hotel, Charlie took off his jacket. Looking both ways, he rolled up the Barbour, and dropped it over the railing. He and Barbara watched as the jacket and the pistol disappeared in the murky water below.

Inside the hotel, Charlie looked around the lobby, but there was no sign of Jonathan. The two of them stared at each other wondering what to do next, when Charlie caught a glimpse of Jonathan exiting a bank of elevators on the far side of the lobby. They quickly joined him. Nothing was said between them, just a nod of Jonathan's head toward an opening elevator door.

It was a silent ride to the eighteenth floor. Once the elevator door opened, Jonathan led them down the hallway towards a room at the very end. There were several drops of blood on the carpet; so small they would have gone unnoticed by a casual passerby.

Jonathan took the hotel's universal key card from his pocket, and slid it into the door lock. A small light glowed green, indicating that the room door was open. They looked at each other, and Jonathan held his finger to his lips in an unnecessary signal for silence.

Now, Charlie regretted throwing the gun away. But it was too late now, and he wished he had kept the Rueger.

Jonathan quietly opened the door, and Charlie burst inside. Barbara followed close behind.

It was immediately obvious that a gun would not be needed. Gross lay curled-up in a fetal position on the floor. Blood trickled from his mouth, and from his side. Documents were strewn about the room, and a large pile lay between him and a small shredder he apparently was trying to reach.

Gross rolled over on his back and held out a plaintive hand to Barbara. She disgustedly pushed it away with the toe of her shoe.

"Need help," he begged. "I hadn't expected that," he added glaring at Charlie. "Please help," he whispered again before passing out.

The phone rang, Charlie leaped for it. "Hercules?" A woman's voice was on the line; Charlie grunted a response, hoping to sound like Gross. She quickly hung up.

"Probably the person who passed him the note," Charlie told them. "His contact."

"We have to get him out of here. Save him if we can." Charlie told them, staring at the man unconscious on the floor.

"You're very compassionate," Jonathan sneered.

"Not at all—well maybe a little, but we need to find out what he was doing, and what he knows." Charlie knew that Gross had the answers he needed to finish his assignment. Without him alive his questions—Riordan's questions really--might never be resolved.

Barbara was already searching through the papers strewn about the floor. She put them aside when she noticed a small digital transmitter and keypad sitting unobtrusively behind the shredder. "Look at this," she told them. He was sending messages to someone, we need to know who."

Jonathan shrugged, and reached for the phone. He spoke in short bursts of Hebrew. Afterwards he turned to them. "Some men will be here soon. They will take him out of here, and see if he can be patched-up. They are good at that. They have a lot of experience with gunshot wounds, but there is no guarantee."

Barbara was trying to contain the bleeding with a bathroom towel.

While they waited for Jonathan's friends to arrive, Charlie looked once again at the note that Barbara had grabbed.

"What do you have?" Jonathan asked.

Charlie handed the paper to him. "This was the note that Gross was waiting for. Barbara grabbed it from the woman who met him on the bridge. It makes no sense just some silly unconnected pictures."

"They're not pictures. Well they are I guess," Jonathan laughed. "They are hieroglyphs. You *are* in Egypt you know."

Charlie knew where they were, but it was not enough of an explanation to understand what he was looking at.

"Egyptian hieroglyphs," Jonathan continued, "are sometimes known as *god's words*. They were a form of writing system used by the ancient Egyptians that combined logographic symbols or pictures, and alphabetic elements."

Charlie was surprised. "How do you know so much about this? Are you some type of a secret scholar?"

"Not exactly," Jonathan blushed. "One of my kids is studying it in school. The government is trying to increase the children's awareness of their cultural heritage by studying hieroglyphics, and I have been trying to help him."

"You can read this?"

"Let me see," Jonathan sat at the desk where the light was brighter.

Before he could say anything more, there was a tap on the door. Charlie opened it and two men entered the room. They nodded to Jonathan.

The larger of the two stood by the door, while the other man adjusted his glasses and knelt beside the wounded man. After studying the wound, he took out a small kit from his coat pocket and removed a needle and a syringe. He tested the syringe before carefully injecting something into Gross' outstretched arm.

Gross shuddered violently, and then fell silent. His eyes popped open, then closed. His face contorted in a grimace and relaxed.

"Is he....?" Charlie asked.

"Not yet, but he will be soon, if we don't get him medical attention," the man replied as he carefully placed a bandage over the wound. He was obviously experienced at the essence of field medicine--doing much with little.

"We have a place," he told Charlie, as he and his companion heaved their patient to his feet.

"Where are you taking him?" Barbara demanded, standing between them and the doorway. "We want to question him."

"I am sure you do. We do as well, but you can't question a dead man," she was admonished. "If we are lucky, we can get him medical attention before he dies."

"Come here tomorrow," he told her, shoving a card into her hand, and brushing her aside. "We have to walk this drunk out of here to our car."

"He's not..." Barbara began, then felt embarrassed when she realized what they intended to do. She stood aside to let them pass.

36

Charlie watched while the two men, with Gross's arms straddling their shoulders, drunk-walked him down the hallway. When they reached the elevator, he shut the door and turned to Jonathan. "How in hell could a man as big as he is be in the hotel without you knowing it?"

Jonathan shrugged apologetically. "Don't know for sure, but I would guess that he paid someone to register for him under some made-up name. Once he was here, he had his meals sent-up and left outside the room; then he put the tray back in the hallway when he was through. He must have lived like a hermit in the hotel. I never saw him come or go—just slipped in and out. It was pure luck I noticed him standing at the bridge each day at the same time. It's when I go outside for a smoke.

"I never even saw him come back, until today. After you called."

Charlie looked at Jonathan. He knew he was talking to a man who was a paid agent. Someone who told lies for a living, but whose income was dependent on the validity of his information. He thought about what he heard, then changed the subject.

"So my Egyptian scholar, what do these pictures tell us?"

"The hieroglyphs you mean?" Jonathan replied.

"Well let's see. The lion stands for *l*. The bird is *a*. The half circle is a *t*. The bird is repeated, so that's another *a*. The circle could be a *k* or an *h*. I would guess a *k* the way this is going. Jonathan rubbed his temples. "Then you have an *i* followed by an *a* again.

"Latakia," Jonathan proclaimed triumphantly.

"Latakia?" Barbara asked. "What is a Latakia?"

"Not what—where," Charlie shouted, remembering what he had seen in Prypyat. "Latakia is the port in Syria where the chemical weapons are going."

Now it was clear what Gross was doing, and with the small transmitter Barbara had found, how he was doing it. This was the information that Ben Widra required to intercept the shipment of chemical weapons. There was just one more thing that Charlie wanted to know.

"Who do you think was supplying him with the information?" Charlie asked, turning once more to Jonathan.

"It has to be the Russians."

"In Egypt?

"Of Course Egypt. Why not? The Russians have been an important ally of this, and some of the other Arab countries, since the 1950s when the Arabs fought Israel in a series of Middle East wars. President Nasser received considerable support from the Soviets for his fiercely nationalist policies that challenged America's role in the region. They have been here ever since," Jonathan concluded. "Underground," he added as an afterthought.

"They play the long game. The very long game," he added emphatically.

Barbara was sitting on the floor, half listening to their conversation as she poured over the cache of highly

273

classified and some encrypted documents Gross had carelessly strewn about the room.

Charlie went into the bedroom, and closed the door. He wanted to get in touch with Karen in Tel Aviv to let her know what they had found. He punched her number. The one that Emmett had given him in Vienna. There was a pause as the number cleared the Egyptian interchange and entered the classified domain of the old man's alternate algorithmic communications grid. He could have used the number Ben Widra had given him, but he felt more comfortable communicating directly with Karen.

"Charlie?" He was glad to hear her voice, and told her hurriedly what had happened. How Barbara Richards, from Langley, was the person in the picture Ben had given him. From there, he went on to describe their experience on the bridge, and finally the note that provided the ultimate destination of the Russian weapons shipment.

"So the port they have chosen is Latakia? That's ironic. Latakia is also the port the Syrians are using as the principal point of departure for their chemical weapons they agreed to give up. They have already shipped out the majority of the lower priority chemicals, and have submitted a plan to ship-out all the remaining ones the international inspectors found."

"And at the same time, the Russians were secretly in the process of resupplying them with the cannisters they had in Ukraine."

"That's right Charlie, at the same time. It is a good thing you were able to find which one of the Syrian ports was to be their final destination. We were able to get a transponder on the Russian ship before it left Istanbul, but the signal is getting progressively weaker. The Mossad was greatly concerned that it would die before we were able to intercept the shipment."

274

"And now?"

"And now we are going to *neutralize* it."

"That sounds ominous," Charlie, told her.

"It is ominous. Things are becoming much more tense between Israel and Syria. Violence along our borders is heating up. Our warplanes just struck some of their military targets in retaliation for an explosion that injured some of our soldiers in the Golan Heights. We have told them that 'we attack those who attack us,' and we can't afford to let that shipment of weapons get through."

"Do you plan to stop here on the way home?" Karen asked, changing the subject. "I know Ben would like to thank you personally for what you have done for us."

"No Karen, I have a few things to clear up, then its wife and family for me."

After a long pause Karen replied, "Well then, till the next time I guess." There was a sadness in her voice.

"Till next time Karen — good luck."

After Charlie finished the call, he stood staring out the window at the peaks of the pyramids in the distance. His mind raced back over the years, and their long relationship. She had a troubled past with the CIA, and he was glad she finally found a home that accepted her for the contributions she could make. But, he also knew the shadow-world was not kind to its members, and he doubted he would ever see her again.

"Charlie," he heard Barbara calling from the other room.

He didn't want her to know that he had been talking to an off-the-books former agent.

"OK Barbara, I'll be right there."

While he was speaking with Karen, Barbara had called Riordan. "I told Ray what happened and what we found. There is so much classified information here he wants me to bundle it in a diplomatic pouch, and bring it to Langley right away. Some of it I can read, but most I can't. He believes that it is very important that I return to Washington ASAP."

As she spoke, Barbara was hastily stuffing pages in a bulging back pack that had formerly belonged to Gross.

"Then I guess it's good-by Barbara?" It seemed he was spending a good deal of time telling women good-by lately.

"I guess so, but Riordan wants to see what you can get out of Gross, and then come to Langley on your way home." She blew him a kiss as she rushed out the door.

"She sure as hell wanted to get out of here as fast as she could," Charlie complained.

Jonathan grinned and said nothing.

Charlie was about to add that he would like to be going with her. He was sick of Cairo, and sick of his assignment. He felt that Riordan and the Agency were taking advantage of him, but he kept his feelings to himself. He knew he hadn't finished his job, and he had to make sure it was actually Gross who had killed Emmett. And why.

He couldn't leave, as much as he would have liked to, without finishing what he has set out to do. Now he had to think ahead, and decide how best to finally complete his assignment.

37

Jonathan led Charlie to the hotel's service elevator and from there to the garage. They walked past a row of expensive imported automobiles and limousines, and eventually into a remote corner where he had parked his vintage English Ford. The door opened with a distinctive creaking sound. Jonathan turned toward Charlie, shrugged his shoulders and grinned.

Charlie got in the car, and searched for the seatbelt. There was none. It was a small car, and Charlie felt cramped in the front seat.

The Ford's engine strained and coughed before finally starting. Charlie's head jerked back at the sudden forward motion, and he braced himself against the dash.

Jonathan carefully avoided the principal streets that were once again filling with demonstrators, but it was impossible to bypass them all. They turned at a corner a few hundred yards from the central courthouse in Cairo's Imbaba district.

The ancient structure still showed signs of a bomb that exploded in the doorway a few days before. At the next intersection, Jonathan stomped on the brakes to let a raucous group from the Muslim Brotherhood pass in front. The demonstrators carried signs identifying themselves as members of the Freedom and Justice Party, and waving banners blaming the Coptic Christian radicals for the explosion.

Finally, Jonathan slid the Ford alongside a crumbling concrete slab in the city's working class suburb of Mattareyya. Charlie looked around the area. The surrounding buildings were badly in need of repair, and the place they parked in front fit in perfectly. Nondescript was an essential element of any safe house anywhere, and this location easily met that requirement.

Inside, it was cold and gray — very gray. The house had an essential emptiness to it, as if it were never really occupied. A musty odor, seasoned with a touch of curry, bordered on the offensive. The rooms were poorly lighted, if at all. The main area had a variety of overstuffed furniture and a tall bookcase, with just enough on its shelves to appear legitimate.

They passed a small kitchen furnished with the bare necessities. An old Egyptian, in a dirty caftan, sat at the table barely glancing at the new arrivals.

As Jonathan led him up a dark flight of stairs, Charlie wondered if the Mossad had a safe house manual dictating the appearance and furnishings for all locations. Charlie sensed, more than saw, similarities between this place and the secluded residence he and Karen visited in Kiev.

At the top of the staircase, the scene through the open doorway immediately focused his thoughts back on the present. Inside the room, Gross sat starkly naked and strapped to a straight back metal chair. His chin rested on his chest where the hair had been shaved and a fresh bandage applied to the bullet wound. The man appeared heavily sedated.

The two Mossad agents sat at a table nearby. They got up when Charlie and Jonathan entered the room. One of them, the smaller of the two, went over to a machine by the table, removed the cover, and began adjusting a series of dials.

Gross looked pathetic, stripped of any resemblance to Hercules. Charlie cast an inquiring glance at the two agents. They shook their heads and shrugged their shoulders. They weren't sure that Gross would be able to survive the wound, and apparently didn't particularly care.

At the sound of people stirring, Gross raised his head and stared at Charlie. "Connelly, Riordan told me about you. Was it really you who shot me? A professional brought down by an amateur. I'm embarrassed."

Charlie had wondered himself if the shot that wounded Gross had actually been intentional on his part, or merely the reflex action of being shoved. At first, he had felt a sense of guilt. Now he didn't care.

"What are these mother f…," Gross barked, then caught himself, as the smaller of the two began attaching a medical cuff to his arm. "These mothers don't need a lie detector to tell if I'm telling the truth. I know I am going to die. I was pretty good at what I do—did. Proud of it really. Fooled everybody. Listen and learn Connelly. Learn about what really goes on behind your expensive paneled doors at your holier than thou Agency."

On the ride from the hotel Charlie thought about what he was going to say when he and Gross finally met. He considered carefully what he would ask, and what he wanted to uncover. He worried that he would somehow have to break the agent in order to make him talk. He wasn't sure he knew how to do that. Now it appeared it was not going to be a problem. He felt greatly relieved.

The Israeli agent continued attaching the wires, and turning the dials on his equipment.

"I tried to warn you, but you wouldn't pay attention," Gross hissed. He was rapidly turning from pathetic to belligerent. Up to that point, Charlie had remained quiet. There was no need to say anything to someone with an apparent obsession to talk.

"Really, when was that?"

"When you were driving away from that old broad's house."

"Marissa?"

"Yeah. Marissa Dolan Anyway, I knew you were going there. I was on my way to the airport, and thought I would stop by. If you were inside, I would have wiped you too, but you had already left, so I thought I would see if I could wreck your car.

"It didn't work, but I didn't care. I never thought that you would ever make the connection to me."

'And you had killed her because?"

One of the agents nodded to Charlie that he wanted to talk. Outside of the room.

His problem was he had a process, a protocol for the interrogation. Start with name. Check the machine. Then ask questions that they already knew the answers for, and gradually progress to the major scope of the inquiry.

Charlie listened, and then rejected the process. So far, he was getting the answers he wanted, and decided to go with the flow. He would deal with the procedures later, if it was necessary.

Stepping back into the room, Gross appeared still eager to talk. "Tell his story," as he described it.

"Why kill a poor defenseless old woman?" Charlie began again.

"One woman, old—young, they're all the same; and this one might have figured out who killed her boss."

"Emmett?"

"Hell yes, Emmett Valentine!" he shouted. "The old cold warrior. The famous spymaster," Gross sneered.

"I slipped something in her tea canister the day before, when she was out. I knew she would drink it that morning. She always did, I had heard."

Charlie surged forward. It was all he could do to restrain himself. The man's indifference for life was stunning.

Instead, he clenched his fists, and moved on to where he wanted to go. "Why kill Emmett? How was he a threat to you?"

"The old bastard had been around too long. His time was past, and he was getting close to discovering the Illegals connection to me. He was asking all sorts of questions about me. He had to go. I went to his place. He invited me in we talked. Then I killed him. That simple. Just one, two and three.

"Got your interest now—huh," Gross laughed derisively. "Now let's you and I make a deal. Get rid of the skinny guy, and the ape. I'll tell you what you want to know, and then you let me go."

"Here's my deal you son of a bitch," Charlie growled. "You tell me what I want to know, and maybe I won't kill you right away. Like my friends here want to do. One way or the other you're going to talk.

"Afterwards, if we believe you are telling the truth—cooperating with us, then we talk deal." Charlie spoke now with an ice-like calmness. "Maybe."

Gross stared at Charlie. He had expected to get a deal after he had offered the bait.

Charlie stared back, and the large guard began to move forward with a butcher knife he had taken from the table drawer.

"What was your question? Why did I kill the old man?" Gross began to speak rapidly.

The Israeli tossed the knife on the table in disgust, and sat down. It was clear to all of those in the room that he would have preferred using the knife, and wouldn't hesitate to pick it up again.

Charlie would have let the man cut Gross's throat, or whatever else he might have intended to cut, now that he knew he was facing the person who killed his friend. But instead, he continued the questioning.

"Yes, why did you kill Emmett Valentine?" Charlie repeated through clenched teeth. "Even if he was asking questions, if he was such an ancient artifact as you claim, why take the chance of rubbing him out, and putting your career on the line."

"You don't get it do you—you corporate son of a bitch. My career was already on the line. I put it on the line the day I met Anna."

"Anna?"

"Yeah, yeah Anna. The one and only Anna Chapman."

"One of the Illegals?"

"That's what you call her. I called her the best bang I ever had." Gross grinned. Then his eyes darted from Charlie to the Israelis, but they sat stone-faced, as if they weren't even listening.

"Go on Ralph"

Charlie thought using the man's first name might create some type of rapport between them. He didn't need to bother. Gross was more than eager to tell his story.

"At first, I didn't know she was a spy. My wife had divorced me a year before, and I was hungry---you know

Connelly, that kind of hungry." He licked his lips and leered. "By the time I found out what she was I didn't care.

"They offered money. She knew that I had blown all my money on lawyers' fees, and even then, my wife got everything. I was broke. Busted. Flat broke."

"Who offered you the money? Anna?"

"Hell no. It was Markoff. Colonel Dimitri Markoff. He was my contact. My control. Now I had the best of both worlds. A red-hot broad, and a big bank account."

Charlie was surprised how the story was fitting together. Earlier, he had been watching the Israeli running the lie detector equipment for any sign that Gross was lying to him, He had given that up long ago. Now he was convinced that the man was telling the truth.

"You know Markoff?" Gross asked.

"I have heard his name." he nodded. There was no benefit in alerting Gross that Markoff was dead, or that Charlie had seen him die in a cramped hotel room in Kiev.

"Now there is a real spymaster." Gross continued. It seemed he couldn't stop talking.

Charlie wondered if it was something the Israelis had given him, but decided it was driven by the man's ego rather than any sort of injection. He didn't care which it was as long as Gross kept talking.

"If he was so brilliant, why was his spy ring in the U.S. rolled-up?" Charlie asked. He was curious, and wondered if this was the point where Gross would begin to lie.

"That was the brilliance of the man. The FBI was getting close to Anna and her *friends*." Gross rolled his eyes, and made a face as he pronounced the word *friends*.

"The Feds were getting close," he repeated. "It was only a matter of time.

"I was working with them," he said proudly.

"The Feds?"

"Yeah the Feds. Our *cousins* with the Federal Bureau of Investigation," he sneered. I was the liaison from the CIA, so I had close contact with them. Besides, most of the Russian Agents had been in the country for a long time—not producing a hell of a lot. Some of them were getting restless—becoming Americanized. So, when I told the Colonel how close the FBI was getting to them, he had me feed the Feds more information. That way I remained safe, and the others got a ticket home a little earlier than Moscow originally planned."

"How did they know they would get sent home?" Charlie was curious. Others had asked the same question.

"They didn't know, but Markoff was convinced they would get deported rather than convicted. He could read you people like a book. He figured your country would want to get them off their hands so as not to antagonize Putin, and jeopardize your precious *reset* policy. He was right. He was always right."

Gross stared at Charlie, expecting some sign of admiration. When he didn't get it, his eyes darted to the Israelis. They appeared indifferent to the whole proceeding.

Jonathan, who had left the room earlier, returned with a tray holding cups of coffee. He set it down on the table and left the room. Jonathan was a ferret and a good one. He ferreted out information and reported it back. The men inside the room were wolves, and it made him nervous to be around them.

"If things were going so great for you, why leave Washington?" Charlie asked, picking up one of the cups.

"Just to be safe. I knew the Admiral was worried about not having a larger presence in the Mideast, so I told him I was an expert, and he sent me over here."

"Didn't Riordan send you?"

"He just does what the Admiral says."

"And you didn't tell Riordan that you set it up? That you went over his head?"

"Why the hell would I do that?"

"I thought you two were friends."

"That's why you are an amateur Connelly. In this business, there is no such thing as friends.

"Once I was here," Gross continued, "I was contacted again by the Russians, who wanted me to radio signals to some ship they had an interest in. I was to tell it where to go. I didn't care where some Russian freighter went, and I was back in the game. The CIA thought I was working for them, sending back senseless reports, and the Russians paid me for sending out some stupid signals on a transmitter they gave me."

Gross seemed proud of what he had done. "So now, you know it all. You try me and everyone will know how they outsmarted you, and there will be hell to pay at the Agency. You are better off just letting me go, and no one will ever know. I give you my word."

It had been all that Charlie could do to control himself when he heard Gross brag about killing Emmett. He was furious, and would have liked to slit the man's throat himself.

His anger subsided. He believed he had obtained as much information as he could. There were many more questions he would liked to have asked, but decided against it. He had found out who, how and why, which were the essential parts of any interrogation. He would have liked to learn more about the man's feelings. Did he have any regrets about betraying his country? Seemingly, he had none about killing Emmett.

Charlie was disgusted with Gross, and everything else associated with him. The whole damn mess made him sick.

He didn't care what happened to Gross after he left. The man's admission of guilt was Charlie's ticket home. Now, he planned to hand him over to the Israelis.

Charlie nodded toward the door, and the two men followed him into the hallway.

Gross watched apprehensively. He was beginning to sweat when he realized his bragging was getting him nowhere.

Outside, Charlie told them he was done with *Hercules.* He used the name derisively in reference to the pathetic man strapped to the chair.

The smaller of the two told him Ben Widra was coming that night to hear what they had learned. They had it all on a recorder inside the lie detector.

"Then what?" Charlie asked dispassionately. He was done with Gross, and really didn't give a damn what they did with him.

"Widra will decide which port to signal the ship as its destination. Then we will either turn him or kill him," they told him. "We would like to know more about the Moscow connection in Cairo, and he could be helpful with that."

"Make him a double agent?"

"If we can, he is no good to us dead. Just another body to be disposed of. Maybe we can send him back to his Bolshevik friends, and get more information on their

286

operations here. If not...." The Mossad agent made a slashing gesture across his throat.

As he approached the stairs, he heard Gross scream, "Charlie---Charlie Connelly — don't — you can't leave me.

"I am an American!"

The screams echoed down the stairway, then reverberated throughout the Israeli safe house. It would be a long time before Charlie would be able to get those screams out of his head.

On the way back to the hotel with Jonathan, Charlie wondered if it was the same with all the world's intelligence agencies. Is there always someone hidden deep down inside the organization who has been passed over, needs more money, falls in love, or is willing to betray his country just to prove he can do it?

He remembered the list of defectors Vincent St. Claire had given him that day in Vienna. What was it the old man said? 'Find the mole and you will find the answer.' That was it.

Vincent had been right.

38

The Egyptair flight to Vienna strained to lift off the runway. The atmosphere was particularly heavy, and the plane was having difficulty gaining altitude. Soon the 737-800 was airborne, and the seatbelt sign turned off.

Charlie was glad to be leaving Cairo; he had never liked it there. It was a city unable to make the transition from past to present. They were proud of their past but unable to contend with their future. The place was interesting enough. The pyramids were spectacular, but the politics incredible. It was the same when he used to go there on business.

His company, Apex Electronics, was on the Arab Blacklist, administered out of Damascus. Their sin was that they did business in Israel, and you couldn't do business with both — according to the Arab League.

In order to gain access to their markets, the League wanted you — demanded actually — that you sign an agreement, which they promised they would keep secret. It documented that the foreign organization would eventually dissolve their business relationship with the Israelis. In return, the League would grant access to their markets. It was morally objectionable, and contrary to U.S. law. Charlie and his company refused to do it, and were never permitted to market or build their products in Egypt, or anyplace else in the Arab countries.

Ben Widra had mentioned that to Charlie when they met the night before. He was aware of the history. Charlie briefed him on what Gross had admitted, and Ben thanked him for what he had done in the past in Israel, and the present in Egypt.

Before he left for the safe house, Ben advised that plans were in motion to sink the Russian ship, as soon as it neared the Syrian coast. The Mossad originally thought it would be best to board the vessel and take control of the weapons, but after Putin swallowed Crimea, they had decided to sink it instead.

Afterward, Charlie called Riordon. It was an open line, and all he told him was that his project had been successfully completed. Riordan understood, and would wait for the details when Charlie returned.

Everyone in Washington remained sensitive to what was communicated, even on their classified and encrypted facilities. Snowden was safe in Moscow, and continued to release information that was embarrassing to the United State. The Agency did not want to provide him and Putin with any more ammunition than they already had.

Charlie looked around the plane's cabin. A woman across the aisle was adjusting a pillow she had packed; and the man in front of her was shuffling receipts attempting to catch up on his expense accounts. None of the passengers seemed to present any form of threat, and Charlie returned to his thoughts.

He would be glad to have all this behind him, and return to a normal life. When he finished talking to Riordan he had called Beth, and told her he was on his way home. *Really* this time. He had just a couple of places he had to stop off on his way.

The first one was Vienna. He felt an obligation to fill Vincent in on the details of his project, and tell the old man he was right — as usual — about the mole.

He was tired, and physically worn out from his recent experience with Gross. Charlie was no Hercules, but as it turned out neither was Ralph Gross. He didn't care what the Israelis decided to do with him after they pumped him dry.

Kill him or turn him, it was all the same to Charlie. Probably the same to Gross as well. Once the man's ego was destroyed, he was as good as dead.

Charlie got a martini. Drank it quickly, and tried to get to sleep.

He must have been successful. He awoke to increased activity in the cabin, and the *fasten seatbelt sign* blinking insistently overhead.

On the ground in Vienna, Charlie cleared customs easily and caught a cab to Vincent's office. Passing the Prater amusement park, he noticed that the Ferris wheel was closed for the season. Charlie paid little attention, he was focused on his forthcoming meeting with Vincent. He was still curious why he was never contacted again, but assumed there was good reason.

The secretary remembered him. "Mr. Connelly, I am surprised to see you," she greeted him with a questioning, but gracious smile. "How have you been?"

"Just fine...," he searched for her name, but couldn't recall. "Is Vincent in?"

"Oh, I am so sorry. You don't know. I assumed you did."

"Don't know? Don't know what? Is there a problem?" Charlie asked, becoming concerned.

"Mr. St. Claire is dead."

Charlie's stomach churned, and he took a chair beside the secretary's desk.

"Who...? How did he die?"

"It was so sad. Pity really. But, it was probably the way he would have chosen to go," she told Charlie, wiping a small tear from the corner of her eye before sitting down behind her desk.

Charlie searched for the right question to ask. The secretary was obviously upset, and he was never very good in such situations.

"What happened to Vincent?" It was not particularly tactful but the best he could come up with under the circumstances.

She wiped her eyes again. Charlie was afraid she would burst into tears.

"Yes?" he prompted her once more.

"It was just a few days ago," she began. "I came into the office. Mr. St. Claire was already here. He always came in early. I opened the door to his office and there he was, his head on his desk—dead." The secretary could no longer restrain herself, and she began to sob.

Charlie reached out to her, but retracted his hand and self-consciously waited until she regained control.

"How did he die? Was he killed? What happened?"

"Oh no Mr. Connelly. Mr. St. Claire just died. He was very old you know. Almost ninety I believe."

Somehow, it had never occurred to him that men like Vincent would ever just die. After the life they led, he always imagined a more vigorous—if not more violent death.

"The funeral was just yesterday," she continued gaining control of herself once more. "It was sad really, he had no family, just some people from the Bank." She paused, before adding, "and those two men from London who flew over for the funeral. I don't know how they knew. They never spoke to me or anyone else for that matter. Just showed up, and left. Very silent type of men. Both of them dressed in gray. They were gray men. Very gray men.

Charlie rose to leave.

"Mr. Connelly." He turned back.

"There was a note he was writing. I think it was for you." She handed a piece of notepaper with his name on the top.

It didn't take him long to read it. Just a few lines really and never finished. "Six says that it was Langley. Look to Langley."

Six, Charlie knew, referred to MI6. Vincent had contacted them after all. Apparently, they knew somehow that whoever killed Emmett was inside the CIA. Ralph Gross of course. It confirmed what Charlie now knew. Would it have helped if he had the information earlier? Probably not, he decided. The important thing to him was that Vincent fulfilled his commitment. He had always known that he would. That type of man—that generation always did.

39

The flight from Vienna was late. It was the season for turbulence over the Atlantic, and Charlie was glad to be finally on the ground. Clearing customs was no problem. There were many people on the flight, and the custom officers didn't have time to waste on a retuning American businessman.

"Mr. Connelly."

Outside the customs area, Charlie turned at the sound of his name.

"The *Company* sent me to pick you up," a tall black man reached for his bag, and led him to a waiting Cadillac parked in a restricted area at the curb. Inside the car, the man removed his brown bowler hat, and introduced himself. "I'm Bernard Thornton, the Agency driver." With that, he rolled up the glass window between driver and passenger, and skillfully threaded the car into the string of exiting traffic.

The guard at the gate checked his list of expected arrivals for the day, looked at Charlie's passport, and peered through the darkened front seat window. "Good to see you Mr. Thornton," the marine guard greeted the driver, and waved them through.

"Been here 45 years," the driver told Charlie. "That gets me a pass at the gate," he chuckled, pulling into a reserved slot by the building's massive entranceway. "Welcome to Langley Mr. Connelly."

Charlie rode the elevator to the seventh floor, and found Riordan's office. The guard had alerted the secretary to his arrival, and she immediately took him into the assistant director's office.

Riordan shook his hand, and waved to a chair facing his desk. "Damned fine job," he roared, shoving aside the organization charts that littered his desk.

Charlie had a chance to study Ray Riordan as he signaled his secretary for the obligatory cups of coffee. In the short time that he was gone, it appeared the man had aged considerably. His close-cropped brown hair was becoming flecked with gray. The creases in his forehead had deepened, and the crow's feet tracked further across his face.

Perhaps he was imagining it Charlie considered. Just a bad day. Tough job. Understandable. But, the tremor in Ray's hand as he raised his coffee cup was undeniable.

Riordan noticed Charlie watching, and quickly shoved the papers aside before setting his cup down on the desk.

"So what finally happened with Gross?" Riordan began.

"I left him with the Mossad," Charlie replied, draining his coffee. It had been a long flight, and he had only a few hours sleep. He was still tired and the strong, black coffee helped — a little.

"The Mossad?" Riordan exclaimed. Charlie suddenly recalled that he had forgotten to tell his boss about the detour to Tel Aviv. About a lot of things actually, now that he thought about it.

"Let me start back at Kiev," he began. Then detoured once more. "By the way, before I begin, I want to put a word in for your man there. Durand provides a strong presence, and would be good in any upward slot you could find.

"And if you need any new recruits in that area, and it sounds like you might, his assistant Nadia would be a person to consider."

"Thanks for the information. I'll keep them in mind," Riordan assured him, looking away. "Now about the Mossad."

It was obvious that a principal concern of the AD's was how much a competing foreign agency knew about the intelligence architecture at Langley. Charlie understood, and proceeded to describe what had occurred while attempting to dispel any fears Riordan might have. He was also doing considerable mental self-editing in order to protect the anonymity of Karen Kincaid. It was a difficult juggling act.

"So Gross admitted murdering Emmett?" Riordan asked.

"Right."

"And, all along he had been working with Markoff?"

"That's right. He had been working as a Russian undercover agent for a considerable period of time."

"That son-of-a bitch," Riordan roared, banging his fist down hard on the desktop, making the coffee cup jump.

His secretary Linda rushed to close the office door.

"I always considered him my friend. I thought that we saw things alike. I had no idea he was a spy," Riordan shook his head back and forth in disbelief.

"And he was also the one who killed Marisa," Charlie added. The poor woman seemed always overlooked in any conversation, and he wanted to make sure her death was not forgotten. She had, like Emmett, given her life to the Agency and died as a result.

Riordan was speechless. He was finding it difficult to believe that all the time he and Gross had worked together, his friend was providing sensitive information to the Russians.

Riordan seemed deflated, sitting with his face in his hands.

Charlie didn't know what he could say that would help, so he kept quiet.

Finally, Riordan rose and looked out his window. After a short while, he turned and stared at Charlie. "That information you sent from Ukraine was very helpful. It gave the first lead on Gross, and some of it also gave us a lead on other Russian agents in the U.S. We have turned most of it over to the FBI, and we are conducting an internal audit here at Langley.

"Ken Madden has the entire IT Department working on the papers Barbara brought back from Cairo. We now have a treasure-trove of names, telephone numbers schedules, bills of lading, and all kinds of crap that we are following up on.

"You do good work Connelly. I appreciate what you have done for us. For me really. No one outside of my--this organization knows that Emmett Valentine was murdered. I guess we will try and keep it that way for a while longer. OK?

"I would like to reward you in some way, but since your assignment was never officially sanctioned there is not much I can do. Not even enter it in your file."

"Try and get rid of that for me would you. It shouldn't be too difficult to lose. What's his name—your file room supervisor—Walter Thorndike. I am sure you can do that so that Walter never realizes it's gone."

"That little pain in the ...." Riordan laughed. "Yeah, sure, I'll be glad to do that for you."

"That will be my reward," Charlie assured him.

Riordan nodded his agreement. "Look, I know you want to get home. I can't blame you for that. Let me get Barbara Richards to drive you to the airport. I'm sure she will want to know what happened to Gross after she left Cairo."

On the way to the airport, Barbara and Charlie did have a lot to discuss. Charlie tried to go over the questioning of Gross as much as he could.

As they neared the on-ramp to the terminal, she turned to Charlie. "Did Ray tell you he was being replaced?"

Charlie was shocked. "No! Why? By whom?" He had more questions, but kept quiet, giving Barbara a chance to answer.

"By his assistant Bill Brady. Bill had been asked by the Admiral to suggest a reorganization of Riordan's group so it would fit in better with the Agency's concentration on the Mideast. The Admiral thought our present focus was too diffused. Too antiquated. Too directed toward the old Cold War. The Admiral feels we should put our entire concentration on Iran, Syria, Libya, and the rest of the Mideast. When Brady finished his work the Admiral put him in charge."

"Also," Barbara continued, pulling the car to the curb outside the terminal, "the Admiral blames Ray for not knowing that Gross was working with the Russians."

Charlie shrugged. "He may be right, but what now for Riordan?"

"Early retirement," Barbara shook her head sympathetically. "Full pay and everything. But, for a man like Ray that's early death. Just another bureaucratic Kabuki dance."

Charlie thought for a moment. "Barbara."

"Yes Charlie?"

Do you remember that day at Langley when you came into my office and I was listening to *Madama Butterfly*?"

She nodded, but it seemed like a very long time ago now.

"Yes, Charlie I remember."

"I told you then that Emmett had said once that, like *Madama Butterfly* was put aside, the CIA often treats its agents badly. Just turns them loose when they have served their purpose, and then coldly proceeds along its merry way."

"I remember Charlie. He may have been right."

"Once again," Charlie added

"And you Barbara? What happens to you?" he asked, opening the car door.

"Back to the field. Station Chief in Dubai. Not bad, I guess. Could be worse."

Charlie leaned through the window, and kissed Barbara on the cheek. "Good luck my friend."

He waved at the departing Agency car.

***

The lights in Chicago's loop were flickering on as Charlie's flight skimmed the rooftops on its final approach to Midway Airport.

He and Beth had arranged to meet, as they always did, at the baggage carousel.

They hugged each other, and Beth studied her husband as only a wife can. "The scab on your ear?" she asked.

His mind flashed back to that night at the Catacombs in Kiev. Markoff's room. The bullet grazing....

"Did it shaving. It will be gone soon," he assured her.

She didn't believe him, but they had been married long enough for her to know when not to press for an answer.

"So, my dear, are you going to be home for a while?" That was what Beth really wanted to know. "When is your next trip?" she pressed.

"No more trips my love. This is the end."

Charlie and Beth walked arm in arm towards the terminal's exit.

About the Author

Russ Miller traveled to over 100 countries as a former international marketing executive. Since retiring, as senior vice president, he has served as an advisor on NGO projects for the UNDP, the Vienna based UNIDO, the World Bank, and the IESC, primarily in the post Soviet countries of Eastern Europe and Central Asia. His previous novel, *The Spy with a Clean Face*, also published by BeachHouse Books, won the Silver Quill Award from the American Authors Association. Miller and his wife live in the Chicago suburb of La Grange, Illinois.

Other Books by Russell R. Miller

Death on the Silk Road

A Spy With a Clean Face

Journey to a Closed City

Doing Business in Newly Privatized Markets

Selling to Newly Emerging Markets

15497156R00173

Made in the USA
Middletown, DE
07 November 2014